CHERRY ELECTRA

MATT DUGGAN

KEY PORTER BOOKS

Library and Archives Canada Cataloguing in Publication

Duggan, Matt, 1957–
  Cherry electra / Matt Duggan.

ISBN 978-1-55263-943-6

  I. Title.

PS8607.U376C44 2010   C813'.6   C2007-901836-X

The Canada Council for the Arts / Le Conseil des Arts du Canada since 1957 / depuis 1957

ONTARIO ARTS COUNCIL
CONSEIL DES ARTS DE L'ONTARIO

The publisher gratefully acknowledges the support of the Canada Council for the Arts and the Ontario Arts Council for its publishing program. We acknowledge the support of the Government of Ontario through the Ontario Media Development Corporation's Ontario Book Initiative.

We acknowledge the financial support of the Government of Canada through the Book Publishing Industry Development Program (BPIDP) for our publishing activities.

Key Porter Books Limited
Six Adelaide Street East, Tenth Floor
Toronto, Ontario
Canada M5C 1H6

www.keyporter.com

Text design and electronic formatting: Alison Carr

Printed and bound in Canada

10 11 12 13 5 4 3 2 1

© Mixed Sources
Product group from well-managed forests, controlled sources and recycled wood or fiber
www.fsc.org Cert no. SW-COC-002358
© 1996 Forest Stewardship Council
FSC

99%

ANCIENT FOREST ™
FRIENDLY

In memory of my dad, J.D. Duggan,
and my friend, Jim Brokenshire

Dear T,

You'd appreciate this, and not just because you've always been such a keen believer in signs and portents. Upon emerging from the communal shower with the rest of the lads this morning, a fellow inmate, with a lightning bolt tattooed on his chest and a red trans-am haircut on his head, threw a cup of urine in my face. But what happened next? Did I pounce on him like a cougar, seize his mullet in my claws, and slam his head on the hard jailhouse floor till blood came out his ears? Or did I make like a rabbit, eyes averted and nose twitching, hippity hopping meekly into the forest thicket, ready to bolt in earnest at the first sign of a more determined attack? Maybe I was like a fox, eyes flashing yellow flame with contained fury, sullenly stealing away while even then formulating my lethal revenge?

Which of god's forest creatures would I be most likely to emulate in the circumstances T? The cougar, the rabbit, the fox? You decide. Such a simple quiz shouldn't present much of a challenge to you, the sharpest little knife in the shed. Especially now that you've had the time and distance for some quiet reflection, and have concluded that I am capable even of murder.

Shortly after having piss thrown in my face—so hot and acidic that at first I thought I'd been hit with a bucket of boiling battery acid—I met with my legal counsel, Mr. Nick Rocolopolous, the softest, most furry, plush-toy pinky-ringed lawyer ever to crawl out from the Yellow Pages. It was then that I learned you were being groomed by the cops and Crown to testify against me.

Having never studied Classical Languages T, I lack the words to properly frame the scale and scope of such betrayal. Instead, I write the following poem:

oh Miss Tease
of the inward curved knees
remember that time, under the trees,
hard by the parking lot of Arby's?
do not do this to me
please

T just for your information I didn't leap up howling and knock over a chair upon hearing of your decision to assist the cops and Crown in their efforts to destroy me. There were no sobs echoing in the close confines of the conference room, no writhing wet-faced with arms flung across the table. There was naught but a sad-sack sigh and a chew on what's left of my left thumbnail.

"Exactly what are the implications of this development?" I calmly inquired, leaning back with a business-like crossing of my orange jail-issue pantsuited legs.

"Well," said Nick, "if true, it's bad news."

"How bad?"

"Superbad. On the bad side of bad. I mean basically,

we're fucked. In fact, if true, one option we might seriously consider at this point in time is to try to cop a plea on a lesser beef, thereby avoiding the whole mind-fuck ordeal of an actual trial as such."

But no T, that will not be. I insist upon the drama and pageantry of my days in court. I want it all—the wigs, the robes, the bailiff, the sleepy but stern old judge, the bosomy court recorder, a jury of my peers. I want a quick-kill sketch artist to render my charcoal image in the *Sun* and *Star* newspapers, depict me as a hard-eyed psychopath with an unshaven asymmetrical face, as Guilty as Shit. After all, what's the point of doing serious jail time if you don't even get to see yourself on trial? Especially when you're Innocent?

At least this news solves the big mystery that's been tormenting me. Why you haven't once visited, answered my daily phone calls, or responded to the two long letters I've written you since I got tossed in here last Wednesday night. Now I know. Now I know that you've been too busy. You've been too busy in some windowless, heavily law-yered room downtown, strategizing over the evidence with those two cologne-soaked dicks, Banning and Marcucci, a trolley of coffee and croissants at the ready. I can't stop picturing you doing this T—you with cops and Crown in closed-door consultation, just conferring away—and it never fails to deliver a bracing jolt of pain, a sickening smack of sad but true.

Before returning to my cell to brood more darkly on these matters, Nick cautioned me not to attempt com-municating with you in any way, shape, or form. My hopes for getting bailed out of this dungeon—the lyrically named Central Metro Detention Centre—before my prelim are already slim to non-existent. Phoning or writing you now would be depicted by the Crown as tampering with a witness, and make many more months of pre-trial incarceration a dead certainty. Much as I'd like to tamper with you T, I'm not that criminally stupid. Yet still I have to write you T, even though I can't send you this and so you'll never read it. I have no choice in the matter. For one thing, how else to keep from going mental in here? And what purpose can I possibly have now, other than proving my Innocence to you, even if only on paper, in the abstract? But more importantly, how else to get you near me here where I need you? My only means of being with you now is to conjure you up in pencil, on the blank pages of a Hilroy notebook.

Here I'm going to recount the facts for you Sweet T, the bare-naked facts of the matter. Much of this story you already know. But there are important bits of it that you don't, specifically the bits of the story that will be explored in agonizing detail at my trial and are germane to my spending the next umpteen years to life in a grey room built for one, with an open-concept steel toilet. These bits of the story will be presented to you here in a narrative of such stunning precision and breathtaking candour that you will, post-ipso facto, recognize that I am telling the Whole Truth and Nothing But, and then you will see how wrong you have been, and then you will cry about what you have done to me and then, yes, you will beg my forgiveness.

What follows are all the things that I'd tell you if only I could.

I mean to break your heart with these things.

But before we get to any of that, you just listen here, little Miss T of Rural Route 3. Here I live a Himalaya of pain due in no small way for want of a small touch of small you, right here in my hands.

Which explains why there will never be any need for you to cry and beg my forgiveness. I already forgive you T. Strange to say, but just hearing your name said out loud today came as such a relief that it feels like I've got you back with me already. So I forgive you. The true torture has been your silence, this void, and my dread that you'd gone from me for good. Now that I've learned you'll be testifying against me at my trial, at least I know that I will once more get to see your face and hear your voice. And that is what I want most of all T. Because I remain

Forever
Your Rabbit,

e.

Dear T,

Let's start on the DVP. We're in the horrible Hyundai, you and I; the day is hot, the air is orange, the car is rusty, the traffic is gigantic, and we have a disagreement on our hands. This is an excursion you are dead set against, but I am cajoling and bantering and promising a fine old time. We're off to the cottage of my friend Teddy's father, on beautiful Red Snake Lake, a place I hadn't been to since my teen years.

Your main objection to our weekend getaway was that Teddy is an asshole. While not exactly disagreeing with you, I do remember attempting to provide a slightly more nuanced perspective on the subject. My position went something like this: Sure, Teddy is nothing short of a total asshole, but he's an asshole I have known and been friends with for many years. In short, he is *my* asshole, and there's not much I can do about it. I even have an explanation for his assholeness, which is that he is not so much an asshole as quite painfully insecure due to his appalling childhood, and this insecurity leads him to sometimes behave in ways that might make him mistaken for the common asshole.

"Insecure is the standard euphemism for asshole," you pointed out.

"Is it? I did not know that. 'Course the other thing about Teddy is he's an artist, a freakishly great artist. And you know what that means—boy can't help it."

"He's not a freakishly great artist. He's a freakishly great asshole, and one doesn't necessarily go with the other. That's just a lame cliché."

"Damn. And here I am thinking I made it up—the Picasshole Syndrome."

"Plus he's mostly a video artist. There's no such thing as a great video artist."

"What a ridiculous thing to say."

"He doesn't do art. He does pranks. He's a prank artist."

"Girl, please. You've seen *Secret Santa*. Tell me that's not great art."

"Bitch, please. *Secret Santa* is exactly what I'm talking about. It's a dirty prank."

"Yeah? Well it's the dirty prank seen round the world. Tokyo, Berlin, São Paulo. That shit went worldwide."

"Which only goes to prove how sadly fucked the world is."

I decided it best to drop it. We'd had this debate before and it always ended nowhere. And anyway, you know the truth—Teddy is a great artist. His inventiveness is boundless, his creative powers terrifying, perhaps supernatural. And another truth is that's precisely why you can't take Teddy. It'd be one thing if he were just your garden-variety asshole, but to be an asshole with such gifts, well, that you just cannot forgive. To you, the gifted asshole is ethically offensive, a moral oxymoron, a crime against the natural order of things.

In addition to which, your position on assholes follows this line of crystal-clear reasoning: Assholes are unpleasant and, since life is already packed full with unpleasantness, why not minimize one's exposure to that which is unpleasant by avoiding assholes whenever possible? Obviously, you are quite correct there Professor T, but at the time my loyalty to this particular asshole made me incapable of appreciating the bulletproof logic of your argument. I won't plague you with the details T, but I will tell you that I've acquired a much surer grasp of the concept ever since finding myself locked in jail, swimming in a tumultuous stinking sea of assholes.

But let's leave aside our learned discussion of asshole theory and get back in the car because we have a long way to go and the traffic is oppressive and the heat is heavy. A four-lane conga line of cars was stopping and starting, starting and stopping, pushing it the hard way out of the hot city. During one such stop I decided I'd be happier barefoot. I took the car out of gear to remove my sandals. Unfortunately, I failed to notice that we were on a gentle grade and that the Pony was still rolling, ever so slowly, but rolling nonetheless, such that it nudged the fresh-cream Volvo in front. Pandemonium erupted in the vexed Volvo. Heads swung around to behold the monster who'd spoiled their air-conditioned enjoyment of the mammoth carclog. The driver's door swung open and a heated cargument was about to ensue, but then the traffic started rolling again and the door was pulled shut. The Volvo folk continued to look back at us with seething outrage and righteous indignation. I waved and smiled in order to convey my most sincere apologies.

"Shee-it," I chortled. "Relax. It was a love tap. People! I meant no harm to the creamy Volvo."

Then you said, "Look. I think there's a baby or something in the back seat. You probably scared it or something."

Sure enough, a woman in the back seat was fussing with a living entity located just beneath our line of sight.

"Oops," I said.

The traffic flowed faster now. The woman in the back seat stole a scorching last glance back and then plucked up a tiny, exotic dog-weasel cross and comforted it with nuzzling snuggles and sloppy wet-dog slobber kisses.

"Ho-ho no," I said. "Far worser yet. I scared their small and ugly dog. Let's hope it didn't go pee-pee."

Then we had another disagreement on our hands. You complained of my careless driving and arrogant indifference to the feelings, concerns, and perceptions of others, traits you see as inextricably bound.

"They're in their own personal space," you said. "It's like they're in their living room or something, and some lunatic smashes into it, like seriously violates their space, then thinks it's funny."

"Who's laughing?" I asked. "Besides, they're not in their living room. They're in their car. They're in their car and they should be alert to that fact and expecting the worst. And I didn't smash into it. I touched it. It's just a touch between cars. Don't mean nothing."

"Cars aren't supposed to touch," you pointed out.

That's when I realized what had truly disturbed you about this minor motoring mishap, and that's why I recount it for you here. It didn't mean nothing to you, my dear dark divining T. To you it meant Something. To you, it was a Sign, as palpable as any highway billboard, indicating Something Bad Ahead. Such is your witchy peasant power to perceive portents. You went all quiet and closed and mopey.

Glancing over, your exquisite pout in profile gave me a sudden idea.

"What say we pull into the first available truck stop and drop the seats back?" I suggested. "We could work on our differences."

"Yeah right," you said "Let's not instead. Let's go home. I mean it. I've changed my mind. Don't be a brat, you bastard. Turn around. Seriously. I don't feel so good."

"No turning back now sweet thing," I said. "We're already having way too much fun, and we haven't even hit the 401."

"Help, help," you said, "I'm being abducted."

Which was so close to true I should have laughed, but didn't. I looked over at you, resisting an urge to take a hold of that blond-pink candy lock of hair that flowed from out your head scarf in a curving compliment to your cheekbone, give it a little yank to ruffle your feathers, apply a noogie, pin you to the seat, and lick your left ear while singing Prince's "Kiss" till you screamed for mercy. You looked so cool and composed, smart sharp eyes hidden behind big black sunglasses, faint regal sideways smile and distant demeanor, but a little pensive too, like you're sitting on a secret. But it wasn't really a secret. It was more like a grim inevitability, the acknowledging of which would only make things worse—like the parking tickets littering the car floor or a hangover or winter or death. So I'd better enjoy this because this may be the last road trip I ever get with you. I'd better make the most of it. I'd better shut up and drive.

See, I knew full well my time was almost up with you T. You were moving on, to Italy come fall if your plans came together or, even more worse and sooner still, back to that fat fuck Byron and his big fat Brain. I had but this one last desperate hand to play T, and here is how I meant to play it: maybe, just maybe baby, getting away from the vapid vapors of the city and all your high-stress preoccupations to spend a

couple of days with me on beautiful Red Snake Lake would
work some powerful crazy Big Magic, and we would
ultimately return together in triumph—me flush with cash
and potential, and us flush with love and promise.

Of course now that notion seems tragic to the point of
hilarity. But how could I have anticipated the sordid horror
show that awaited us? Do you think I would have brought
you north had I foreseen how bent things were going to get?
Never in your life T. The determining factors then were that
I had to go to Red Snake Lake to attend to some vital self-
interests, and you had to come with me because, at that
point, I wasn't about to let you out of my sight for a second,
lest I never see you again.

So yeah, right—help, help, you're being abducted.

Having resolved to enjoy the road trip, I proceeded to do
just that, even though the freeway was a no-flow stop and go
stinking river of sun-sparked metal, a turgid endless turd
stream of fully optioned vehicles in all their market driven
variations, an overkill of horsepower all pent up and
pointless. Crawling along like babies. On one side of us a
silver Silverado towed a boat behind an indigo Infiniti with
smoke-tinted glass; on the other, an orange tanker truck's air
brakes hissed insults at my head, its chrome wheels rolling
with slow menace, mere inches away. In such company, the
standard-equipped 1986 gunmetal grey Hyundai Pony felt
vulnerable and out of place, as basic as a barn-built go-cart.
Unlike the other motorists comfortably ensconced in their
cool leathered cocoons, we were actually out there, with
windows down, rolling slow on the fucking Four-O-One. You
might have preferred a more refined automobile—or ideally,
say, a helicopter—but I liked it like that. Our crude little ride
gave the whole trip a frolicsome, holiday vibe.

Better still, we were leaving behind a city stunned stupid with heat, abandoned by all who could escape it, all but the surly scavengers pushing shopping carts down greasy back lanes. We were fleeing it like a disaster, and heading for the simple but thrilling promise of trees and rocks and sweet-water lake. Is there any place on earth you would rather be than a late July lakeside cottage in Shield Country? Me neither. I smiled in anticipation of falling into that lake. I twiddled my bare toes in anticipation, savouring the dirty, hot freeway breeze blowing up my t-shirt-sleeved arm dangling out the door. I was loose as a goose for the lake.

Best of all, I had this here spooky little gypsy girl at my side, her pretty little legs and magpie tattooed bare shoulder, her smooth skin flirting with the cotton whisper of a Summer of Love yellow flower-print mini-sundress, her Japanese perfume mixing it up with the diesel fumes. T. Rex's "Telegram Sam" squalled faintly from the classic rock station on the radio. I sparked a joint, and later we stopped and stood in line at Timmie's for glazed sour cream doughnuts and sickly sweet Ice Caps. How could things be any better?

It took us only five hours to get there.

I suppose from the very moment of arrival at our destination—"Harry's Hide-a-Way" says the burned-in script on the oil-stained plaque at the gated entrance—we both realized that this wasn't going to be a weekend for res-torative retreat. This wasn't going to be one of those healthy, wholesome cottage weekends when everyone is so exhausted from the fresh air and vigorous swimming in the chilly lake that we're all in bed asleep by ten, and when Sunday afternoon comes around, the abundance of food in the fridge provokes a dispute over who's to be foisted with all the leftover cheese, cold cuts, or pasta salad. No, this wasn't going to be like that at all.

For one thing, Teddy's dad Harry Chup was there.

I think I'd already told you about Harry Chup—that he was a money-mad multiply divorced manic-depressive alcoholic Lithuanian who'd made a mountain of money selling automatic garage door openers. All of which accounts for why, upon our arrival well after dark, we found Harry Chup applying a fresh coat of fluorescent white paint to the fieldstones lining the driveway, bathed in the Las Vegas glow of halogen stage lights, and clad only in dazzling white Reeboks and a simple black Speedo avec cellphone fanny pack.

The car lurched to a stop at the spectacle, and the engine belched and stalled.

"We must have crossed into Quebec," I joked lamely.

"Oh my god," you whispered. "He's naked."

"Yeah, what the?" I said, all confused. "I didn't know he was going to be here."

Which, as you now know, was a lie.

Of course I knew the sad, mad, bad Lithuanian dad was going to be there. The whole deal had been meticulously arranged by his insecure son Teddy, and I was well aware of these arrangements, since I'd helped to arrange them. There is abundant email and phone message evidence of these arrangements—evidence that lead those two smug chuckling dicks, Banning and Marcucci, straight to the door of my mom's condo, bright and hot last Wednesday morning. Evidence that you have probably been shown by now, and which is presently being cooked to perfection by the sleazy Crown for presentation in a Court of Law. I know this evidence looks bad on me T, but the truth is, in my village idiot innocence I was oblivious to the darker game in play.

All I knew is that Teddy was banned for life from the cottage and could only visit because I was with him, and that the arrangements I'd assisted with were meant to accomplish one simple goal: Get Teddy's dad Harry to front us a substantial amount of cash to finance our film. Failing that, the default goal was to get Teddy's dad Harry to drunk-drive into a ditch in order to set him up for his third impaired driving infraction of the century (the hat trick we kept referring to) so that he'd get real jail time and we could thereby enjoy summer-long, Harry-free access to his luxurious cottage on beautiful Red Snake Lake.

But my role pertained almost entirely to Goal One. Teddy needed me there because, as you soon saw, he and his dad aren't exactly on speaking terms. Actually they do speak, but it's in the Esperanto of the Dysfunctional, with Teddy shifting rhetorical gears from grotesque respect to tragic-comic verbal abuse to horrific tenderness and back again with swift unpredictability. Obviously such a pattern of communication is not conducive to a meaningful discussion of money. That's where I came in. To put it plainly, I was needed there to Talk Turkey with Harry because Teddy could not.

There's much more to it than that, though, T. What you need to understand is that Harry has always been fond of me. In fact, Harry loved me like the son he always wanted, as grotesque as that must seem to you now. It all goes back to the early teen years (what doesn't?), when I first met Teddy and began hanging around the Chup household. Back then, Harry warmly welcomed me into the inner inferno of their family circle. It could be because I was fatherless, poor, polite, and played hockey. Or it could be because I first became friends with Teddy following a schoolyard brawl—ye old fist fight being the surest way to cement a lifelong bond—and Harry digs that kind of thing. But most likely it was because by showing his fondness for me, Harry was able to inflict pain and humiliation on his youngest son, for whom he showed no fondness whatsoever.

To grasp the dynamic at play here T, try to picture me as a fully feckless, lightly freckled youth, and then imagine the kind of impression Harry made on me back then. Harry was as dynamic and elemental as the weather, always doing something, going someplace, moving things around—race cars, boats, company trucks, people, events, shrubbery—with the potent charisma that money bestows upon an older guy, especially to a kid from a home with no money and no older guy. To me, Harry radiated a force field composed of raw energy and cocksure confidence. Even his comb-over seemed sexy. When I first met him, I was a scattered and searching thirteen-year-old, and he was sockless in tan loafers and a pale blue seersucker, stepping out of an Arctic white Cadillac Seville in front of his four-stall garage, reeking of Brut, booze, and Belmont Menthol Special Milds, and carrying a stainless steel briefcase that looked like a chunk off a fighter jet. He made me think of a Bond villain.

"You are the boy that give Teddy his two black eyes, yes?" he asked me.

"Yeah. But, like, that was like a misunderstanding," I answered, looking him sly, right in the eye.

Harry laughed. "No, no, is good. That's how it goes with boys. Now you will be friends forever. You see? What is your name—your family name?"

I told him and he asked, "What is that? English? Irish?"

"I don't know. It's on my mom's side, from Newfoundland."

"Newfoundland?" He smiled. "And your father? He is
from?"

"States. But he's dead."

"Oh sorry to hear that. But is good to be from
Newfoundland. Is good people. I know so many Newfies
from the trades. You are good boy. Part Newf is good."

I soon found myself cast to play a dual role by the family
Chup, an acting job that was at once calculated and un-
witting. With Harry, I played the aw-shucks, always say
thanks twice for dessert neighbourhood stray—sporting,
well mannered, brave, and true—a real man's real boy.
Flattered by his attention and keen to please, my three-and-
a-half star performance of this role was rewarded by Harry
with lifts to my hockey games, March Break holidays in
Florida, fishing trips up north, Sundays at Cayuga where
he'd drag race his collection of Olds 442s, weekends at the
cottage, and, best of all, spontaneous (drunken) fistfuls of
walking-around cash. Meantime, Teddy spiraled into a lying,
thieving, destructive, sneaky, malicious teen mayhem artist.
With Teddy, I assumed the role of the loyal sidekick and
reliable point man on his criminal capers. For this I was
rewarded with a lifetime's supply of thrilling true crime
adventure stories and a bone-deep paranoia of police.
What's pathetic is that I've been stuck performing these two
roles vis-à-vis the Chups ever since, and I was reprising
them even as I climbed out of the Pony to greet Harry at the
cottage late that Friday night.

"Dives!" Harry called me, using that baseless nickname
I'd acquired as a struggling early-cut Junior B hockey
player. I put an eager bare foot onto the welcoming black

grit asphalt of the driveway. You remained sitting in the car, pensive and pouting.

"Why, if it isn't Mr. Harry Chup," I said. "What a pleasant surprise."

When we shook hands I recoiled at first, thinking he held a gag trout. But no, that was indeed the precise texture of the man's living palm flesh. What medication (when mixed with vodka) has that remarkable effect, I wondered. Then Harry hugged me and farted. He felt moist and fragile, yet shockingly vital in my arms.

"You brought a little friend?" Harry asked, squinting over my shoulder at you in the car.

"Yeah," I said. "She insisted."

I walked back to the car and leaned into the window for a quiet word with you.

"Come on babe. Come say hello to Mr. Harry Chup."

"Not till he puts on pants. I can see his thing from here."

"Don't worry about his thing. I bet it doesn't even work anymore."

"Are there any firearms on the premises?" you asked. (Such awesome instincts you!)

"What the fuck," I gently scolded. "Don't be stupid. Come on."

"I mean it E. I don't want to be here. Please. Let's just go."

"Why you being so weird? Relax. Check this place out. It's wicked beautiful. Seriously. Tell me you'd rather be stuck in the city."

"I'd rather be stuck in the city."

"We can't drive back now, it's late. Just one night. Okay? Have a swim in the morning, and then we'll leave first thing. Promise. Remember: July is Truth Month."

It was only after I'd made that false promise and lie,

along with the equally bogus guarantee that there were no
guns in the cottage, that you grumpily gathered up your bag
and frumpily followed me inside. I remember, too, that the
presence of a female of the species (that being you) had a
most unsettling effect on Harry. It was as though I'd
brought along my pet lynx for the weekend, and Harry only
looked at you, or the parts of you that interested him most,
when he was sure that you weren't looking back. Perhaps he
feared that direct eye contact might provoke an attack from
such a wild little hellcat. Your demeanor did nothing to
dissuade him of that impression.

By now, of course, you realize that Harry is the source of
his son Teddy's insecurity. Harry had been, as the generic
term renders it, an abusive parent. With that in mind, you
must appreciate my reasons for agreeing to assist Teddy in
his dealings with his problematic pater. You must appreciate
that my motives were noble, humane, and largely altruistic.
And also that I owed Teddy a lot of money. Several thou-
sands of dollars plus, to be exact, a debt I mostly accumulated from that time so long ago that I sort of told you about
when he and I headed out West for a season of tree-planting
and poker-playing and coke-dealing in soggy tents on the
sodden B.C. coast so that I might earn enough money to
drop out of grad school properly. You know all too well of
my chronic cash flow concerns T, so it should come as no
surprise to you that I leapt at the opportunity not only to be
forgiven my debts to Teddy, but also to acquire some crucial
seed money for our film project. All just for visiting beautiful
Red Snake Lake, having a little powwow with Harry, and
maybe helping to facilitate his drunk driving into a ditch.
What fun! I figured.

That I owed Teddy serious money will come as no big

shock to you either. (And, just by the way, don't think for a second that I've forgotten I still owe you six hundred dollars for Pony parts and labour, plus half the first and last month's rent on the shotgun shack.) You always suspected something of the sort. Remember that time last fall, not long after Teddy first entered our life like a suicide bomber boarding a pleasure cruise, when I dropped by your place, somewhat shaken to tell you vaguely of the episode at a motel in Mississauga where I'd been compelled to play the role of the armed heavy while Teddy negotiated his way out of a way-past-done drug deal with a crack-fuelled faux Rasta called Fry Pan?

"Why?" you asked me at the time. "Why do you get involved in his shit? What do you owe Teddy?"

"Nothing," I lied. "He's just a friend in need."

Or that even worse time this spring, when I arrived at your tiny perfect attic flat in the Annex at three in the morning, even more severely shaken, and only vaguely told you that I'd been chased and indeed actually shot at by a teen gangsta on a bicycle behind a schoolyard in Parkdale, again on Teddy's behalf?

"It's nothing. I'm totally okay," I totally lied when you sprang up from bed to see what all the clatter was about.

"Then why are you almost crying?" you asked.

"To keep from almost laughing," I cried.

"Baby," you said. "What happened to your leg? Look at your arm. Your hand. You're bleeding."

"I dropped my bike turning onto Dundas. Caught a streetcar track in the rain."

"What in the fuck is up with you and Teddy?" you demanded to know. "Why do you keep getting in all this fucked-up shit with that asshole?"

"It's not Teddy. I'm the asshole," I admitted, searching

the cupboards for something, anything, to drink, finding
only a third of a bottle of Peppermint Schnapps, which I
instantly drained.

The truth is T, I did these things for Teddy out of loyalty
as a true friend. And also because I owed him a lot of
money. But more than just money. I owed Teddy a much
deeper debt, a debt that I've never revealed to you.

Okay. My dearest T. The admissions that follow may cast
me in a less flattering light than what I explained above, and
that is why I never shared them with you before and do so
now only to demonstrate my complete, almost stupefying
honesty. So here goes.

Also in B.C., while powerfully drunk and coked to the
hairline, I was driving a rented pickup truck away from a
scummy little bar in a soggy little town when a scruffy little
man lunged out of the rain and into the path of the truck and
was accidentally struck. The truck was travelling very fast, and
its left front fender clipped the man very hard, such that he
flew like a booted ball, up and up and then down and down,
hard to the pavement, all in a wet flashing black blur out the
corner of my eye in the side mirror, with a thud and a grunt
and my groan. (Such freakout freaking terrible nightmares I
have of this incident T, unto my very last night.) I slammed to
a stop and sat there, rocked in shock, muttering my top-secret
mantra (*in-finite, in-finite, in-finite...*) while Teddy got out to
inspect the damage. He ascertained that while the truck was
okay, the pedestrian wasn't (although not dead) and that,
significantly, no one had witnessed the accident.

Teddy got back into the truck and this is what he said to
me: "Go."

Teddy really had to talk me through this one. My
instincts told me to tend to the injuries of the accident

victim as best I could until the paramedics arrived, and then
throw myself at the feet of the local authorities for whatever
punitive measures they saw fit. But Teddy would have none
of that. It's in times like this that Teddy's life force emerges
at its most potent, and in this case, it easily overpowered my
puny inner altar boy. His resolve was frightening to behold.
He was utterly and awesomely committed to fleeing the
scene, and would entertain no alternatives to this plan of
action. He admonished me with shouts and vigorous
downward glancing slaps to the head—"Get [slap] Fucking
[slap] Going [slap] Right [slap] Now." And then slap slap slap
again. When that didn't work, and I remained sitting
slouched at the wheel in stunned, slack-mouthed shock,
Teddy wound up and punched me smack in the face with a
rock handed right fisted haymaker. (So there—now you
know the truth about my broken tooth.) I yanked open the
door and spilled out of the truck, spitting blood and tooth,
and Teddy slipped behind the wheel.

"Get in!" Teddy ordered, yanking the door shut.

Teddy was already pulling away, and I just managed to run
around to the other side of the truck and fling myself in before
he left me there, my only resources being the fight or flight
messages emanating from the most primitive reaches of my
brain stem. I was but a simple hunter-gatherer at that point, or
maybe more like a naked and panicked Australopithecus.

"What the fuck?" I demanded to know. "What the fuck?"

"What the fuck?" Teddy whined in cruel imitation.
"What the fuck?"

By then we were already flying past the motels and
equipment dealerships marking the outskirts of town,
gathering speed as we headed on out and up the rainy black
mountain highway.

"Okay then," I said, having at last begun to organize my brain. "Okay. Let's think about this. I'm thinking about this Teddy. Okay? I'm thinking very seriously man. Teddy. Listen. I'm thinking we should swing back and report an accident."

The windshield wipers flip-flopped fiercely at the steady, stupid rain.

"Think about this, shit-for-brains," Teddy announced over the rental truck's high-winding V-8 engine, "I got four fucking eight balls on me, you're totally fucking pissed, and we're both totally fucking fucked if we get pinched. So fucking think again."

"No, no, listen, we dump the blow and go back. I'll take the tumble. That guy, man, shit. What if he's dead?"

"Attention. Attention. This is your captain speaking. Remain calm, motherfucker. I repeat. Remain calm. No one is dead. All survived the event. We go back, we go to jail. Over. Motherfucker."

Then he cranked up the radio and suddenly we were enjoying that one Weezer tune I always liked. Of course Teddy sang along.

Turned out Teddy was right about jail. Only it wasn't *we* who went to jail. It was just Teddy. That's because when the police cruiser loomed up behind us, lighting up the rental truck's rear-view mirrors and interior like an alien spacecraft—that is to say, when the siren-wailing, horn-honking, roof lights-popping, high beams-flashing RCMP Ford Interceptor came flying up from behind to bully bumper us off the road just as Weezer finished that tune—it was Teddy who was at the wheel. And it was Teddy who had to be Tasered (twice) before complying with the trim young moustached officer's instructions to shut up and lie on the wet shoulder with his hands behind his head (I obeyed like

an eager lab retriever), and it was Teddy who was discovered
to have four neatly packaged eighth of an ounce quantities
of cocaine tucked into his Civil War boots, and it was Teddy
who spun, swung and refused to submit to a Breathalyzer
back at the station. Consequently, it was Teddy who had to
bargain his way through a stunning buffet of charges,
including reckless driving, leaving the scene, speeding,
resisting arrest, carrying a concealed weapon, assaulting a
police officer, uttering a death threat, refusing a Breathalyzer, and possession of a narcotic for the purpose of
trafficking. Thus it was Teddy who ultimately had to spend
eighteen-and-a-half months behind the stone-cold walls of
Stony Mountain Federal Penitentiary.

Whereas I walked.

And Teddy will never let me forget it. His so-called "lost
years."

Okay T, so now do you see, my dearest, sweetest, ever-
ready little T, why I did all this amazingly stupid shit for
Teddy? Can you comprehend why I felt a heavy burden of
debt to this man? Can you understand how the guilt and
loyalty I felt for my insecure friend Teddy convinced me that
I had a duty to act at his behest? If so, I wish you could
explain it back to me so I can get it too. Because none of it
makes sense to me now. The fact is I owed him nothing. He
was always the sole *auteur* of his *noir* nightmare, and I was
but a hapless dupe, tricked into playing a supporting role. I
should have done what you urged me to do after the very
first time you met Teddy—ditch him pronto. We should
have done what you urged me to do the moment we arrived
at the cottage—flee the scene. Because look at me now T.
Having ignored your advice, I am in jail facing murder
charges and have probably lost you for good.

All at once I'm completely bored with thinking and writing about insecure people and their unfunny follies. I've had more than enough of the dysfunction, desperation, and destruction wrought by the Harrys and Teddys of our world, as I am sure you have too. Now all I feel like writing about is Love. About our Love. More exactly, about my Love for you Miss TKO, my little Cossack supernova.

The next thing I'm going to write is a Love letter.

But a final note before I finish—fittingly, a note about you.

I remember taking you by your cool, smooth hands and searching your sly smart smiling downward gaze on the stone deck in the dark behind the cottage soon after our arrival. You looked quite impossibly beautiful T, my little T girl there in all your perfection, the poised frame of your dancer's body, so confident and lithe, and what with the perfume of the pines and being free from the city and about to get high in a luxuriously decaying lakefront cottage—it all conspired to make me idiotically happy and catastrophically insensible to what you so powerfully sensed: this was all headed for hell in a hurry. I was too busy pretending to be rich and accomplished.

But by then, spent from the long hot drive and weary of trying to penetrate my thick head with the obvious, you'd become resigned to what fate was sending us Special Delivery. You'd given up. I looked into your sad, sweet, indulgent smiling eyes as I put my lips on your neck, my hands caressing your gunslinger hips.

"What exactly did you bring me here for anyways?" you asked.

I could only sigh in reply.

Because I don't know what I'd brought you there for. I had decided on a whim. To dig a little deeper though, I might suggest fear, for one thing. Fear that if I'd gone away without you, I'd have returned to the city to find our shack in the Junction empty and T-less. Hope, for another thing. The hope that a couple of days together at Red Snake Lake would reverse our trajectory, and that I could get it all—the money and the girl—and would soon be riding the Pony back to town with both.

As you know, I couldn't have been more wrong about that, and things went way different from what I'd hoped. Obviously you know it, since you are apparently ready and willing to testify about it.

But I'm going to put that all aside for now T. I've got a love letter to write.

Love,
e.

Dear T,

So much for that love letter. It got thieved.

Let me tell you a thing or three about jail. You are vulnerable to every form of injury, insult and indignity imaginable in here, including having a love letter that you lovingly wrote to your lover stolen and used as a masturbatory aid by some loveless deviant. I toiled long and hard over that letter too, working through several drafts and a subsequent final polish, all in circumstances that are impossible for you to imagine. You can try though. You can close your eyes and picture the men's washroom in a downtown big city bus depot, featuring a multicultural spectrum of self-soiled psychos, scores of scared and angry young boy men, a cross section of solvent sippers, fatherless fetal crack gang affiliates, run-of-the mill retards, plus a few normal type guys who just happened in to take a leak. Then triple the number of occupants you had initially visualized and lock the door. Now open your eyes and try to write a love letter.

So the loss of that letter pains me deeply. I want it back. Believe me, there were some truly fine bits in it, and I don't mean just the erotic bits, which proved infuriatingly tricky to write. Sex famously eludes pencil and paper, and its description in words tends toward lame and lazy metaphors ("your silky smooth thighs," "the pink petals of your moist flower," "doggy-style," etc.), so I soon discovered that the description of doing those things does not even come close to delivering the dizzying intoxication derived from those precious transformative moments of actually doing those things. And eight empty days and nine emptier nights in jail have made me come to truly appreciate just how precious those transformative moments are. If I ever get out of here, I don't plan on wasting even one single second of my freedom writing about sex, but I do plan on wasting every single second of my freedom either having or trying to have sex. Or, at a minimum, jerking off, something I haven't accomplished since early two Wednesday mornings ago, believe it or not, mainly because I'm too bashful to attend to those needs in my current circumstances. (Would that my cellmates were as coy; it sounds like a combination massage/exorcism clinic after lights-out in here.) Because writing about sex convincingly is just not possible. I tried. And I failed. So although there were some graphic bits in the letter, I sought and found God and Satan in the margins, in all the subtle, sumptuous details—those turquoise cotton sports panties around your tiny ankles—my slap-happy boyfriend boner in the back seat of the Pony; those sky-black formal silk panties around your tiny ankles—my slap-happy boyfriend boner in the washroom at Club Plastique in Montreal. And so on. You get the drift. No actual penetration scenes as such. Except for that time on the picnic table behind the sewage filtration plant in Scarborough.

Luckily, your full name does not appear anywhere in the text of that letter because I fear you've become somewhat of

a virtual porn star around this here Central Metro Detention
Centre. But don't worry. All that the reader can discern of
your actual identity is that you grew up on a farm in
Manitoba, occasionally work late at a hair salon on Queen
West, are of Ukrainian heritage, and once fainted during
cunnilingus in a hair salon on Queen West after closing,
while engaged in a session of frenzied post breakup sex.
Which is a relief, because god only knows how many goons
have read and used the letter by now. I'm pretty sure I know
who stole it in the first place too, because this one guy (not
the actual guy I suspect, but a friend of his) keeps asking
me if I could write a love letter to his gender-conflicted
girlfriend for him. That's when I realized that I could
actually make a career of ghosting porn letters from jail,
because the guy said he'd pay me ten bucks if I made it
"hot." The extent of illiteracy in here is nothing short of
appalling. I would estimate it at well over ninety percent, so
you can easily see my potential for profit. Looks like all that
book learnin' could finally pay off. (Just imagine how proud
my mother would be!) I told him I'd have to think about it,
that I was too far into my current writing project to consider
taking on any side jobs at present. But now I realize that I'm
going to have to do it, not so much for the money, but to
earn props and respek from all my homeboys here on the
range. Already they call me Harry Potter merely because I
wear glasses—or used to, till Captain Lightning Bolt, Sir
Manfred Mullet himself, the gentleman who thought it
amusing to throw a cup of his piss in my face—knocked
them off a table and performed this weird mincing jig on
them—and also because I stay aloof and alone while writing
morosely yet fiercely at every opportunity. And, by the way,
what you did to my hair hasn't helped matters much. It's

only made me more difficult to categorize, in a place where categorization rhymes with survival.

My new jail name should give you some indication of the illiteracy pandemic in here. They must think it was Harry Potter who wrote the famous series of books that goes by that name, no doubt the only books most of them have ever heard of, aside from the famous texts ghostwritten for God, such as the Bible or the Koran or *The Killer Inside Me*. Perhaps back in some distant Golden Age of Literacy, the inmates would have named their jailhouse scribe Shakespeare, and they'd have paid him to write love sonnets or epic outlaw ballads instead of horny doggerel to their transgendered street meat pals.

I don't want to go on and on about that lost love letter, but there was one part in it that I still want to tell you about T, because—well, just because. Because I enjoyed writing that part so much T. And don't worry: this one will not fall into the wrong hands. Promise. I've made an arrangement with Nick the Greek Attorney-at-Law to collect and keep all my notebooks now. He thinks I'm making notes for my impending trial. In fact, don't worry about nothing now sweet thing because you're never going to read any of this anyway. Just don't worry baby T-bird girl. Relax as I tell you that...

...it was so hot that afternoon, a sultry first flourish of spring heat Sunday, not long after we moved in together. Together at last, in the Secret Smell shotgun shack in the Junction, with a view through the broken fence of the mainline railway tracks out back, just enough for a flash of graffiti on the boxcars rolling past. You had so many things to do that day, what with working two-and-a-half jobs and sorting out the decor in our tilting rented flat, all the while scheming all your futuristic schemes. Even then already

halfway gone to Italy, I reckon. At last you finally had a full
day off, one complete day, and you had planned on doing so
many busy important things, things like last year's taxes and
sorting out your portfolio for that monstrous application for
your grad design schooling thing in Florence. Plus dealing
with Ronnie's intestinal worms. And what was that Secret
Smell you searched for so desperately but never found? Oh
so many busy important things you had to attend to T.

You were taking a little break from all your busy important
things, making yourself a refreshing fruit 'n' wheat grass
smoothie in the blender when I sauntered into the kitchen.
And there you were. Like a cool little cocktail, clad in flimsy
cotton housedress, your hair in a strictly-for-business bun.

"Howdy ma'am," I said, in a southwesterly drawl.

I was wearing the greasy straw cowboy hat I'd found at
Value Village, with no shirt or shoes, but looking for service
anyway. The crude layout of the shotgun shack flat meant
that the afternoon sun was at my back, blasting through the
open sagging porch back door.

"Sure is hot, ain't it?"

"Go away. I got so much shit to do."

"Well I gots shit to do too hon, but alls I'm 'a doing is
sitting out there in the parlour, jus' by myself, watching the
NASCAR on the TV set."

I cracked a beer and sighed wearily.

You stifled a sputtered laugh and looked away, but it was
too late. I'd caught you.

"There's a new baby calf in the barn, ma'am. Thought
you might like to come out and have a look-see."

"I mean it. I'm up to my fricking eyeballs here. Can you
seriously please just go see about getting that shit for
Ronnie? Please and thanks?"

"Looks like your daddy's done gone to town little girl. Looks like that leaves just the two of us here. All alone on this great big spread. Ain't no one else around, not for miles and miles. And that old Ronnie's fast asleep."

I took a long, slow, sloppy pull on my long-neck beer, spilling backwash down my naked chest and onto the floor. I suavely swabbed the spillage from my glistening body with a tea towel.

"Uck," you said. "Gross. Chuck that in the laundry. Actually, you know what? Do the laundry."

"It's the humidity. Not to bore you ma'am. With the obvious."

By then your eyes were in play and dancing and your mouth was muckled. I sat up on the kitchen counter, feeling all mopey for myself.

"Yeah," I sighed, "you can say whatever you want little girl. Call me gross. Whatever. I'm just a hat full of shit as far as you're concerned. Ain't that right? Dirty old hired hand Hank. Just on account 'a I ain't some big rich fancy-ass rancher, like your daddy."

"Okay then. Hank? Would you please go to town and get some medication for the cat's intestinal worms? Do it now. Just go get on your fucking horse or whatever."

"Is that all I am to you ma'am?" I asked, as I found and opened the cookie can atop the fridge and rolled us up a midday twister, taking charge of the situation. "Just some fella you can order around? Tend to the cat's intestinal worms and whatnot? Get on my fucking horse? Or whatever? Let me remind you of something here little missy. I'm a man. I'm a man and I have needs. And I don't mean just my basic needs for beer and stock car racing neither."

"I'm gonna tell my daddy to fire your ass if you don't do

what I say. Hank. So finally I learn your real name. Hank, eh? You are the worst hired hand ever. Hank. Shiftless, shifty Hank. Look away Hank. Hit the road Hank."

By then I'd rolled us up a trim and perfect reefer, complete with match-pack filter. I lit up and you reached out, twiddling your fingers to take, so cute on the kitchen chair, left foot tucked under right butt cheek, left eye squint shut to take a toke.

"Ma'am, I reckon a man's free to look where he wants," I said. "Ain't no harm in lookin'. Say, what you got going underneath that fancy frock of yours anyhow? I must say. You are one sweet little cupcake. Case you didn't know."

"Get away from me Hank."

"See this here is what you call the master-slave dialectic little girl."

I said this from my knees on the kitchen floor, with your slim calves in my hands.

"I've been reading all about it at nights, all alone in the bunkhouse. It's in a big book by this ol' German feller called Hegel. And it is precisely that historical paradox what puts me down on this floor, kissing your fine feet."

"Oh. My."

"And then licking them. Between your fine toes. Like this."

"No. Oh. Don't. Stop. Hank."

You resisted, but you are small and I am tall and soon I carried you down the hall.

To the barn
On a bale of hay
Thrice we did it that hot day
And then we dined at Swiss Chalet

Love,

e.

Dear T,

Wow. That sure was fun. I hope you enjoyed it as much as I did. Until I had to stop writing about you before you made me cry. Then Manfred—the aforementioned piss-throwing mullet head—hastened over to see what was the matter, having spotted me forlornly closing my Hilroy notebook and casting about for an empty place in jail to rest my weary gaze.

"Awww," Manfred cooed. "What's the worry Harry Potter? Feeling sad 'cause you can't fuck your mom no more?"

"No," I said. "I'm feeling sad 'cause I can't watch you watching your dog fucking your grandma up the ass no more."

Or at least that's what I should have said. Instead I said something about my allergies.

"Fuck, you are a pussy."

"Sorry?"

"You are a pussy. Agree?"

"Well, I—"

"Or disagree?"

"Sorry?"

"Say it."

"Say what?'

"Say 'I, Harry Potter, am a pussy.'"

"What? I mean—"

"Just fucking say it!"

There's no point in transcribing the rest of that conversation T. You can already see where it's headed (me saying, "I, Harry Potter, am a pussy") and it must also be becoming obvious to you by now that I've got a serious quandary on my hands in the form of this vulgar, impulsively violent redheaded vermin called Manfred. He's the only guy who's giving me any grief in here. I avoid or find a way to fit in fine with all the other misfits in this place. Manfred's the only reason why I now come equipped with a specially shortened, ultra-sharpened pencil that fits into my fist just so, like a stealthy secret spike. I'm not sure what Harry Potter would do in the circumstances (use his Invisibility Cloak? or perhaps the Porthole Key?), but in here I have no choice. There's no place to hide, nowhere to run. I have to step up and assert myself. Direct confrontation isn't the answer. I mean to call in an air strike, U.S. Marine style. I'm thinking next time Manfred's sitting there enjoying my caramel pudding, I might have to sidle on over and pop a hole in his neck with my custom pencil. Hopefully, I won't have to resort to such drastic measures to defend my just desserts. But such are the depths of desperation that my current circumstances have brought me to.

This place is starting to seriously fuck me up T. I doubt I'll ever be the same.

But it's not all stress humiliation boredom caf-food constipation mental illness and rank stank body odour in here. There is humour to be found too. On the lighter side, for example, I recently learned what Manfred's in for. I'd assumed that he was some kind of major league crime guy involved in international biker drug smuggling, or a daring-do casino invasion, or some plot-heavy gold bullion heist. But it turns out he's facing a slew of charges related to a bungled insurance fraud attempt. That's right. Insurance fraud. Apparently, he torched his garage in an effort to collect the insurance on a pair of snowmobiles, but the fire got out of control and burned down two neighbouring garages, including his father-in-law's. The best part is his favourite pregnant British bulldog was destroyed in the process, plus he was two years behind on his child support payments and was wanted for questioning in regard to uttering a death threat at his kid's baseball tournament.

See what I mean? Even in jail one can find levity, a little something to smile about. Such is the human condition. And just compare his lame sitcom circumstances to the beefs I'm currently confronting. Who's the pussy now Manfred? Just fucking say it.

On the other hand, there was no levity or smiles this afternoon when I had to tell my mom that, on the legal advice of Mr. Nick R, I was forgoing my God-given right to a bail hearing. Knowing that I am Innocent, my mom can't understand why they won't just drop me off at her new condo and call it a house arrest until my trial. She showed up today clutching an attaché stuffed with my university transcripts and curriculum vitae, with the intention of introducing these yellowing documents as proof of my good character at the bail hearing. Mostly though, she wanted me to see her in her new pearl-grey Chanel suit, a recent score at Holt Renfrew's Last Chance Outlet at the Vaughan Mall. It's just the thing for her appearance in court. I could have cried.

"You want to make the correct impression, prior to decisions being made and all," she said, pretending not to notice the three hundred pound white baby-momma in a baby-blue terry tracksuit and corn rowed hair, faking patois at her sulking husband slumped at the next booth.

"Make the judge think we don't belong here," she added, "like it's all a big mistake, like we just wandered into court by mistake. Speaking of mistakes, don't wear that plaid teal suit of yours. It's ridiculous. I'll get you one. Black's the only way to go."

She looked so fragile skinny blonde my mom, like a prematurely aging teenager. She asked me if I'd resumed the Transcendental Meditation we'd learned together when I was a youth.

"I bet meditation could be a big help for you in here. To keep you centred. And prayer. I've been praying. Have you thought at all about praying baby? Doesn't matter to who or what. God doesn't care anymore. You really should just pray baby."

"What mom, are you *trying* to make me cry?" I asked.

She's been asking about you T. You know how she feels about you. She loves you to the bones T Bone. It really would be sporting of you to take her out for lunch—some place trendy, not too expensive, may I suggest Thai?—and explain where things are at with you. I can't do it. I haven't had the hard heart to tell her that the "peculiar little beauty" about whom she speaks so fondly has up and slipped away (where are you T? No one knows, or at least no one who knows will tell me where) and is said to be in cahoots with the cops and Crown. It's going to flat out kill her when she learns about that.

How exactly did that happen anyway?

Let's go straight back to the cottage to see if we can find out.

I believe that when I last left off we had just arrived to the (for you) disturbing surprise discovery that Harry Chup was joining us for the weekend. Your next unpleasant discovery was that father Harry and son Teddy had both been drinking persistently for six hours straight, and that there wasn't a crumb of food to be had in the cottage, aside from a container of antique olives in the crisper. I quickly mixed us up a couple of stiff g and t's in order to tune into the program already in progress.

"I assume you've met my father?" Teddy asked you. "The Mad Count Drunkula?"

Oblivious to us, the man in the black Speedo was wandering on- and offstage, muttering and mumbling, singing and humming, all the while carting tools and whatnot, as though under the direction of some invisible demonic director.

In addition to a grinning gust of booze breath, Teddy had greeted us with big gooey black cocaine eyes, like a demented doll, and his chilling brand of cheerful exuberance. He was simply elated to have us there. You weren't buying it though. It's always fascinating to observe you and Teddy together, the way you two seem to understand and loathe each other on levels so deep that others cannot ken. One might think you were family or something. You instantly assumed your respective battle stations—you with your humorously knowing contempt, concealed by a sardonic sort of supercilious sociability, he with his unappealing attentiveness, overtly anxious generosity and creepy condescension. As always, I assumed a diplomatic stance, and used my warmest and most facilitative language in order that we could all get along nicely and start right into chipping away at Teddy's high-quality blow.

Harry stumbled up the back deck and into the kitchen, humming Lennon's "Imagine."

"Dad, you fucking freak," Teddy said. "Put on pants already."

"Where is extension?"

"What extension?"

"You know, red one. Thirty-foot one. It's not in thing, garage, where I put last."

"How should I know? It's probably up your ass. Have a look."

"Oh Jesus Christ," you quietly complained to me.

"Harry," I said, "we're talking about going to town to get something to eat. Want to come?"

"You go ahead Dives," Harry answered. "I got to go finishing that fucking thing there."

Wielding a large orange power tool, Harry wobbly weaved his way out of the kitchen and back outside. Two beats later, said power tool was heard ripping into a sheet of plywood, tearing asunder the deep dark woods silence of the night.

"Jesus Christ," you complained again, this time more loudly.

"He's got to go finishing that fucking thing there," I explained.

Then Teddy and I had a great big laugh, which I think helped you to recognize the high-quality comedy of the scenario, because you laughed too. Together in the kitchen we laughed and laughed. Long and hard we laughed. And you must admit T, it was pretty funny. Until Teddy got weirded out by all this hilarity at the expense of his dear old dad. He became suddenly serious—always a danger sign—and proceeded to make an artificial heartfelt show of the deep respect and high esteem in which he held his dynamic dad.

"You know," Teddy said, in a tone of solemn reverence, "he's actually an amazing man, when you seriously think about it."

I seriously thought about it, staring at the floor, trying not to laugh. Outside the saw screamed at the dark.

"When you think about all he's done I mean," Teddy added. "I mean the guy came here with dick."

Yes, I knew the saga well—Harry Chup: Man and Myth—arriving a penniless refugee from the East Bloc, fleeing the legacy of his extended family's extensively evil past to thrust his dick into our innocent young country, where he cauterized his surname and swiftly established himself as a successful bipolar businessman, competitive quarter mile race car driver, prolific killer of animals in the wild, peeler bar cocksman, suburban subdivision political fixer, serial husband, doomsday dad and recreational boater. Yes, the very template of success for the Old World Man in the New World. And let us not forget that it is thanks to Mr. Harry Chup that no one residing in the Golden Horseshoe region ever has to get out of his or her vehicle in order to open the garage door.

"Come," Teddy said gravely. "Check this out."

That's when he showed us the thing that ended up being the catalyst for all or at least many of our problems that weekend. The first problem being, I'd promised you there weren't any firearms in the cottage when in fact the place had more weapons than Fort Apache. Not that the specific weapon Teddy showed us was anything other than a horrific collector's item.

We'd left the gleaming track-lit expanse of the kitchen, with its hanging copper pots and aircraft carrier-sized granite island counter, guarded by a triad of stern stainless steel appliances, journeyed down the tropical hardwood hallway, past the six sumptuously appointed bedrooms— three with ensuite cans, two with Jacuzzis—and then taken the three steps down into Harry's den, where we entered a different world. Harry World. Here was the original trapper's cabin Harry had preserved, restored, and built around instead of levelling, back when he'd first purchased and developed the entire bay back in the seventies.

The space was small and low and dark, with thick log walls glazed like honey doughnuts, upon which hung giant fantasy puke-epic oil paintings of Whitey's first encounters with the Red Man, alongside the stuffed dead heads of massive mammals and freakishly fat freshwater fish mounted on varnished plaques, and all around there were non-fun furs flung about the stone hearth and rough timber floor. The two La-Z-Boys and matching couch were in blood red leather; the warm aroma of fur and flesh was sweet and moist. In terms of theme, I've always thought of the room as a celebration of historic Eurotrocities in virginal America North.

Teddy put down his drink, opened the (unlocked) gun locker and carefully removed Harry's most recent acquisition, suitably and sinisterly wrapped in a piece of thick black velvet.

"Holy fucking shit," I said, when Teddy told us of its appalling provenance.

"Exactly," Teddy said. "Freshly purchased at auction, in Boca Raton."

"How much?" I asked.

"He outbid Marilyn Manson."

"Really? Shit, guy. How much?"

"Fuck knows. He's completely lost it. Hundred grand, easy."

"How can we know it's real?"

"There's paperwork to authenticate. Check the initials."

"Jeez. May I touch?"

I took it in my hands. It felt small but heavy and dense with evil. What made it somehow worse were the obscenely ornate decorative flourishes festooning its gold plating, making the thing look more like some obscure Victorian gynecological implement than an actual gun. The Art Deco font initials in gold—A H—on its sour yellow ivory butt were the most shocking thing I'd ever seen with my own eyes. Just knowing that at one time that vexed vegetarian had held this very thing in his clammy little hands chilled me to the marrow. I fell into a contemplative mood.

"Make a great stocking stuffer," I said. "Care for a feel?"

"No," you replied, astonished that I'd even ask, no doubt sensing that the mere touch of such a thing would contaminate you with some horrible curse.

By then all our previous hilarity had evaporated, and you wouldn't even look at me, so dismayed were you with the abundance of weapons in the cottage, and that one weapon in particular. From outside, we could faintly hear the power saw sing and ring and then stop.

"Well," I said, trying to lighten the mood, "let's dress Harry up in his best formal ss uniform and head to town for cheeseburgers. He can pack his new Hitler gun if he likes."

"Fuck 'im," Teddy said, replacing the collector's item in the gun locker. "He'll forage in the forest if he gets hungry."

"Wait—shouldn't you lock that thing?" I asked, referring

to the gun locker, just to show you how attentive and
responsible I can be when I try.

"Can't. Numbnuts lost the keys," Teddy explained.

Harry was there all of a sudden, appearing out of
nowhere like a pop-up ghoul, browned and moist and
seasoned with sawdust, now with safety goggles around his
wattled leather neck, and wearing work gloves, but sadly
nothing else, save the sad black Speedo and the sadder still
fresh white Reeboks. He smiled knowingly because he knew
what we'd been fondling.

"Everyone thinks it is Luger," Harry said, beaming with
bashful pride of ownership. "But is not. Is Walther P.K., his
personal favourite."

He adjusted his nut sack in the sticky Speedo with a tug of
his gloved hand before adding, "You seen the initials, yeah?"

"Yeah," I said. "Sweet."

"He got in 1939. On fiftieth birthday. For giving so
much business to Walther."

Which instantly reminded me of a very unfunny joke I
once heard (Q: What did Goebbels say to Hitler? A: If I'd
known it was your birthday, I'd have baked a kike.), which is
why I snickered—not because it's funny, but because it's
funny to think of the unfunny mind that would come up
with such an unfunny joke and find it funny.

"What's funny?" you asked.

"Nothing," I replied.

I was hoping you wouldn't demure from sharing your
perspective with Harry, and you didn't disappoint. With
head cocked cutely you said, "You know what? Sorry, but I
think that's just plain straight-up fucking sick. I mean, why
would anyone want to own something like that? Seriously,
you know what? Can I throw it in the lake? Or I could give it

to someone I know to melt it down and make jewellery out
of it or something. Do the world a favour. Honestly. What a
sick thing. Makes me want to puke."

Harry grinned, his watery blue red-shot eyes splashing
with amusement. "It's collector's item. Something of
interest, an historical artefact. I am only collector. It is
disturbing for you?"

"No," you said. "I mean yes. 'Course it is. Is that what
it's for? To, like, disturb normal people?"

Harry laughed. You'd broken the ice with that, and
Harry was beginning to enjoy himself, finally at ease with
your presence.

"This is interesting to me how you are feeling about it.
May I ask your last name Miss?" Harry asked.

"What's that got to do with anything?" you replied.

I knew exactly what that had to do with anything. Harry
was of an era and sensibility that files everyone according to
his/her race, religion, and/or ethnicity, like so many breeds of
dog, and believes that one's actions and reactions are entirely
predetermined by one's kennel of origin. My barber's the
same way. That's one reason why Harry's always been so
taken by me, with my half-blank ancestry, the mystery
mongrel stray at your back door.

You told him your last name anyway, and he smiled,
satisfied, although I have no idea what insight he'd gleaned
from that.

"Aha, Ukrainian?"

"Ya figure?" Cheeky you.

"So is this the gun Hitler topped himself with?" I asked,
hoping to change the subject to something more pleasant.

"No, no. That gun does not exist, but actually was also a
Walther. His favourite, you see. That gun was destroyed,

probably in the bunker, but you know this one joker, this fake Irish Jew in Australia, he tried to sell forgery of it on market a couple of years ago. This piece here in fact is only ceremonial, only for show. So-called 'presentation model.'"

"Not suitable for suicide?" I asked.

"Well, could be used, but. . . ."

"So, like, you're some kind of major collector of Adolf Hitler shit?" you asked.

"No, no," Harry smiled, savouring your interest in him. "I collect all kinds of objects. Many, many different kinds of shits. To me, this is just for curiosity. Probably I give it away to some Holocaust foundation or some place. You see so I will do world a favour. B'nai Brith maybe. To keep out from the hands of the wrong people. So many people would kill to have it, so many Nazis around these days, you would not believe. Or maybe I should give to you, for putting in the lake. Ha ha ha. So, well then. You would care for drink Miss?"

"No," Teddy answered for you, "she would not care for drink. She would care for food. For eating? There's no food here you crazed old prick."

"Teddy," I said. "Come on boy, stay onside."

Harry only laughed.

"Okay. Dad?" Teddy continued carefully, as though talking to a slow dog. "Our guests cannot eat guns. Understand? Buy food for fuck's sake, no more guns. Or cars. Or shit. And please. Would you please try and wear pants when there's company?"

Harry folded his arms in a frown, his stance combative.

"I bought food. Is in the car, in the Buick, help yourselfs. I told you—trunk is full with food. Everything I bought. I told you five, ten times already. People coming to stay, I know what to do. Check the car you don't believe.

Everything, steak, everything is there. Is sitting in the trunk all the day in the hot sun, rotting by now. All you took was the booze bottles of course, but nothing else. Why?"

"Don't lie, you mad bastard," Teddy said. "You never said anything about food."

"Why? I will tell you why. Because you are clown, that's why. Always being idiot, like clown, never thinking."

"Dad, God just phoned. He's got a pair of pants he wants you to try on."

Harry directed his twisted grin at you. "In Lithuania there is saying—'Everyone loves the funny clown at the wedding party, but his father only smiles in his beard and waits for later, to hang him in the barn.'"

He chuckled at this bit of folk whimsy, but no one else seemed to find it funny. Except for Teddy.

"That's beautiful dad," Teddy flashed happily. "Can we hear it in the original? I bet it fucking rhymes. Drop us a beat boy."

"Harry," I said. "Come on, let's go to town. We'll get something to eat, it's too late to cook anyways."

"But wait. I don't think they'll serve insane old drunk naked guys," Teddy pointed out. "Dad, why don't you relax here in the nude, hanging clowns in the barn, while we go to town for something to eat?"

"Bah, eat my shit," Harry said, waving his hand contemptuously, turning to leave. "Was small joke only."

"Harry," I called after him.

"Fuck 'im. Forget 'im." Teddy said. "Let's do a quick bump and go."

I thought he'd never ask. I wasn't sure if you'd be into it, though, given the circumstances. As it turned out, we were both more than ready to hitch up the reindeer by then, what with the stress and strain of the long, hot drive, followed by a series of (for you) unpleasant surprises. Teddy chopped and served several fat lines on a big game hunting magazine on the mantel, while travelling back and forth to the kitchen to mix drinks and sort things out with Harry. We could hear their loud fake talking and frightful forced laughter, the hate-drenched acrimony of seconds ago magically forgotten, and all was swell between father and son.

"Brother," you said as you circled and swooped in for an additional line, "scene's too freaking weird for me."

And now T, a word or two about drugs and alcohol.

As you no doubt recall, there was a lot of both going down that weekend, as there always is whenever Teddy is around. And clearly, they were an important contributing factor to what ultimately transpired there. My judgment wasn't quite as sharp as it might have been had I not been more or less shit-faced for pretty much the entire weekend. A more lucid me, for example, would have bundled you into the Pony at first light next morning instead of going for that ill-advised boat cruise. But that's not what I want to discuss presently.

Instead, what I would like to confront here is your claim that I have been a corrupting influence on your character, a claim that you have made countless times before and will probably make again soon, in a Court of Law, under leading questions from Crown Council. According to this for-mulation, before meeting me, you were in essence a good and dutiful farm girl, as pure as the spring rain on a Prairie morning, and raised a devout Catholic to boot. Clever and plucky, you'd ventured into the wide world with a farm family's golden girl promise of accomplishment. Then I happened in your life. It was I who taught you how to smoke cigarettes and stay up late in torn stockings, cultivating a taste for old time reggae and certain kinds of drugs, especially Rock-Steady Reggae and the Hard Powder Drugs that you came to enjoy so much—the soothing soulful heartbeat of those great old tunes, and the wicked potent power of those great old narcotics to clarify everything, and make life itself ten thousand times more vivid than life itself.

Remember the illuminating surprise of your very first time?

"Oh my," you said, illuminated by surprise. "Now I see."

As another example, remember last Christmas? You'd cashed in your gift plane ticket home for the holidays, and we holed up at Chris and Sandy's flat for a couple of days, like some nascent cult cell, pinned indoors by a thirteen-hour blizzard, feeling too fragile to leave, alternating lines of junk with lines of blow, singing "Let it snow, let it snow, let it snow," all four of us snuggled together under a duvet on their living room floor. Until the pale dawn of Christmas morning reminded you of family and friends back on the farm, and made you miserable for want of them. You blamed me then for everything—for toxifying the Yuletide season, for how raunched-out dirty you felt, for despoiling the little farm girl you and making her lose her way. Most of all, for dashing your dreams of a springtime farm wedding with the stout Lord Byron of Brampton.

Later we watched the Queen's Christmas address live on television, which made you yet sadder still because your mom—an anti-Bolshevik, pro-monarchist—would be watching it too, back home at the farm on the Prairie. I felt terrible for you T. So much so that I ran you a bubble bath and then set out to hunt down an open corner store for eggs and milk to make guilt ridden griddlecakes. But when I got back, you'd dumped me (for the first of three times) via a hasty half-page scribbled note, and you were gone.

I had to leave too because Sandy's mom and stepdad were on their way in from Niagara Falls for a family dinner, so all I could do on that bright white Christmas afternoon was wander around in the melting snow by myself. You'd locked down your attic flat in the Annex and gone into hiding, and my mom was home in Nfld. for the holidays, leaving me to stagger about aimlessly and alone, under the bleak black weight of a ten ton high-regret hangover that only a two day cheap red wine and expensive white powder binge can deliver, until I was eventually forced back into Brent's for somewhere to shelter, the whole time knowing that I fully deserved my suffering for all that I had done to you. For wrecking your life and all.

But now I'm not so sure T. Now I see that these things can be looked at from an entirely different perspective. Come, stand over here and check out this view for a bit.

It was you who were the corrupter of me.

You exploited my genetically predetermined disposition to alcohol and substance abuse, an inclination that was encoded in my mom's family's DNA way back when her earliest prototype ancestors got up on hind legs, picked up a stick, and started walking around, looking for a way to get high. And then steal a horse. Admit that I was so right for you T. Not only was I there to provide you with the intoxicants and occasions to use them (which you wanted), but I was also there as a convenient receptacle (which you needed) for all the guilt you felt after the fact, especially if you had to call in sick. In short, you had me working both sides of the street, you bad Catholic girl who wants a spanking.

You never just said no T. Not even once.

I have to leave off here. This line of thinking has made me miffed. I've completely lost the thread on the cottage story, and I find myself still stumbling the streets alone on a sunny snow melt Christmas Day,

Madly Aching For You,

e.

Dear T,

Happy Anniversary T-bird!

I'm not so good with dates, but I'm almost dead certain that this weekend marks one year since we first officially met.

Remember? I sure as shit do. It happened at a party.

The first thing I said to you was, "How much you weigh kid? I bet I could lift you right over my head."

The first thing you said to me was, "Rocking. Try it guy and I'll fucking kill you, swear to god."

Do you believe in love at first sight? Me neither. It must have been something other than that then, something about—forgive me—old souls, bearing vital news from another time and place, a deja-luv, that made me mad for you from the second I saw you, unable to keep my eyes and hands off of you, watching and wanting to touch your every move and gesture. That sly sexy sideways smile and chippy tilt of the head, your boyish stance with left hand on girlish pelvic bone, the straight cut blue-black bangs and pert ponytail, that slight compelling overbite. You T, altogether so small and fine that you'd fit just so in my pocket, like a slim stolen jewel. And such smart eyes you. The Asian cast of your cut stone blue-green-grey Slavic eyes. Fresh familiar you, plus a tasteful tat or two—the lovely long-tailed Prairie magpie lurking beneath your right polka dot sleeve, the crop circle as yet undisclosed—and all the while the way you pretended to not like being looked at.

How did I look at you then? Here's how I looked at you then. I looked at you so brazenly that I saw beyond your blatant beauty to discover your tiny flaws and imperfections, and finding them, I was happy. Why? Because each tiny flaw and imperfection gave me a better chance to have you for myself, I strategized, since they might be seen to discourage competition. That's why it was your very tiny flaws and imperfections that I loved most deeply of all.

You were in big trouble T.

Did I care that you then had a fiancé named Byron? Not especially. Because no fiancé named Byron could ever see what I saw when I looked at you. Your flawless flaws and perfect imperfection. I already knew all about them.

Boy did I need a drink.

It was a swell party on a sweltering hot summer night, with pretty party lanterns and the miracle of a backyard swimming pool. Not long after you'd left to go home with Byron, I fractured a rib lawn wrestling. But I didn't care about that. I lost my glasses too. But I didn't care about that either. I'd seen you and met you and talked to you, and that was all I could care about.

I for sure didn't care about your fiancé named Byron whom I met informally in the pool after you and I had fallen in, which, by the way, was technically not my fault even though I shouldn't have been trying to lift you over my head since you'd plainly asked me not to, several tequilas earlier. I told you I was pushed. Then when you swam away in a huff, like a livid little dolphin in black and pink polka-dot blouse and green Capri pants to curl up beneath the surface in the deep end, so stunned was I by the dreamy vision of lovely mad you, a perfect angry little ball afloat in the turquoise pool light, that I went under to join you. My goal was to stay in the deep end with you forever, just the two of us together. We'd begin by spawning. That's when I met your fiancé named Byron. There he was, also in the deep end, having jumped in to save your life, I suppose. No words were exchanged by way of introduction (after all, we were underwater), but I remember that we briefly checked each other out eye to eye, like two hungry predators from opposite ends of the ocean, meeting by chance at a kill site.

I resurfaced in time to catch a glimpse of your slanting wet panty line as you slipped out of the pool and was wishing that I hadn't. Then Byron popped up and flopped out and took you home.

Luckily, before falling into the pool, we'd had the opportunity to acknowledge our special connection. Or at least I had. It was never my style to be so relentless T, but fuck style I figured. Style is for pro players, and I was but an inspired amateur in need of a number. I cornered you once, twice and then a third time. That's when I gathered your data. But not until after you'd informed me of your fiancé named Byron.

"I don't care about that," I said. "I could be like, your girlfriend."

"Oh yeah? I bet you'd make a terrible girlfriend."

"No I wouldn't. I'd call. We'd talk every day. I'd make a great girlfriend."

"I got tons of girlfriends, boys and girls. I don't need another one."

"Not even a super great girlfriend? Like a favourite cousin girlfriend?"

"You could do that?"

"Be like your best cousin girlfriend? Shit, girl. Just watch me."

Generally speaking, a best cousin girlfriend doesn't stalk, and I wanted to be your best cousin girlfriend ever. It wasn't easy. Because even when I wasn't seeing you, there you were. You were every true blond blue-black dyed hair with strawberry streaks in a ponytail sporting a poor-boy peaked cap, smoky mascara-eyed petite chicky-boo gliding by on a bicycle or checking her cellphone or jumping into a cab or waiting at the corner for a light to change. The city was suddenly teaming with you. And all the things of the city became connected with you. A streetcar losing its cable sparking blue-white in the rain made me fear for your safety; I looked into the eyes of panhandlers, jealously wondering if they'd looked into your eyes that day. Some nights in bars I couldn't stop drinking about you. Moreover, a cat snoozing in a storefront window, the smell of perfume or pork roast, the click of heels on a polished floor, a mailman whistling a tuneless tune, the sun, the moon, an empty sky—who knows why?—all these things and about a billion others conspired to make me think of you.

Admit you were stalking me too.

In addition to some light stalking, there was also a lot of sweet-talking. At first we were all talk. You said you loved the way I talked. And talked. Yet the first time we necked

was because you wanted me to stop talking. We'd met by
happy semi-fluke at The Duke of Cannot with some mutual
semi-friends. I offered to accompany you home, and on the
way, we walked and talked and (deliciously) held hands
before deciding to stop and talk at The Red Neck's Son, just
the two of us, for a nightcap. That's where we first started
necking, to make me stop talking.

We were talking at the time about my twin brother
Douglas. I told you about how Douglas and I, when we were
twelve, climbed the roof of a garage to watch the May two-
four fireworks from the lakeshore, and that he'd plummeted
to the pavement attempting to leap onto the roof of the
garage beside us, provoked by a double-dog dare by a mean,
older, fat, red-headed white kid named Craig. The roof was
rotten and a board broke so Douglas tripped and plunged
headfirst into a coma, followed by death after two weeks in
Intensive. This you called my "Holden Caulfield thing."

"How do you mean?" I asked.

"You know, in Catcher in the Rye? His little brother dies
and he goes all nuts and punches out the windows—the
windows of his garage by the way, coincidentally. It's the
standard motif in the alienated boy coming-of-age type
thingy. Someone dies and the character is all traumatized
about it but doesn't realize it, but of course the reader does."

"Really? I don't even remember that part. All I
remember is this kid moping around Manhattan, getting
hammered, staying in a hotel. Firing a hooker. Like to me
the whole thing seemed like a Richie Rich comic, only for
some reason Richie's acting like some cranky fucked up
war vet. And wait—doesn't he stalk and kill John Lennon in
the sequel?"

"You should read it again. It might actually resonate

with you. Because I mean, that's horrible about your brother. I can't even imagine. What kind of sadness is that?"

"Yeah, it's pretty weird and all, especially 'cause he was like, you know, my twin, my identical twin. It's like I can get this feeling, even now, that someone's missing. I'll look around and go, who's missing? But no one's missing. It's just Douglas. I sometimes sense like he is around, just hanging out watching me, you know, living through me."

"Oh my god that is so sad. It's sweet. But sad."

And that was that. I knew I had you, right then and there. Because what actually resonated with me was that this was in fact your Holden Caulfield thing. You suddenly saw me as some sensitive damaged boy in a book, and you couldn't help responding to that, despite your best interests. In typical T style, your way of revealing this was cunningly coded.

"You know what's weird? I always thought if I ever met some guy who tried to pull some Holden Caulfield shit on me? I'd for sure end up throwing a drink in his face and running away screaming."

"Good thinking girl. Well then. Shall I freshen your drink?"

I can't speak for Holden Caulfield and what kind of shit he was trying to pull. But I will admit that I was determined to take full advantage of this gigantic hole in your armour. I should be ashamed of myself for exploiting the tragic death of my twin brother in order to get into your green Capri pants. But I'm not. Dougie would've been totally cool with that.

I was halfway into my third in a row Douglas and me story when you said, "Quiet. Just for a second. Okay? Shhhhh."

"Sorry. I'm boring you."

"Yeah. No. Just for a second."

We sat there in a quiet corner, necking till last call. I
remember you being kind of sad just then, and I vowed to
myself that I would never make you sad ever again. There's
a vow I failed horribly to keep. Soon after, I made another
vow I didn't keep. I vowed that I'd leave you alone since
you told me you feared that you might be falling for me
and yet you had plans of spending your current lifetime
with Byron, and you just weren't a double life kind of a girl.
Our occasional chaste hand-holding sneaking about was
serving mainly to make you miserable.

We discussed the matter in depth over our last lunch
summit at the Saigon Palace, and then parted on the street.
I remember it being a splendid early fall day, sunny and
windy bright, with low scudding clouds sailing downtown
off the lake. I was riding my new favourite bike that
afternoon, the orange '76 Peugeot fixie I'd just fixed, and
clad completely in battling plaids. You were in a slim,
structured coal-black wool skirt, pastel blue stockings, with a
pink silk headscarf, saddle brown gloves, and (I'm guessing
here) French-cut red wine panties. We looked simply
smashing together, and clearly meant to be so. Yet I smiled
in sad sage acceptance, and we hugged quickly, like
travelling siblings wishing each other happy-trail fond
farewells in a foreign city. Then after I watched you walk
away, I ducked into a lane off Spadina and went behind a
dumpster to throw up my Number 32 Lunch Special—
vermicelli and shredded pork with spring rolls and a Sprite.

Sorry, but there was just no possible way I was going to
keep that vow T.

I'm sorry about almost everything T.

T-girl, I'm most of all sorry I ever made you come to
Red Snake Lake.

However, I'm not at all sorry about those nights I made you stay up late, my dream girl party doll T. Generally speaking, it was fun. But was it fun that Friday night at the lake when we stayed up late and went to town with Teddy? I'd give it a qualified sort of, in a way, in retrospect, I guess.

We each toot one last line and now we're all frisky fresh and raring to go. It was agreed: we must head for town immediately. We burst outside, feeling it big now, aloft in a mood of fun-seeking fearlessness, far and away above it all. What a beautiful night it was too, with the forest stars dancing in your bright eyes and the fresh lake air lustering your silky skin.

"Quick, to the Pony," I said.

"Oh ho, no, no," said Teddy. "Style over substance. Always."

By that he meant we should deploy Harry's big solid gold seventies Buick Electra for the ride to town.

"Right this way," he said, keen as always to impress.

But then he missed, tripped, and fell over a white painted boulder on the lawn, thereby partially impaling himself on his car keys. Which made it obvious that I was the designated driver for the night, and also that we should be using a less flash ride for the occasion. It took some wrangling and wrestling to get Teddy away from his dad's car, another questionable collector's item, that hulking heavy, gleaming golden barge in the driveway, so long and low and wide it was hard to picture as a transportation device, like the first time you saw a 747 on the tarmac. It looked like the wheeled burial sarcophagus for a disco-era Aztec king.

You watched impatiently while Teddy and I did battle

over the fallen car keys on the lawn, and then decided things
by going to the Pony and hopping in the front seat.

"Hey!" you honked, "fuck heads!" you honked twice
more, "Let's go already!"

Sometimes common sense will prevail, even with Teddy,
so we were soon on the highway in the Hyundai Pony,
zooming for town.

With windows down and cigarette smoke swirling in the
highway breeze, I remember our discussing a wide range of
subjects—the human impulse to collect shit, the Hitler gun
and Teddy's rapidly diminishing inheritance, your girlhood
collection of Beanie Babies, my dead daredevil brother's
collection of bird bones, which I've somehow managed to
lose (by the way, have you happened to find them anywhere?)
and again, the Hitler gun and Teddy's rapidly diminishing
inheritance.

Here is a perfect illustration of why blow is so godawful
stupid. It couples a world-beating attitude with a very
narrow agenda—basically, the need to set the agenda. You
chew your lip while waiting sweetly for whoever is talking to
shut the fuck up so you can say whatever amazing thing it is
you need to say, even though you know full well that no
one's truly listening, that they're just chewing their lips,
waiting sweetly for you to shut the fuck up so they can say
whatever amazing thing it is that they need to say. And so
on and so forth. How stupidly boring. That's why coke's the
choice of Fascists everywhere. And it's also one of the
reasons why I've resolved never to do blow ever again. In
fact, since arriving in jail, I've resolved never to do any
drugs ever again. Except, of course, for reefer, ecstasy, some
of the friendlier cousins in the synthetic Opiate family and,
on very special and rare wilderness camping occasions, acid.

But for sure not blow. It's a stupid drug. Fun, yes. Big fun.
But big stupid fun.

So by the time we got to town we were all talking in
German accents all at once, sparking with that brash and
flash, rock star ready and willing, big hearted warm vibe that
blow brings at first, supersmart on the stupidpowder. I
wheeled into the only establishment still open—Larry's by
the Lake—the kind of place that self-respecting cottage
families would have carefully avoided for however many
generations they'd been cottaging in these parts. I slid the
Pony to a styling sideways stop in the gravel lot, and we
leapt out like late arriving action heroes.

Larry's looked like a former gas station because it was,
and since the nowhere-near-the-lake back deck was packed
beyond capacity, we were forced to find a table in the
steaming guts of the place, up against the white brick wall
of what was once a service bay. I could swear I smelled
gasoline. The sign out front claimed Larry's was "World
Famous for Food," but instead of ordering something deep-
fried delicious (our appetites gone, another blow by-
product), we ordered a bucket-sized pitcher of margaritas on
special, and signed on for some karaoke.

The sights and sounds from the stage were kind of
blurry from where we sat, but it appeared as though a series
of rotund drunk rural folk were taking revenge on the New
Country Music trend for ruining their lives. At last your
name was called, and up you went. You'd changed into
tavern-in-the-town wear before we'd left the cottage. So
when you took the stage, in dark pencil-legged jeans rolled
once at the cuff, suede boots, and black and yellow checked
pearl button cowgirl shirt, your blond hair tinted pink and
tight in pigtails, the entire crowd, men and women alike,

were transfixed, so dazzling diamond-bright were you. Your
sly rendition of "Ring My Bell" started shyly at first, but
soon found its pace, and eventually brought at least three of
the tavern's dancers to their knees. Literally.

You were followed by Teddy's obvious and horrible
"House of the Rising Sun," presented in a mash-up Tom
Waits growl meets Prince falsetto that prompted the droll
and chubby bearded DJ to question the very Meaning of
Existence when it was finally finished, Teddy spent and
sprawled flat on his back at the edge of the stage, freestyling
about hanging clowns in the barn. Unhappy with the
selections available, I eventually settled on the Jim Morrison
classic "People Are Strange," which I delivered with
adolescent conviction to scattered applause. For that I blame
Teddy's heckling—"show us your tits!"—since it totally
alienated my audience. On paper I was committed to sing
"Sometimes When We Touch" directly at you as a special
surprise treat. But meanwhile I was beginning to become
concerned about Teddy's deportment, and the negative vibes
it was engendering among Larry's staff and patrons alike.

Part of the problem was basic presentation. Teddy's
never been able to adopt a thematically whole or halfway
convincing mode of dress. He always pretends to be one
unlikely thing while hedging his bets by simultaneously
pretending to be something even less likely. Dork is his one
consistent style note. For that evening's outing, Teddy had
selected a slacker surfer dude meets horny folk-troubadour
look—open blue Hawaiian over a wife beater, crudely cut,
way too short brown corduroy cut-offs, black cowboy boots,
and a summer beard of dirt. Regrettably, he'd chosen to
accessorize with orange tinted cycling glasses, some sort of
flak jacket bush vest, and one of his dad's Tilley's adventure

hats for retired teachers, which, taken altogether, made him look like a hillbilly foreign war correspondent on a crack binge, trapped behind enemy lines. This alone could have caused trouble, but what made trouble certain was Teddy's insistence that he was well known and warmly admired by all the local rustics when in fact everyone there seemed to regard him as some shit-dipped man from Mars. He worked the room like a car-lot Kiwanis recruiter, backslapping and yee-hawing around, oblivious to the baleful glares of his imaginary friends.

"Is he autistic or something?" you asked. "Like is that Asperger's?"

"No, no," I explained. "He's just a little insecure."

Anticipating trouble, I set myself a challenge: prevent Teddy from getting seriously killed, which, if you remember, I more or less succeeded in doing.

My tactic was simple. I got Teddy to sit down at the table and focus on our ostensible mission for the weekend.

"So what do you figure?" I asked. "Think old Harry Chup is amenable to our business proposal?"

"What business proposal?" you asked.

"Well, aren't you the sleazy motherfucker?" Teddy asked rhetorically. "Aren't you just the sleaziest of all sleazy motherfuckers? Know why?"

"No," I answered. "Why?"

"'Cause you are, that's why. You are one dirty, low down mofo you. Think about this whole thing and all you think about is money. It's that fleeing with the stolen watermelon survival instinct you got going. Us plain honest white folk simply don't think like that, do we girl?"

"That's 'cause you all are devils. Admit it. Y'all here should come clean about that right tonight. The whole room

should come clean tonight. Promise I won't tell no one
'bout it."

"Why are your people so angry?" Teddy asked. "Why?"

"Wait. Think about what whole thing?" you asked.

"Think about money's not what it's about at all. Fuck
the money. It's about belief baby. It's about faith.
Commitment. The goddamn golden touch. I need him to
hook hard."

"Who hook what hard?" you asked.

"Well actually, Teddy," I said. "Who gives a fuck? Long
as he signs the fucking cheque."

"The fucking cheque for what?" you asked.

"See, that's exactly what I mean. You may well be
incapable of comprehending this deal, and this makes me
feel sad for you," Teddy said, in a tone so gallingly
condescending that I might have hit him were he not the
one carrying. Which reminded me—our blow levels were
plummeting rapidly. We'd need to freshen up soon if we
hoped to remain friends.

"Like not capable of comprehending what?" you asked.

"Yeah," I said. "Not capable of comprehending what?"

"Basically," Teddy continued, "first off, admit you're
basically a skeezy cunt. I mean you think of Harry, all you
think of is a big shit sack full of money. That's all he is to you."

"Wait," you said. "Why is he basically a skeezy cunt?"

"Yeah, wait," I said. "Why am I basically a skeezy cunt?
And by the way, I have never said anything of the sort about
Harry. Ever. You are so chockfull of shit Teddy, it's fucking
mortifying. Anyways, drop it—let's do a bump before I have
to hurt you."

"Don't get me wrong," Teddy clarified. "I love you my
brother. I love you to death—you're brilliant, you're the best,

you are my one true gallant Black Knight at the fucking round table. But you just don't get it."

"Okay," I said. "So explain Sir Knight. What don't I get? Anyways, actually fuck it. Instead let's do a bump and compete in feats of strength. Right here. Right now."

"Let's don't," you said.

"What you don't get, see," Teddy explained, "is that Harry is an evil miserable shit sack full of money. That's all he is, that's all ever he was. What you don't get is he's just pissing it away. I believe he's terminal with ass cancer so he's just blowing the whole wad, buying cars and guns and property and fuck knows what—dirty fucker—he's got three ex-wives and three kids and what the fuck is it? Four, five grandkids. And no one is going to see a nickel of all his bazillions by the time he finally checks out. But I will promise you this. When it's all said and done? At the end of the day? I will shit on that man's grave."

"Nice," you said. "Okay cool let's go."

"It's last call," I pointed out.

"Yeah," Teddy said, "it is last call," as though those words had some deep metaphysical resonance for him and him alone, and no one else could possibly comprehend the profundity of his awesome existential dilemma.

The waitress passed by then, pushing through the spinning-thinning crowd of rip-roaring drunks. To get her attention, Teddy reached around to grasp her hand, but missed, and accidentally groped the distressed denim housing her family discount detergent box-sized behind.

"Hey there Marnie," Teddy said, "another pitcher for my friends—on me as per usually."

"Don't touch," she replied curtly, adding, "You're cut off."

"Mary, sweet Mary," Teddy said smiling. "You can do us

one more, can't you? For little old me?"

"It's Marie asshole. And you heard me. You're cut off. Good night."

Marie plucked up our empty plastic mugs and jug, efficient and swift, making no effort to conceal her want to be done and home.

And I saw it coming already.

"Hey! Martha! You slatternly cow you," Teddy called after her, followed by a shockingly foul and lengthy invective, not a word of which will be repeated here.

"Holy fuck dude," I said. "What a bad idea."

Marie sensibly pretended not to hear. But, unfortunately, some of the tavern's patrons, who had been studying Teddy's act and not enjoying it very much, heard it loud and clear, and they didn't pretend otherwise. In fact, if I'm not mistaken, a number of folks there had been hoping for Teddy to make precisely this kind of grievous social faux pas, so eager were they for an opportunity to correct him.

Presently, a low and wide lobster-faced fellow in a Cat hat appeared at our tableside, with a number of his compadres crowding in behind him like curious cattle.

"What in fuck did you just say there bud?" the lobster-faced fellow asked, his tone polite, measured and affable.

"Nothing," I said, with a rueful smile. "He's just pissed, and we're just leaving." I realized that getting to my feet might be misconstrued as provocation, so I chose to remain seated while addressing his concerns.

Teddy was grinning in another direction, muttering a song.

"Eh? Come again?" the lobsterman inquired of Teddy, ignoring me.

Teddy then asked the musical question: "Did someone

74 CHERRY ELECTRA

say Tillsonburgh?" singing it loud, eyes blazing black behind the orange cycling glasses. "My back still aches when I hear that word."

"Oh dear," I chuckled, in an effort to reframe reality for lobsterman. "He's fucked and we're leaving. Dude, let's roll."

I sat forward slightly, still unwilling to stand up just yet, not wanting to be the hapless dink who gets nailed first, merely for being the first dink to make myself available for getting nailed first. I felt Teddy should take the lead in that regard.

Teddy removed his sunglasses, revealing eyes as bleak and blank as sewer holes, and he and lobsterman stared at one another, locked and loaded. I knew then that there was no avoiding a melee, that at this point it could at best be mitigated slightly. Teddy does love a good fight. Actually, that's not true. Teddy loves a bad fight, one in which he gets to hit his opponent hard and first, preferably by surprise. There was no chance for any such surprises now though, and even if Teddy were to strike the lobsterman by stealth, it had better be in the sweet spot with a crowbar, judging by the impressive thickness of the man's cranium. I was keeping an eye on lobsterman's hands, and noted with concern that they were those of a worker—meaty, red and ringless. It occurred to me that he could well be Marie's husband or cousin or both, and that Teddy had opened up a whole new world of experience for us, a world of complex interconnecting webs of blood bonds and loyalties among families and friends, of hard toil in resource extraction and tourist servicing, of bench clearing hockey brawls and snowmobile fatalities on half frozen lakes. A world where the resentment of smug city assholes is an essential component of one's very identity. Most salient at the moment, a world where the tale of how two smug city assholes got

thoroughly pounded in the parking lot at Larry's-by-the-Lake
would provide righteous entertainment around broken home
kitchen tables and Camaro on blocks in the backyard barbeques for many months to come.

I had no choice but to play the chick card.

"Come on babe," I turned to you, "let's dip."

It may have seemed cowardly of me to employ you as a
human shield at that point, but you must admit that it was
also completely necessary, the paradox being that by
appearing to protect you, I was in effect protecting myself.
No man of honour would strike another man who is
(pretending) to protect his girl, especially a sweet petite girl
who had earlier charmed the pants off the entire tavern with
her karaoke stylings. And anyway, it was Teddy who was the
big bone of contention.

Teddy managed to slip in front of us, so we left the bar
in a defensive wedge formation, with him lustily singing his
way through a medley of Stomping Tom numbers, you and
I following behind, my arm about your shoulder. I could
sense the human wrath close on our heels, trailing along
after us like a tropical storm. The moment we were out the
door, down the steps, and out on the open gravel parking
lot, the storm broke. Lobsterman seized the opportunity
he'd been waiting for. That is, he came around from behind
us to seize Teddy by the scruff of his collar and swung him
around to meet his fist. But he hadn't calculated how
spinnable Teddy was. Lobsterman took a swing and a miss,
and Teddy spun right around him, one cowboy boot in the
air, before sprawling out on the gravel. A portion of Teddy's
Hawaiian shirt remained in lobsterman's hand. He glanced
at it in disgust before dropping it like a dirty diaper.

"Get up," lobsterman said, contradicting these

instructions with a hard swift kick to Teddy's face, knocking the cycling glasses and Tilley's hat sideways.

Down and stunned with nose gushing blood, Teddy smartly rolled away from a supplementary kick to the face, while reaching into his pocket in search of that something sharp and surprising he carries. I saw where this was headed. The lesson Teddy took from the events of 9/11 is that one should never be without a box cutter. And now that he had his box cutter out, Teddy was crabbing around the gravel to find his feet, with the clear intention of using it on lobsterman, but not before taking a second swift kick in the face.

That's when I stepped in and saved the day with the Hitler gun.

I know you won't like this part T, but I have to include it anyway.

To prevent a third-man-in violation, an earnestly bearded drunk bachelor couch uncle, rocking his best big-night-on-the-town leather vest, had been pinning my arm to my back in some kind of an improvised Navy Seal sudden death grip. I'd easily jolted his hairy jaw with my free elbow, broke loose, and jumped between lobsterman and Teddy.

Instantly I had the Hitler gun out and levelled at lobsterman.

"What? Wait! Don't!" you loudly went, which I think helped lobsterman to recognize that it was in fact a real live gun pointed at his face, and not an antique curling iron. Tumbling to the realization that it was an actual handgun, he reeled back, amazed.

"What the fuck bud?" he asked, hands out wide, backing away, bouncing on the balls of his feet like a corner-back, as though thinking he could dodge a bullet.

"Don't!" you said again. Which sort of annoyed me. I

mean obviously the thing was but an unloaded toy. Or what? Did you think I was going to just stand there and shoot that guy point-blank in the face? Seriously T. Please. Come on, think about it.

"Step off," I said, shakily. "We're leaving. I already tried to tell you that."

"That's right bitch," Teddy said, now upright and angling toward lobsterman with box cutter in fist. "Now I fuck up your shit."

I might have anticipated this—that Teddy would expect me to hold the entire town at gunpoint while he went to work on lobsterman with his box cutter. Luckily, Teddy was so sloshed that when I straight-armed him as he tried to charge by, he slipped and crashed backwards to the gravel, prompting fans of physical comedy who'd been watching the proceedings to laugh heartily.

"Forget it Teddy. Let's get out of here," I said, holding the pistol pointed high, in fleeing bank robber Dust-Bowl era style.

Teddy picked himself up off the parking lot, part by painful part, and then all three of us crab-walked sideways, warily watching the crowd as we made for the car. Seconds later we were in the Pony and speeding away. In the mirror I caught a glimpse of a major mob forming and fuming in the parking lot. Would someone call the cops? Likely not, I figured. Everyone had to drunk-drive home now, so they probably weren't any more interested in police involvement than we were. As we hit the highway, I made a mental note to never again ride into that town in my distinctively rust ravaged gunmetal grey Hyundai Pony.

You were silently simmering in the back seat, glaring out the window, furious about the turn of events, but especially at me for having that evil Hitler gun on my person. I knew how shocked and pissed you were by that T, and I was looking forward to the opportunity to explain myself. See, when you'd gone to change before we left for town, I'd snuck back to the gun locker and slipped the Hitler gun in the inner pocket of my green linen jacket. As a joke. My intention was to use it as a prop for a gag I had planned—to be honest, I forget exactly what the gag was now, but I bet it was a good one. Perhaps it was for use when we were all riding buzzed back to the cottage, at which point I might have pulled it out and said something explosively comedic. It hadn't worked out that way, but I still had some hope to salvage the joke. Once we were back in the cottage in our room alone together, you'd be mad at me still, but then rendered helpless with laughter when I pulled out the gun and delivered my joke, which would make you momentarily madder still. And then we'd have mad sex. What I had in mind was post-mad, partially clothed sex atop the armchair in our bedroom.

But then the car struck an animal.

First there was a vivid flash of fur and mirror bright yellow eyes caught in the headlights, then a plush thump bang, followed by a baby-like blood-curdling shriek scratch and a rumbling tumble beneath, and finally, the lusty roar of the engine freed from its muffler.

This then was Portent Two—the car accidentally running over an innocent woodland creature who'd made the mistake of crossing the road at the exact time and place that we happened to be travelling.

I realize I took the long way to get to Portent Two, and I'm sure you were beginning to wonder why I bothered to depict the context for this event in such unrewarding detail. Perhaps you thought I thought that some of the other events of the evening—Harry in a Speedo, Teddy singing karaoke, the confrontation with lobsterman, the Hitler gun in the parking lot—could be characterized as portents. But I know better. I know how your mind works with regard to portents and the like. All of that was just some amazingly stupid random shit that happened, all a mere prelude to Portent Two. Which was obviously the hitting of the animal by the car.

I have no idea what kind of animal we hit. Of course, Mountain Man Teddy assumed to easily identify the species of the luckless beast—I forget what he said—but all I know is that it was somewhere between a very small bear and a very large beaver, and that while rolling under the car, the wily critter succeeded in tearing the exhaust pipe loose from the muffler in revenge. Instantly, the happily humming Hyundai Pony became a wounded, howling wwii Spitfire fighter plane looking for a French farm field to make a crash landing. But I daren't stop to assess the damage to the car's undercarriage, or even to see if we could perhaps nurse the unfortunate animal back to health for fear that an opp cruiser might chance by and invite me to provide a roadside breath sample. Not to mention my concerns about the onboard drugs and weapons, and that highly charged negative scene we'd left at Larry's-by-the-Lake. Perhaps an armed posse had already formed up and were by then in hot pursuit.

I had no choice but to return swiftly to base.

The unmuffled roar of the engine now made com-munication impossible, aside from monosyllabic shouts and singing (Teddy), so little was said on the rest of the drive home. I sensed there was slim hope for sex now, mad or otherwise, because I knew what you were thinking T. I adjusted the mirror so that I could study your hard little face fixed in foxy frown, glaring at the dark bush gliding past.

That's Number Two, you were thinking, and Number Three will be the Big One.

The ultra most stupidest thing about blow is that no one quits with it until every last line is blown and all blades and surfaces licked clean. Not for you though T, at least not that night. You wisely went to bed soon after we got back to the cottage.

But I can't bring myself to write about that now.

It's taken me all day and night to write this far, and now the lights are low but never fully out in jail, and the nighty-night jailhouse noises—the banging and clanging, the barking and braying—are rolling through here like foul weather, and I'm stretched out on my styrofoam pad on the floor of my overcrowded concrete sleepover cell, wishing and imagining that I'd gone straight to bed with you when we got back to the cottage that Friday night.

Don't mind me if I do now anyway T, even though it's too late.

Don't mind me if I slip under the covers and spoon in right beside you and whisper in your ear,

Good night sweet T-bird deluxe. And so good night my tiny perfect T.

Love,

e.

Dear T,

Great news from the Central Metro Detention Centre. I quit smoking. Because you cannot smoke in the Central Metro Detention Centre. I also quit drinking. Because you cannot drink in the Central Metro Detention Centre.

Well then there you have it—at last some small ray of good pierces the bleak dark bad of my dismal incarceration. The withdrawal from nicotine was a mind-bending, soul-shaking, body-battering ordeal, during which I met myself coming the other way as a non-smoking twelve-year-old boy, all clear eyed, tender and pure. I have to admit though, soon as I get out of here, the first thing I'm going to do is take that boy directly to the crusty tree shaded patio out back of the Dog Gone Inn, to relax and enjoy with plentiful pints of St. Andre's Special Amber and a pack of Du Maurier Extra Light King Size, plus Jäger shots and a half-gram of toot. Just writing that sentence made my mouth water. The kid will have to carry me home.

The far greater good news today is that I've succeeded in containing the Manfred menace. This might not seem like much to you, out there rocking in the free world, but in here it's a very big deal indeed. Small things can become quite big in here. Small things can be life and death in here.

It all started, ironically, with Manfred in a foul mood. He'd just returned from some court proceeding, and I could tell at a glance that things weren't going so good in Manfredland. He appeared stressed, his manner manic, and his overall demeanour that of a red-headed incendiary device, one toe-tap from exploding. To the uninitiated, he might have seemed merely jocular, in what could be perceived as an especially expansive mood. But I wasn't fooled. He was yapping way too loud, blatantly on the boil. I'd characterize his condition as Code Red Lethal. I don't want to sound racist here T, but I have to admit that angry white people in jail scare the shit out of me.

It was just after the seventh inning stretch out in the yard, and we were back inside milling about the range, waiting for evening chow. Attempting to attain invisibility while at the same time keeping myself informed of Manfred's whereabouts, I found a corner of the range from where I could pretend to be watching "Friends" on the TV bolted to the wall in the opposite corner, about twenty yards away. It looked like Chandler was dining out at a restaurant with a swimsuit model burn victim, but I couldn't be certain without my glasses.

And then it happened.

"Harry Potter, you soggy douche bag, how's it hanging?" Manfred brayed, striding my way.

Usually I say nothing to his open-ended inquiries, faking a face of stone cold detachment, all nonchalant, just gazing at the blurry TV screen. It's my new jug mug frown—someday I'll show it to you. But this time, I opted for the snappy retort.

"Fuck you," I snapped.

"Eh?" Manfred replied, his pale freckled face bursting into a zany mix of delight, rage and stage surprise. "Well, that's a fine fucking how-do-you-do. Feeling a tad cranky this eve, Miss Potter?"

"Yeah, as a matter of fact, I am a tad cranky."

"Oh no. What's making us cranky then?"

"See, I'm trying to watch 'Friends' on TV, but I can't, 'cause some fucking goof broke my glasses."

What you need to know is that, for some reason, "goof" is a fighting word in jail. There are, of course, many fighting words in jail, all for the most part quite predictable, so there's no need to consult a glossary. Who knows how "goof" got pride of place on the list, but it did, especially when it's preceded by that particular modifier. In fact, "fucking goof" may well be the most frequently heard last two words uttered by the countless fucking goofs who've ended up maimed or worse in the system down through the ages. Even the Somali guys know not to use it.

Manfred was taken aback. He had no way of knowing that it was likely just a combination of nicotine jag and several quarts of backed-up seminal fluids that made me say that thing.

"Oh really?" Manfred said, stepping up close and treating me to a sample of his sour stanky rot-in-hell jail-mouth breath. "What fucking goof would that be?"

It was his breath that did it. What had I ever done to deserve the pong of such bad breath? It was worse than a slap in the face.

All at once a white-hot shock of rage shot up my spine to the top of my skull. I'd been pushed into a corner and badly used, thrown into these horrific circumstances through no

fault of my own, abandoned by all but my mother and this
really weak shitty lawyer she'd hired. Betrayed by you. Given
all of that, Manfred's turbine-powered turd breath was
simply beyond endurance—the forced intimacy with this
sleazy scumbag I'd normally have nothing to do with
crystallized everything in an instant. It was time to push
back, lash out like a god of destruction and kill the whole
world. Strike a blow and die. I looked Manfred square in the
eye. My customized pencil was in my right shoe, in the grips
of my wet clenched toes. The time had come to use it. One
word more and I'd kick off my shoe, draw my weapon, and
put a hundred holes in Manfred's chest and neck area.

"To be honest?" I said. "Some fucking goof who looks
sorta like you."

It must have been that something in my face that made
Manfred step off just then. He must have seen what would
come next. He chuckled a raspy chuckle.

"You're not such a bad shit in the long run, Harry
Potter," he said, winking, "but then again, who likes long
runny shits?"

Next thing you know, we're standing there chatting
pleasantly, like two like-minded individuals who'd met by
chance at some tedious government sanctioned obligation,
renewing our car tags or some such. As we shuffled into
line for our sweatshop lasagne, Manfred asked me about
what I was writing, and we talked about books. He was
surprisingly well read, especially in the history of Medieval
Britain, with an emphasis on the Scottish clans. He's also
an avid downloader of movies, so it impressed him to learn
that I myself worked in the film industry, not realizing that
as a grad school dropout with zero real-world work
credentials, I have no choice in the matter. Or that my

occasional actual paid employment in the business mostly involves the movement of orange traffic cones and white cube vans, meanwhile asking around town that sad, oft heard query: "Had a chance to read my screenplay yet?"

By the time we'd finished dinner I'd gained a completely new perspective on Manfred. He's a much more sophisticated and erudite individual than I'd presumed. Although he does subscribe to conspiracy theories (apparently 9/11 was choreographed by the Oval Office, the Illuminati and the Military-Industrial-Pornography complex) and his taste in films is highly debatable ("Mel Gibson's a true fucking genius"), Manfred's overall take on reality is informed and stimulating. It's refreshing really. What's more, I learned that, like me, Manfred is largely a victim of circumstance.

"I was doing okay on the street," Manfred explained. "Nice little place, couple of kids, solid house-painting business, along with, you know, a little dealing on the side, right? Loved my wife four or five times a month. Leasing a fucking fully optioned Explorer. Then I got stupid, right? Got a girlfriend in the east end, this dirty whore Crystal Meth. Let me tell you something bro, that's one crazy bitch you might want to try to avoid. I look around one day and it's all gone—kids, house, business, wife, Explorer, along with half my fucking teeth."

In addition to accounting for why his breath smelt like an abandoned port-a-potty at a classic rock reunion festival, Manfred's hellacious love affair with Mexican bathtub speed revealed his essential humanity. Like most of us, he is weak. And like almost every single one of us in jail, he's an addict. I'd estimate that about ninety-nine percent of the lugans in here struggle with three forms of addiction or another. It's like every guy in here has his dog that needs walking, and some guys' dogs are bigger and more demanding than others. By way of comparison, I'd say that my dog is relatively manageable, something along the lines of a frisky Yorkshire terrier. Whereas Manfred has to contend with a rabid, starving, three-headed rottweiler yanking on his chain. His dog-walking stories are, as you might expect, hilarious.

Since Manfred—whose jail name is, of course, Red Fred or Red Man or simply The Red—had been so forthcoming with me, I thought it only right to reciprocate in kind. I have to admit I was slightly less than honest with him. In recognition of the prevailing status hierarchy in here, I decided to embellish my role in the crimes I've been accused of, and my thumbnail sketch of events suggested that I was both mastermind and perpetrator of the caper. Much as seen on film and television, the social order inside is the inverse of what it is outside. Meaning that the more spectacularly violent your history—as long as it doesn't involve children or animals, especially dogs—the more respect you are bestowed. Positing myself as a stone cold killer was a stunning strategic survival move on my part. Not only did I impress Manfred, by this morning I already noticed that some of my fellow inmates had become watchful, even deferential around me. Soon they'll be calling me Mister Potter.

And my status will only be further enhanced now that The Red is going to be my cellmate.

"I'm going to pull rank with the bulls and see if I can't cell with you," Manfred told me over breakfast this morning. "I need someone with some smarts who I can at least talk to while I'm canned, otherwise I'm gonna go completely spare. I've had it with all the loons and dirtbags in this slam—we gotta start looking out for each other in here bro."

"Right on bro," I said to my new best bro Manfred.

I'll tell you what T, a bro like Manfred is simply invaluable in here. In addition to being generous, considerate and a stimulating conversationalist, Manfred's a violent psycho with biker connections. Being his bro thus renders me untouchable. What's interesting to note is that Manfred conforms completely with my theory regarding the redhead of the species. In my experience, red-headed guys are either timid, pathologically shy types, or else gregarious and pugnacious loudmouths, deadly dangerous to a foe, but mad loyal to a friend, ready and willing to give the shirt off a back or an organ from within if called upon. Manfred clearly falls into the latter category, and I'm therefore proud and grateful to call him bro.

So all and all, it's been a pretty good couple of days here in jail.

The point being, I'm feeling considerably more on top of things now, and not a mere pawn of the powers that recently assumed control of my destiny. There've been times when I thought I wasn't going to make it T. But now I know I'm going to be okay. I can handle this. Since getting tossed in here, it's been all shock and confusion, stress and constipation. I'm past that now. I can see clearly now the rain has gone. I can see all obstacles in my way. Gone are the dark clouds that had me down. It's going to be. Well, it's going to be a bunch of long lonely bleak deadly boring days in the slammer until my trial. But fuck, whatever.

Oddly, what I'm seeing most clearly now, as though for the first time, is that I stand accused of murder. That's why I'm here. Until now that somehow hadn't registered with me. It was like a joke with a punch line I didn't get. But it's no joke. A man is dead and the cops and Crown say I did it.

That's serious. What's worse, you say I did it. Think about
that for a second T. Think about me committing murder.
I'm in a weedy ditch and I'm taking the life of a sixty-nine
year old man by standing on his neck with my sandalled
foot. And you can see me doing this thing. Where T? Where
did I find the requisite hellfire to commit such an act?

The truth is, you know little about the main events of
the weekend, and you understand even less, and that's why
I'm compelled to write you T.

Remember what a relief it was to be swinging off the
highway and onto the familiar side road, tacking in for the
safe harbour of the cottage? All at once all of the bad was
behind us, done and gone—the karmic trauma of hitting
that animal, the sordid drama of the parking-lot dust-up,
the tawdry bathos of our cocaine karaoke—all of it all over
now. It just fell away, forgotten in an instant. I geared
down to second and slowed to a crawl. The muffler-less
engine dropped to a low guttural growl. The narrow gravel
road shadowed the contours of the unseen lakeshore.
Towering trees formed a wall on both sides, making it
seem like we were moving along the bottom of a deep dark
canyon. The little engine echoed rudely in the treed
corridor. Every fifty yards or so, the gatepost of a luxury
lakeside cottage would appear, and I sensed their
occupants sitting suddenly bolt upright in bed, awoken by
the unwholesome report of the hurting Hyundai.
Something wicked this way comes. I reached back to find
your foot.

Safely home at the cottage, my first move was to tuck the
Hitler gun into the gun locker for the night. But the door to

Harry's den was shut and locked, so I was stuck holding the fucking thing, that slimy evil pistol now jammed in my shorts pocket, where it felt warm and weighty, like an extra phallus. Hitler's extra phallus, since his original one apparently didn't work, hence the invasion of Poland.

"Let's go to bed," you said. "We're leaving early early, first thing, yeah?"

"Yes ma'am," I said. "Sure am."

Your mood had shifted. Your anger seemed spent, your edge gone, and you were soft and sweet, in want of a cuddle perhaps. Maybe you sensed that, since we'd made it back to the cottage alive and well, without criminal charges or further mishap, things might go okay after all. If we left early enough tomorrow, we could be back in the city by noon. No need to stick around and see how this shit played out, not after Portents One and Two had served ample warning. Message Received. All we had to do now was enter our bedroom and close the door, let nature take its course, then hit the road home at first light.

We were in the kitchen, just the two of us, drinking ice-cold water from the fridge tap, pressed close together at the counter, deconstructing the evening's karaoke sessions and debriefing our highway mishap, speculating on the species of the accident victim. You feared a pregnant fox; I reckoned a rabid raccoon. I kept saying I was so sorry. Through the open sliding glass door we could see Harry and Teddy lounging on the big stone deck out back. Harry had stayed up waiting for us with pricey cigars and pricier Scotch. The fact that he wore shirt and pants—a metallic silver Polo and burgundy plaid golf slacks—confirmed the atmosphere of placid sanity that had descended on the cottage at Red Snake Lake. The satellite radio was sending silky smooth

big band oldies through the speakers out back. All was
serene, all was cool.

While we talked, I took to touching your cheekbone,
and then went to tracing a line with my fingertips to your
jaw then to your neck, to your shoulder, across collar-
bones to the other shoulder, then down, all the way down,
to your hipbone, where I found skin under your shirt,
and you started with a catch of breath. My other hand
went to that place on the small of your back, due north of
the Pantyline, where a fingernail graze shuts your eyes
and makes you shudder, as though a secret switch is
hidden there. I followed up with a sloppy wet kiss, and a
boozy bite of your overbite. But when you reached down
to find what was happening in my shorts, I had to twist
away. What if you touched the Hitler gun? The mood
might be lost.

"What?" you asked, eyes sparking just for me.

"Nothing."

"Damn," you said, taking my hand, "you are fine boy.
Fuck, I hate you. Such pretty eyes, like a girl. Come. Come
to bed."

"Yeah but. What say we do a little something something
first? I got to shake some of that out of me, all that stress and
shit. Nurse, I think I may need something for my stress."

"What's say we don't. We want to wake up tomorrow—
early early."

"One more won't kill us."

"That's like your motto. One more won't kill us. You
should get that tattooed on your forehead."

"Yeah, in Latin. What'd that be in Latin?"

"What's this in Latin? And so, to bed."

"Listen, you go ahead babe," I said, giving your hand a

squeeze and then letting go. "I really should wish the Chups goodnight. I'll just be a sec."

"Don't bother. What for? Come. Come to bed. How can you even cope with those dickheads?"

"People skills. Won't be but a minute. You go ahead."

You sighed, dismayed. "See what I mean? You're a brat. You bastard. Okay, you know what? If you're going to be doing anymore, you got to bring me a taste. I'm waiting for you, for a bit, so don't be long, okay?"

"Okay."

"Promise?"

"Promise."

My conundrum being, with you being so adamant about leaving early the next morning, now was my only opportunity to work the deal with Harry. I figured all I needed was ten, fifteen minutes, tops.

"Why not warm up that Jacuzzi?" I suggested.

"Yeah, sure thing sailor boy. Me love you long time."

You tossed me a look over your shoulder as you walked away, just to make sure I was checking you, which of course I was. What is it about your ass T? I mean, beyond its qualitative and quantitative correctness, it's peach-perfect proportions and heartbreaking heart shape? Can we call it personality? I would argue yes. Because your butt has personality to spare, girl, a real mind of its own, so clever and cunning one might think it could be taught to talk and perform tricks. To roll over and beg, for example.

A more pertinent question is, how I was able to resist following your coyly pencil-jeaned ass straight to our guest bedroom right then and there? I'd never once even tried to resist its allure before. What made me watch it twitch 'n' flick from my grasp that time?

Money is to blame. Harry's money. I had to choose
between Harry's money and your sweet little ass and I opted
to play for the cash. In fact, I was playing for both. Getting a
slice of Harry's dough might be the very thing to secure
some sort of future with your ass, I calculated. Of late your
sense of me as an over-educated semi-criminal layabout
with a small but sagacious wardrobe and a charming bike
collection, which at first you'd found kind of louche and
sexy ("Ever think about pulling like a real armed robbery?"
you seriously asked me once) had gone stale, and now you
were beginning to see me as little more than an indolent
jerk-off with some nasty habits and a rusty Hyundai ("Ever
think about getting like a real job?" you seriously asked me
once). I was your dark back road detour, and you'd long
since mapped your reroute to the well-lit expressway. If I
was going to reverse all that, I'd better get something
happening, and for that I needed money. In resisting your
allure in order to go scam Harry out of some dough, I was
deferring immediate gratification for long-term access. To
your ass I mean. It was an uncharacteristically adult
decision on my part. It was also among the stupidest
decisions I've ever made in my life.

"Dives, how you doing boy?" said Harry when I came
out smiling to the big back stone deck.

"Great. Good. Beautiful. How's Harry this beautiful
night?"

"Beautiful. Harry is always beautiful."

"Well isn't that just beautiful."

"Let's go down to the boathouse," suggested Teddy. "It's
even yet way more beautifuler down there."

Harry was game for the idea, but he was also pretty
plastered, so the steep stairs down to the lake presented a

challenge. Likewise for his son. I was nowhere near their states of inebriation, and trace elements of that night's blow were keeping me alert and nimble. I could handle the stairs no problem.

"Careful boys. Insurance says these stairs is four drinks maximum," Harry said as he negotiated his way down the wooden steps expertly crafted into the steep rock face, zigzagging the fifty feet or so to the boathouse and dock below. "So watch how you go."

Teddy, clutching a pail of ice with both hands, tripped along close behind his dad, while I followed well back with bottle and glasses. Looking down at the dark duo below, an image popped in my head, a quick film clip featuring Teddy giving Harry a push from behind. It didn't take much. Just a nudge between the shoulder blades with the ice pail, and Harry was launched and tumbling, head bashing rocks and steps, arriving on the dock a splayed bloody corpse. The whole sequence flashed like lightning in my mind's eye. Then it was gone and I blinked and forgot about it.

We set up on the deck atop the boathouse. The air was cool with a rotting sweet lush lake smell. A sour candy lemon moon was sneaking around behind the black trees across the bay. The frogs chirped steady and deep, in a heavy breathing rhythm that seemed to come from Mother Earth herself. Expensive Scotch was poured. Fine cigars were lit. The Scotch tasted like velvety seaweed. The cigar tasted like a warehouse fire.

"Cheers."

"Where's the girl?" Harry asked. "You lose her?"

"Not yet," I said.

"Don't lose her," he advised me. "She's good girl. I like

her. Very smart, I think, your little Ukrainian friend. Funny looking thing, such a beautiful ugly girl."

"Say?"

"Interesting to look at. Small eyes, big nose. Face like bird. Stick legs. Funny looking, but in beautiful way. Something to her. Her smile. You want her smile. Every time you look, she is looking somehow different."

"It's his thing," Teddy said. "He's always been into them freaky looking bitches."

"I what?"

"Sorry, what I meant was, exceptional looking women. Dat's da flava."

"For me," Harry mused, "all of young women are beautiful, same like racehorses."

"Yeah. With tiny men riding them," Teddy added.

This was not the conversation I'd been angling for. Discussing women with these two seasoned misogynists would be like taking a seminar in African history with a pair of Klan Wizards. I felt like downing my drink and packing it in for the night, especially when Harry got on the topic of Teddy's mother, the second of his three wives. It's not a topic Teddy is comfortable with, which explains why Harry brought it up. As a youth, when I'd first started hanging at the Chup household, Teddy's mom Rita was in some kind of trial separation mode with Harry, and she was there only sporadically and sullenly. I remember the stunned confusion I experienced the first time I met her—she was ridiculously beautiful, femme but feral, brown eyed but blond, her face a striking Miss Universe version of Teddy's. She went to Florida over Christmas holidays that year and didn't come back. Teddy was thirteen at the time. He hasn't seen her since.

"Rita she could not even put gas in car at self-serve," Harry reminisced, with sparkly eyes. "Could not understand how to do it. Something wrong upstairs with her. All the time she is believing Madonna talks to her in songs. Sending secret messages, just for her, in the music. Crazy, crazy woman. Sex was fantastic, of course. But everything else? Ridiculous. Terrible."

"Yeah? Well, anywho," I said, "women, eh? Can't live with 'em; can I have another Scotch?"

I couldn't take the sick riveted look on Teddy's face— fixed yet flummoxed, absorbing every word, needing to hear all but incapable of hearing any. I hated Harry for doing this to him. It was the kind of hurt only a true sadist could indulge in. A dad sadist. I felt duty bound to stick it out for a while more, just to make certain the Rita talk was done, for Teddy's sake. I poured triples all around.

"Any fish left in this lake Harry?" I asked.

"Plenty. Brown trout. No ice," Harry said. "Scotch this good does not deserve ice. By the way, the girl, your little friend? I think she took the Walther. It's not in locker. She took I bet, maybe for throwing in the lake. So what? I don't care. I don't care about nothing now. Teddy told you? I'm dead?"

"No," I said. "He didn't."

"The cancer is up my ass. Teddy didn't tell to you?"

"Dad, you're not dead," Teddy said. "Get it straight. Remember? First the chemo, then you die."

"Fuck chemo. I treat only with best Scotch, then put bullet right here," Harry said, pointing at his forehead. "Pow."

"Now now Daddy. Let's not be talking nonsense," Teddy said. "Obviously you're gonna live forever. What would we do without old Harry Chup on planet earth, making it happen? Hey but thanks for saying suicide 'cause that reminds me—

fucking golf. I think I left my sticks up here."

Teddy lurched to his feet and reeled across the deck and down the exterior steps to the rarely used fitness room beneath the roof deck of the boathouse. The mere mention of his mother was reason enough to go cut a line of blow. I was feeling similarly inclined.

"Jeez Harry," I said. "That's rough about the cancer. I'm sorry to hear it."

"Ah fuck it. Who cares? Everybody now has it. The big C. Everybody. Probably you too. So! Teddy tells me you are in film business now, looking for investors. Tell me about it."

As keen as I'd been to deliver the pitch, when the opportunity so abruptly presented itself, I was at a loss. The whole notion suddenly seemed ludicrous. How could I possibly make the prospect of investing money in an ultra low budget dystopic indie art film sound appealing to this ruthlessly capitalistic captain of the automatic garage door industry with rectal cancer? I rambled around the business plan for a bit. Then I stumbled into the premise of our feature presentation, *Galvanizer 2067.*

"It's set in the future," I explained. "It's about a gang of rickshaw pullers living in an abandoned house in the suburbs. They hit on a scheme to kidnap this girl, this pharmaceutical company heiress, so they can get her dad to give up the secret formula for this next-generation drug he invented, this mood enhancer. One of those nanobot drugs, you know?"

"No. What is nanobot?"

"They're like super-tiny computer chips, like these miniature cellular robots they can inject in your blood. This drug's called Galvanizer. Basically it turns you into a psycho-path, so that way you're loose to do anything you want, whatever it takes, no guilt or worries. Pure results.

The idea is, like, the world is so entirely fucked up by then, it's the only way you can survive and get ahead. Without moral compunction or compass or whatever. You just don't give a shit. So everyone wants this drug, which is why they kidnap the girl."

Harry closed one eye in an effort to keep my face in focus. "So what happens?"

"Well, so our guy, the main character, after they kidnap the girl, it turns out he knows her, he's met her before, at this futuristic club called Sticks and Stones. It was a love at first sight thing. And she's into him too. Or so it seems because the thing is, what if she's on that drug? Cranked on Galvanzer? Like, what if she's only playing the guy to escape, or to get the formula herself? Could be she's just a manipulative but extremely hot psychopath."

"So. Is she?"

"Come on Harry. Can't give up the ending. And maybe we never find out. Maybe it ends with, you know, we're not sure about anything."

"No, please. Not that. I hate these fucking endings like this. European-type ending. Is garbage. You want to know, to leave the theatre happy. To be in your car driving home happy. Proper Hollywood ending. With nice song playing."

"Yeah you're right. So no, it doesn't end like that exactly. Because it's a, you know, a love story."

"Love is good," Harry said. "World needs love story."

"Yeah, and see, the beauty part is Harry, like I said, we're going to use found locations, pure guerrilla style, in and out fast, on digital with amateur actors. We got a couple of rickshaw kids from downtown. But none of that improv dialogue shit and making it up as we go. The script is tight. And for sure no fucking zombies. No public arts funding, no fucking zombies. We're approaching private investors only. Plan is we do it cheap, quick and dirty."

"Dirty is good," Harry said. "But what in fuck, why gorillas?"

I needed Teddy's help. This was a shared vision, a duet, and it only came to life when Teddy was there to sing along. Plus he's the visionary, the director, the one with the talent; I was but the writer/producer, the one with nothing. The paradox here being that Harry wouldn't listen to a thing Teddy said, whereas he'd happily sit there and listen to me sling this shit till dawn.

"Present some scene from it," Harry said. "Show me the story. How the acting goes."

"Harry, I can't act. No listen, we got this kid to do the lead. He's perfect. He pulls a rickshaw downtown, you know, one of those punks ripping off tourists from Rochester?" And retailing brutally cut coke in the club district for Teddy, I might have added.

"You should be doing acting. You look like actor. I've always thought this. You could be big star. I would invest money for that."

"But. Really?"

"Yes of course. Try it, just one scene, when boy meets girls. I love these parts."

I needed to do a line immediately. It was imperative that I get into a more aggressive, closer's state of mind if I was going to get the deal done.

Teddy emerged from downstairs and marched across the deck like a chipper first mate reporting for duty.

"I am the walrus," Teddy announced.

"Koo-koo-ka-choo," I said.

"Son, what is it you are putting up your nose all the

time?" Harry asked. "Hey? Bleeding again. All the time is bleeding."

"T'aint nuttin' Daddy-o," Teddy said, sniffing and testing his bloody nose with a fingertip tap as he took his seat. "Like I told you. Buddy here kicked me in the face, for absolutely no good reason."

"Blame the karaoke. He left me no choice."

Harry laughed. "Kick him again."

"You should check out the vintage canoe Harry bought," Teddy advised me. "Peterborough. Cedar strip. How much that thing cost you Dad?"

"Don't know. I saw, I liked, I bought."

"You use?"

"What? Fuck no."

"Hold that thought," I said. "I gotta take a leak."

I slipped down to the fitness room and hoovered the two fat lines Teddy had left on his pocket mirror sitting on the bow. He was right. It was a vintage canoe. Thus emboldened, I hastened back up to the deck, hoping that Teddy hadn't squirreled the pitch in my absence. I was all ready to act that scene.

Too late. I arrived back on the deck to find Harry and Teddy in a heated argument. About fucking cars. Harry wanted it known and appreciated that his 1976 Buick Electra was the single biggest sedan General Motors had ever produced. Ever. Teddy wasn't buying it.

"Is true," Harry said. "This piece, Electra has wheel base exactly 234 inches, almost twenty feet long. Is biggest four-door sedan GM ever make. Ever. Also first ever car equip with airbag."

"I call bullshit," said Teddy.

Teddy had inserted wads of tissue into each nostril to

staunch the bleeding and prevent coke leakage, and I noticed the dark crescents forming under his eyes. By morning he'd have a pair of proper shiners, his nose busted by the lobsterman.

"What bullshit? You bullshit."

"What, bigger than a fucking sixties Caddy?"

"Yes fuck bigger. Why you think I bought it?"

"Penis envy?"

"Dives," Harry said, turning his attention to me. "Sit. Have a drink. You look like you going somewhere. Sit! Have a drink!"

I sat. I had a drink.

"Thing would make a great derby car," Teddy said. "When I was tanking it up in Betterham the guy told me they're having a derby at the fair next weekend. Said I should enter it."

"What derby?" asked Harry.

"You know, demo derby," Teddy said. "Bunch of beaters go into a pit and mash it up, mostly shit-kicked taxis. Last car moving wins. With that monster V8? The size of the trunk on that motherfucker? We be beating those bitches down yo."

"Shame about the Cordoba," I said. "I'd love to see that fucker in a derby."

"Cordoba was garbage car," Harry said. "Driving it all the way here from West Coast. What for? Why? Leaking shit car. First thing I told you, engine is shot. No, listen to me. Buick Electra is cherry. Cherry Electra. Mint condition. In total less than ten thousand miles on it, all in Florida. Put in derby, my ass."

"Good idea," Teddy said. "We should put your ass in the derby."

"Agreed," Harry said. "Superior method to chemo treatment."

We all had a laugh and started talking about death.

Harry wasn't afraid of death, he was afraid of dying, which is understandable, given the terrifying advances made in medical science. Nowadays you can be subjected to all manner of excruciating and humiliating life-threatening interventions on your way to being dead.

Likewise, you can be subjected to all manner of vicious, cruel and underhanded attempts at murder on your way to being killed. Just look at what happened to Harry. You think it's easy to kill someone? It isn't.

Here are some things you don't know about T, things I didn't know about either until a meeting yesterday with my lawyer, Mr. Nick Rocolopolous.

"Word is," Nick confided to me, "down at the Coroner's they're calling him 'The Man They Couldn't Kill. And Then They Killed Him.' Body had enough pharmaceuticals in it to take out a three hundred pound trucker, plus all kinds of unaccounted for bruising and contusions. Collapsed lung. And then there's the matter of that mystery bullet fragment they found in his skull. They're calling it the 'magic bullet,' figure it must have been fired from the grassy knoll. It's all good. For you, I mean. Not so good for Harry, obviously."

I think you get the import of this. The murdering had commenced before we'd even got to the cottage. But it's way more complicated than that, and only at the end did I get a sense of the whole play. Some of it I'll never get. For example, I'll never get the thing that happened just before we embarked on our boat cruise.

A smudge of pale light appeared by surprise on the eastern horizon accompanied by sweet birdsong all around, signalling the end of one day and the start of the next. By then we'd emptied one bottle of Scotch and seriously dented another. A host of world problems had been aired and solved. Clearly it was time for a boat cruise. But before our departure, while I was in the exercise room of the boathouse putting the finishing touches on Teddy's blow, from outside on the dock I heard a confused cacophony of shouts, crashing, bashing and splashing.

I tooted a last long line, licked the pocket mirror and blade clean, and then hastened down the stairs to the dock to investigate. There I came upon a most unsettling tableau. There'd been a tiff of some sort. Both Chups had just pulled themselves out of the lake and lay sprawled on the dock, wet and gasping for breath. Blood was everywhere, but I couldn't tell if it was just the same old blood that had been leaking from Teddy all night, or new blood from some other source.

"What the hell?" I asked.

"Teddy is playing silly buggers," Harry said.

"Harry is off the chain," Teddy said.

Baffled, I could only surmise that one Chup had fallen or been knocked into the lake by the other Chup, following which one Chup had jumped in to save or to drown the other Chup. But that's all pure theory. I'll never know what happened there.

Both Chups rolled over and sat up, turned away from each other on the dock, wiping their faces, testing limbs for loss or breakage, breathing hard as they collected themselves, neither saying a word. It was as though they'd just come to an understanding of some sort, and nothing more need be said. I felt stranded outside the scene, like I was the only one there who hadn't read the script.

"Well!" Harry finally said. "Now is time to change and take the boat out. Looks like to me."

"Fucking A yeah," said Teddy, inspecting a soggy wad of tissue he'd pulled from his nose before flicking it into the lake.

It may seem odd to you that in the aftermath of such an event there was still the mood for a boat cruise. But such is the way of the Chups. They always try to normalize things by doing something normal in the wake of things sub-normal. As for me, I was pretty high, and felt I had no option anyway, since I doubted you'd be exactly welcoming me into bed by then.

What's more, I had the deal with Harry to consider. Having initiated a dialogue, it was essential that I stay on top of the situation, especially in light of the delicate nature of negotiations at this crucial juncture. See, what happened was, not long before we boarded the boat, while Teddy was off on one of his frequent trips down to the exercise room, Harry announced his commitment to the Film Project. But with one very firm proviso: No Teddy.

"I'm finished now with Teddy," Harry explained. "Is over. Completely. No more money. He uses money for only drugs and making his dirty shit fuck so-called artworks. And anyway for this type of movie you don't want him, for this you are making nice and normal type movie for the people to come and watch to enjoy it. This is kind of movie I would put money to. A love story. You I believe. Teddy, no I don't believe. Never. It can only be you, otherwise no. Sorry I can't."

"Well," I said. "I bet we can work something out here Harry."

"Is up to you entirely. Maybe we can. If you think, you should put in writing. For my lawyer to see. How much?

When? What it's for? Like that. Contract. Simple, yeah? Do it tomorrow to show me."

"Cool, Harry."

Then there was more booze, blow and bullshit, followed by that incident on the dock I told you of, and finally, a boat cruise on the lake.

You can see my dilemma T. I had to play it down the middle, position myself between the Chups like a friendly firewall for the sake of all involved, lest everything and everyone burn to the ground. It'd be tricky, but I felt up to the task. And the prize was too great, too real and too near at hand now to let slip away. My screenplay was to become realized in film. It was that simple, that wondrous. Harry's money would make it happen, like magic, with that pixie dust called cold cash. I boarded Harry's boat in an exalted mood. To see my words made real, on the screen, to dream the impossible dream. This was the greatest thing that could ever happen to me. Or so it felt then. Of course now, not so much.

Now is where I have to end this T. With me about to board Harry's boat for a pleasant outing on the lake to pay homage to the sunrise first-hand. Even at that point it wasn't too late. I still could have avoided all that was to come, simply by returning to the cottage, waking you up, and blasting home in the noisy Pony. But I didn't, and there was no turning back once I boarded the boat.

I have to tell you about that, but I can't now. Truth is, I can hardly remember why any of this ever mattered to me.

Love,

e.

Dear T,

This morning when I woke up as usual at 3:33 in the AM, I had that Thing on my mind again. That Thing being an image of you, in conversation with those two heinous dicks, Banning and Marcucci. Of course, that Thing's been plaguing my mind for many days and nights now T—you, Banning, Marcucci, just the you three, having a little chit-chat, a pleasant powwow, a cosy closed door threesome. But of late that Thing's become an all-consuming obsession with me. It's become the Thing that I think about for hours at a time, often to the exclusion of all else. For example, from 3:33 this morning until now I've been thinking about that Thing pretty much non-stop. And do you smell that smell? That smell means lunchtime: Denver sandwiches, mealy dry inside, soggy wet outside, with creamed corn soup cooling on the side.

What exactly did you tell those two dicks T?
What exactly did those two dicks tell you T?
Nick has to keep reminding me that we've got to wait for Disclosure to find all that out. Meanwhile, I'm left to construct your discussions with Banning and Marcucci by

myself, piecing it together from the fragments they
dropped me while under interrogation, just before I got
popped for Murder.

I don't know about you T, but when they first picked me
and brought me in, I tried but failed to take them seriously.
The airless silent cologne cloud ride downtown in the back of
the unmarked Crown Vic; the blatant theatrics of their self-
adoring stroll through Homicide HQ—"Morning Mavis. My
goodness, you are positively glowing girl." / "Yeah, look at
you. What are you, five months now buttercup?" / "Six, but
just keep talking boys"—parading me down the grey carpeted
corridor like some giant stuffed Care Bear they'd won on the
midway at the Ex; their lame game of leaving me alone to
stew in the interview room for half an hour, wondering how I
looked on tape, overtly aware of body language. Their whole
approach seemed too transparent to be of any threat.

Even after the questions started. In they came and
closed the door, opening fat black notebooks and hunkering
down to business, hulking over the table bulked in black
business suits. Formalities over, they commenced with a
series of soft lobs, in a just-getting-to-know-you sort of way,
feigning disinterest. Then they tested my balance with some
harder higher inside pitches, before trying to flatten me
with the bean ball (surprise!) that Teddy had fingered me as
the sole killer of Harry Chup.

All this I was able to laugh off. At first.

"What's funny?" Banning asked. "You should probably
know forensics is having a look at your sandals. They're in
the lab as we speak."

"Really?"

"Yeah, really. Anything you want to tell us about your
sandals?" Banning asked.

"I'm not sure. I got them on sale at Winners?"

"Funny. You're funny. Is this funny? We're treating them as a murder weapon. I think you know we know why," Marcucci said.

"No. Actually I don't. How do you know I was the one using my sandals?"

"Using them for what?" Banning asked.

"Should I have a lawyer here?"

"You tell us," Marcucci said.

"Tell you what?"

"Which word you having trouble with?" Banning asked.

"Listen, I just hope forensics is checking other shit too."

"Do you? Should they?" Marcucci asked.

"Yeah they should."

"Checking what?" Banning asked.

"Should we have a lawyer here?"

"I don't know," Marcucci asked. "Should we?"

"I was hoping you'd tell me."

"Tell you what?" Banning asked.

"I mean what, am I actually charged with something here?"

"Charged with what?" Marcucci asked.

"Charged with sandal-wearing?"

"Think you're funny?" Marcucci asked.

"No."

"What's with the limp bro?" Banning asked. "Hurt your foot?"

"Yeah, stubbed my toe. On a rock. Up north."

"Rock, eh? We'll want to get some pictures of that foot," Marcucci said. "You mind? How come both your feet are messed-up? Look at that."

"Do I need a lawyer?"

"What happened to the gun?" Banning asked.

"What gun?"

"What gun. You know what gun," Marcucci said.

"No. I don't."

"Hitler's Happy Birthday gun. You were flashing it around all weekend," Banning said.

"Who told you that? I don't even know what you're talking about."

"Have any idea how much that thing's worth?" Marcucci asked.

"I think I might need a lawyer."

"Why? Need some legal advice about that gun?" Banning asked.

"What gun?"

"The fucking Hitler gun, smart ass," Marcucci said, smacking his meaty hand flat on the table, hard and hairy side up.

And so on—the tag-team bad cop/worse cop interrogation travelled along those lines until it went from vaguely amusing to somewhat troubling to deeply unsettling, before arriving at full-stop flat-out full-on fucking horror show.

They're quite the shiny sharp straight from their morning squats in the weight room pair of hard-ons, wouldn't you say T? Packed tight into their handsome black just for homicide suits (Armani? Boss? Moores?—you'd know) and their already pissed with people they haven't even met yet demeanour, freshly barbered and thoughtfully accessorized, what with their high school grad rings, platinum birthday bracelets and so forth. I must admit, though, that shit starts to work. I was soon feeling a right bad dirty bird, sitting there unmade, unshaven and increasingly unmasculated, in a pair of flip-flops, shabby shorts and musty Madras shirt, getting picked apart by those two alpha roosters. The sheen of their preening polish ground me down, made me feel weak and diminished. A failed human.

Then they punched me in the nuts.

It started with me suggesting—hilarious in retrospect—that it'd be helpful if they could show me some of the evidence that their suppositions were based upon.

"I'd like to see the dossier or whatever you call it. Crime scene photos and statements and whatnot."

"Dossier?" Banning asked. "There's no dossier. That's not how it works. What, do you think you're on TV or something? Fucking dossier."

"No I knew that. Cops on TV are way cuter."

Banning chuckled, Marcucci didn't, for obvious reasons. Seriously T, what kind of a man at his age and ugliness feels compelled to treat his thinning bum fuzz hair to such elaborate streaking and product placement? And what is one to make of the matching gold hoop earrings and goatee? How could you keep a straight face with that guy T? I couldn't. Which is probably why he punched me in the nuts with your name. No doubt they'd been holding your name in reserve for effect, waiting for the opportune moment to deploy it so as to maximize its nut punch impact. It worked. Just hearing that asshat Marcucci mispronounce the proper mispronunciation of your sweet and sexy Slavic surname was enough to knock the living daylights out of me. Like a swift surprising shot to the nuts.

"Why you bothering, I mean, what are you talking to her about? It's got nothing to do with her," I said, my voice shaking all over the place.

Banning looked at Marcucci; Marcucci looked at Banning.

"We're just talking," Marcucci said. "You know, about this and that. About you and her. Filling in some of the blanks. What she knows. What she doesn't know. Et cetera."

"She doesn't know nothing," I said.

"No? Still, she knew enough to give us a statement. Twenty. No, what? More like thirty pages long," Banning said.

"Really?"

"Really? Why you smiling all the time boss? Finding this amusing?" Marcucci asked.

"Not particularly."

"So what's it going to be? Any closer to giving us a statement?" Banning asked.

"Currently no; not at present."

"You'll feel better, I can promise you that. The truth heals brother," Banning said.

"Not in my experience. Brother."

"From your point of view," Marcucci said, "your relationship with little Miss O., how would you characterize it?"

"Little Miss? What the. Close. I would characterize it as close."

"Close," Marcucci said, flipping pages in his notebook, with a dainty fingertip grip on his gold framed and chained, weirdly oversized reading glasses. "So you wouldn't call it a kind of a, you know, casual sort of a fuck buddy kind of a deal?"

"A what?"

"Let's back it up here," Banning said. "Were you at anytime over the course of the weekend behind the wheel of Mr. Chup's Buick Electra?"

"No. I already told you that like ten times. Wait, hold up a sec. Where exactly did the term fuck buddy originate?"

"I don't know," Marcucci said. "It's probably a thing the kids say in high school."

"You know what I mean."

"So at no time did you drive the Buick Electra?" Banning asked.

"Correct. Jesus. Fuck buddy."

"We understand you were trying to do some business with Mr. Chup that weekend," Marcucci said. "Trying to get some money out of him to make a movie of some kind. How'd that go? How would you describe your negotiations with Mr. Chup?"

"Productive? I don't know. Cordial?"

"Yeah?" Banning said. "That is not what we heard."

"Why? What'd they tell you?"

"What'd who tell us?" Marcucci asked. "Your little fuck buddy?"

"Guy. Please."

"You use her computer to send your emails and so forth?" Marcucci asked.

"Yeah?"

"You send emails from anywhere else, or just her place?" Marcucci asked.

"It's *our* place by the way. And what do you care where I send emails from?"

"Why do you think?" Marcucci asked. "We've gone through Teddy's computer. It's all there. The whole deal's mapped. Subject line—'Project Harry Drop.' Let me tell you something here chief, you fuck heads aren't exactly Al-Qaeda. Stop smiling."

"I'm not. It's just my face."

"What do you think?" Marcucci asked Banning. "Why we playing around with this dildo? He's wasting our time.

Doesn't want to help. Doesn't want to talk. Won't swear a statement. We got Teddy Chup, we got the girl, the computer, the sandals, the dead body—fuck it, let's roll with that. Stitch him up. Murder in the First Degree, Accessory, Interference with a Human Body. What else we got? What about the gun?"

Banning sighed.

"You know what? He's right. We don't need you to close this here. It's disappointing. I'm disappointed. In you I'm disappointed. You seem like a halfway intelligent individual, yet here you are, playing the fuckwit. Like this is a joke. What I can't understand is why you don't want to help yourself here, especially after what your two friends gave us. They gave us everything. They gave us you. Meanwhile you give us sweet fuck all. So alls we can go on is what they gave us. Unless you got anything else to contribute. An alternative version of events. How's about the truth? Why not tell us the truth?"

"I am. I don't know what you want. Ask me anything. I'm sitting here. Telling you the truth. Ask me anything."

"Okay," Marcucci said. "For starters, why exactly did you kill Harry Chup?"

"Right. That's it," I said, getting to my feet. "I'm out of here."

"You're what?" Marcucci asked. "You tripping son? You're not going anywhere. Sit down."

"You said you just wanted me to come and talk. I'm done. What the fuck."

They both chuckled.

"Yes and thank you for your co-operation," Banning said. "We certainly do appreciate it. Sit down."

"I think I need a lawyer."

"Fucking rights," they chimed in unison.

"Jinx," I said, still standing.

The System took over from there. I was handcuffed, processed and tossed into the massive meat, mind and soul grinding machine that is the Justice System, stripped of any and all decision-making powers and personal agency. Since then, all doors lock from the outside, electronically, and I haven't so much as controlled a light switch in weeks. I miss my clothes, my bikes.

I have to tell you this has been pretty freaking weird T.

Made all the more so because you apparently helped put me here, while you remain on the outside—remote and mute, untouchable. That's why I find myself obsessing stupidly about your confab and eventual Sworn Statement to Banning and Marcucci. But it won't be until the Disclosure stage that I finally get to see your stuff, and that's many months away, a year or more, even. I can't tell you how anxious I am for that part of the proceedings. Of everything in the Crown's case against me, it's the paperwork pertaining to you that concerns me most. In fact, it's pretty much all that concerns me. I want to hold it in my hands. I want to bring it to my cell and sleep with it under my pillow. It's gotten so bad that I've taken to fantasizing these documents might contain some tangible memento of you—an example of your distinctive lefty backslash handwriting, an image of your lovely fingerprints, your graduation portrait perhaps, or how about a whiff of winter on your neck, fresh home on a frosty night? A stray hair? Any small sample of your lovely DNA would be most beneficial to me here in jail T.

And it's all because of you and your apparent decision to act as a Witness for the Crown that I haven't been able to focus on what's really important here—collaborating with

Nick to develop an effective defence strategy so I don't end up squandering my most socially productive and personally rewarding years pacing around a very small cell in a very big Federal Penitentiary. Instead, when I met with Nick yesterday, for example, all I did was badger him as usual with questions about you and this goddamn Disclosure deal and how soon I can finally get a hold of your file to have and hold in my cell.

"In point of fact," Nick pointed out, "at this point in time we don't for certain know what she's going to do, or how her statement reads, and we won't know any of that until Disclosure, so forget it. Put it out of your mind. Capiche? Or do I need to walk you through the whole entire freaking process again?"

I begged him not to, but because he's a qualified lawyer and therefore duty bound to bore and pulverize people with procedure, he did so, anyway. I blanked out for sanity's sake, although he did get to me in the end by closing with this provocative metaphor:

"Picture running a marathon. I mean like a really fucked up marathon. Picture running a fucked up marathon in a river full of shit, and you're running it with like an eighty-pound sack of shit on your back. Picture you're getting set to run a fucked up marathon in a river full of shit with an eighty-pound sack of shit on your back, and there's a crowd of people there, raining shit down on you from all sides. And there's no finish line in sight. Because that's at least two years away."

I exhaled carefully, my head heavy in my hands, elbows sharp on the table.

"Unless, like I said, as per my earlier advice, we opt to cop a plea."

Suddenly keen to return to my jail cell for some quiet reflection, I thanked Nick for the edifying visualization exercise and said my goodbyes. There was, however, one more thing to deal with.

"Don't forget this," I said, indicating the Hilroy notebook I'd filled with my dense dark pencilled lines to you.

"Oh good," Nick, the courthouse dump truck said, "Still compiling the notes, eh?"

He glanced at them as though he'd just been alerted to some sick the cat had made on the carpet, irked now that he'd have to clean it up.

"Yeah. You been reading them?"

"Well, not as such," said Nick. "I had a look but when the time comes, maybe what I'll get you to do is, I'll get you to go back over them. Do me an executive summary."

"Fine by me," I said. "It's just I can't keep them here 'cause for sure some whack job will boost them to wipe his ass or something."

I don't care that Nick isn't reading any of this. Almost none of it would be of use to him anyways. Because it's not for him. It's for you. Nick suggested I write point form "bullets" in a strictly chronological order—think: who what where when why. Focus on the facts and stay on the surface, use the active voice. That won't do T. Not for you. For you I need to go deep to the bones and dark meat of the matter, sometimes in the passive voice. Upon this your understanding depends.

Beginning with your understanding of what happened while you were in bed sweetly sleeping early that Saturday morning.

I waited in the boat while Teddy and Harry went up to change out of the clothes that had been soaked and bloodied from whatever that tussle was on the dock.

Despite the big buzz I was carrying, as soon I flopped onto the cool white plush leatherette curved lovebench at the stern of Harry's brand new two-storey two-tone blue and white Sea Ray, a weighty wave of fatigue washed over me and drowned me in semi-sleep. Moments later, the knock of footsteps on the dock rocked me back out of it.

I don't know what kind of drugs Harry was on, but whatever they were, they seemed to be working. He'd changed into a nautical themed ensemble—crisp white pants and matching short sleeve shirt, a captain's hat and jaunty red cravat—and he appeared lively and fresh, whistling away as though a whole new Harry had arrived to replace the old spent drunk Harry to greet the new day. Teddy had changed too, into track pants, flip-flops and a baggy burgundy Just Do It t-shirt, but nothing else had changed about him. He was three day binge high—fiercely, determinately, perversely high—hanging bare assed off a cliff by a thread high, flip-flopping around the dock clutching a plastic shopping bag with a half dozen tallboy cans of Heineken. The orange tinted cycling glasses sitting askew on his face could not conceal the dark purple welts now in full bloom under his searing red eyes. In fact, they only magnified matters.

I studied Teddy as he stood swaying on the dock, surveying the scene like he'd just discovered joy in the simple beauty of an early morning on the lake—the creamy yellow glow of the approaching dawn, quickening behind the line of dark trees across the bay, the thin layer of powder-soft mist lolling on the glassy green water. Sadly, I

knew that such raw sources of joy were inaccessible to
Teddy Chup.

"Hey, here's a thought," Teddy said. "Let's grab the skis,
why not?"

"Let's not be stupid. Is not even light," Harry said. "Get
in the boat."

Teddy untied the lines, steadied himself to step into the
boat, tossed the bag of beer into the mid-deck cooler, took
one for himself (I waved off the offer) and then sprawled
into the swivel bucket co-captain seat beside captain Harry,
swinging around to face me as he snapped open a tallboy.

The boat bounced off the dock twice before Harry found
reverse and pulled away. We made a slow curve out into the
bay, the motor jet-smooth and insistent, like a powerful
kitchen appliance, churning the mirrored surface a creamy
dessert topping foam in its wake, whipping up that fresh
green misty lake smell. The silky motion of the boat
skimming the water coaxed me back to sleep. It was a thin
sleep, poised between the inky dark of night and the pearly
glow of dawn, in and out of consciousness, with little
difference between the two. The kind of thing that passes
for sleep when you've done way too much blow but you're
massively fatigued from a long hot drive and being up all
night drinking a wide variety of beverages on an empty
stomach and you find yourself lying in the back of a boat
skimming across a lake—now asleep, now awake, never
fully either.

I dreamed a dream. Or what I thought of then as a
dream but I realize now was more like a memory. I have
such vivid dreams now T. These past few weeks of forced
clean living here in pre-trial detention have worked wonders
on my dreaming faculties. I'm even keeping a separate

Dream Notebook. But don't panic. I wouldn't dream of
inflicting its contents on you. Write a dream and lose a
reader, I know. My memory faculties have likewise been
rehabilitated. Cold sober clean jail time has acted like a
power hose wash for my memory. I remember things now
with a clarity and precision that is nothing short of horri-
fying. All thanks to my monastic-ass lifestyle.

What I now remember remember-dreaming as I lay in
the back of the boat was about a different time at a different
lake in a different boat on a different drug, but with the
same two Chups. There were two additional Chups involved
as well—Teddy's half-brother Thomas and his sexy stunning
six-foot-one former track star wife Donna, in short-shorts
promoting the University of Texas all across her big bum.

Teddy and I were fifteen at the time, and Harry had
brought us up for a weekend visit to Thomas's dazzling,
newly built cottage on Georgian Bay.

All five of us were in the boat together—a sleek candy
apple green metal-flake speedboat christened *Sex Toy Too*,
the proud possession of Thomas, a proud Scientologist. We
were all in the boat because it had been decided what a fine
idea it would be to head out and picnic on some uninhabited
island in the bay. This decision had been made despite the
weather. It was a crystal clear sunny day, but a wicked wind
was blowing from the south, a steady flat relentless blast that
felt false and forced, as though manu-factured in hell's own
factory discount wind outlet, freighting freeway grit all the
way from downtown Detroit.

Compounding the wind was the fact that Teddy and I
had dropped acid that morning. Yes I know—write an acid
trip and lose another reader. So I will tell you only this: we
were on the rocky beach waiting for Thomas, who was

bringing the boat around to load it with the picnic things, when the active ingredients of the LSD arrived first and the scene melted down. I will add only that the sun was a neon beach ball; the wind was an intergalactic jet stream from distant stars; the water was a living quivering mystic green Jello; and although there was no God, all things were connected by the now discernible shimmering silver gossamer threads lacing the big blue sky, and a truly awesome Power was at work in the Universe— unfathomably ancient, yet fresh and vital beyond reckoning.

Such is the gift of acid.

Once we were all aboard, Teddy and I shared a glance. We were instantly smacked stupid by the horrific, hair-raising, hilarious beauty of it all. Laugh? We laughed till our brains bent. The laughter was impossible, explosive, compulsive—I thought I would die laughing. I mean it—actually die. I thought it was all over if I couldn't stop laughing. I turned away from Teddy and tried to contain the laughter inside my face and make sense of the living lake.

"Must be comedy hour," Harry said.

Compounding matters further was that Teddy had poured Mountain Dew in the gas tank shortly before we left.

I was there when he'd done that—emptying an entire two-litre bottle of Mountain Dew into the boat's tank while it sat on a trailer behind Thomas's cottage—and I asked him why and what he said was, "Pure jokes."

Although neither of us had been especially keen on a picnic, Teddy's sabotage of the excursion wasn't motivated by his resentment at our being forced to go. He did it because he wanted to see what happens when you put Mountain Dew in the gas tank. It was that simple. Teddy's always had this need to create situations, to throw a tilt into things and make the commonplace day-to-day a little less mundane, a little more sparky, with the bracing edge of uncertain outcomes. Ever since I've known him, Teddy's been producing these high stakes, compulsively entertaining real-time mini-dramas for his own amusement in his life as much as in his art. Most of the crime he's done over the years is likewise marked by an absence of rational motivation or serious intention for tangible gain. He just wants to disturb shit and see what happens. It's all pure jokes.

Sometimes—many times—the joke goes too far. Like this time.

Thomas backed the burbling boat off the beach, punched the throttle hard, and swung about smartly in a steep banked turn that directed us straight at the open smiling face of the big bay. Then the engine died.

The thing about a speedboat is that it's engineered for speed, designed to have a powerful motor strapped to its backside, with a high winding prop biting hard into the water. Without power, we were instantly at the will of the wind and waves, the speedboat itself now nothing but a metal-flake candy-apple green farce, a frivolous party boy, as goofy and useless as a rodeo clown at a house fire.

As a top-ranking Scientologist, Thomas felt confident in his ability to rectify matters. He began by attempting to restart the engine. After killing the battery, he and Harry constructed a clever makeshift sail using bungee cords, a vinyl boat cover, and a pair of skis. When the sail was hoisted at the stern of the boat, the wind laughingly ripped the vinyl cover from the skis and flung it at the sky, sending it cartwheeling toward the Arctic Circle.

"Hey," I said, "I can swim for it." By which I meant that

we weren't yet too far out, and if I went in now, I could still make it to the rapidly disappearing shore for help.

But no one heard me due to some kind of a drama eruption among the grown-ups. Donna was crying. Thomas was raging. Harry was nonplussed.

"What's wrong?" Harry yelled from the back of the boat.

"She's pregnant!" Thomas yelled from the front of the boat.

"What?" Harry yelled.

"She's pregnant!" Thomas yelled.

"What?" Harry yelled.

"She needs a drink!" Thomas yelled. "Get her a drink!"

"What kind?" Harry yelled.

"Sprite!" Donna yelled. "Diet! Or Grape Crush!"

"What?" Harry yelled.

"Oh my god!" Donna sobbed. "Fuck whatever!"

Recreation becomes survival when someone puts Mountain Dew in the gas tank. It soon became obvious that we were in serious trouble. Even the two snickering teens on acid were starting to get the picture. Teddy and I huddled on the floor while the boat plunged up and down the canyon deep troughs and razor sharp peaked waves that threatened to flip it just for fun. There was nothing else for me to do but thrash at the rash that had suddenly exploded on the hinged areas of my body—behind my knees, in the crooks of my elbows, around my wrists and ankles, between my toes—a case of poison ivy so severe I might have murdered myself to make it stop. Even an area behind my eyeballs itched. The only other thing I could think of doing was to wish that there really were a God. A real God. Not that amorphous, conceptual LSD blob god experienced earlier, but a kind and caring bearded God in a robe, sitting on a throne in the sky, watching anxiously over all of us like a caring Father. I used to love that Guy when I was a kid.

The opportunity to swim for shore was long gone. We were too far out, although I was still tempted to try. Every wave was an event. A bleak panic ensued. Teddy found the whole scene terrible good fun. I didn't, mostly because I was sure we were all going to die. As our predicament worsened, I came to resent Teddy for conspiring to kill us. I decided to ignore him and turned my attention to Donna, who had joined us on the floor to cry. I wanted to comfort her in some way, but knowing that she was pregnant, I was uncertain as to how. I'd never met a pregnant woman before, let alone a pregnant yet sexy stunning six foot former track star Scientologist in an out of gas speedboat in a windstorm while on acid. What was I supposed to say? "How's it going?" I wondered if her being pregnant tipped the odds of our survival one way or the other. Either way, it seemed like pretty good headline material. She was sleek and groomed, expensively bejewelled, her long nails painted shiny pink, and her skin, smooth and golden brown, vast and fertile, smelled of cocoa butter and pulsed with life. I would have very much liked to climb inside her skin and wait out the ordeal in the soft brown quiet. She wore white gold ankle bracelets.

"How's it going?" I asked.

"What?" she asked.

"How's it going?"

"How's it what?"

"Are you? I mean. Do you?"

"What's all over your legs?"

"What?"

"You're all blotchy. Look at your face."

"I know. I'm itchy as shit."

"Keep away from me."

"What?"

"Don't touch me."

Then she started vomiting over the side of the boat, followed by a spell of violent dry heaving. I tried not to stare at her bum (University of Texas) but couldn't help it.

After endless hours of tedious terror I spent clawing my poison ivy, enlivened by plenty of pointless yelling on the part of the adults on board, it appeared that salvation was at hand. An island was dead ahead. It wasn't so much an island as a bunch of scraggily wind ravaged trees on some rocks with a sandy point at one end. We were headed straight for it and it was coming on fast.

What happened next took mere seconds, but those seconds were packed with content. Thomas was at the rear of the boat, working a water ski as a paddle, while Harry was at the front doing likewise, with no discernible effect.

"Push it left!" Harry yelled. "Hard right!" Thomas counter-yelled.

Then Harry called for Teddy to get up on the bow and take the line. The idea was for Teddy to jump in and tie up to one of the wrecked trees that reached out to us from the island like the beckoning arms of an anxious grandparent. The problem was, as we neared the island, it became apparent that the wind was going to blow us around it, not at it. And that's just what happened. For a heartbeat the water was bottle-green clear to the bottom, with the comforting sight of rocks and wood and pirate treasure on a floor of soft golden sand, and then it was deep and dark again, and the island was no longer in front of us, but instead travelling hard and fast in the opposite direction, to our left.

"Jump! Go! Now!" Harry yelled.

And then Teddy did something he rarely did and which I'm sure he wouldn't have done then were he not baked on acid. He obeyed his father.

Holding the line in one hand, Teddy slipped off the bow of the boat and into the lake. And disappeared. We were momentarily shielded from the wind by the island, and then the boat spun around to face back as Teddy tugged at the line before the wind resumed control and away we went.

I have to pause here to remind you that I'd taken some wickedly potent blotter acid just hours earlier. I'm too lazy to do it for you, so you'll have to fill in the sensory impression details for yourself, impressions that were raking me like so much machine-gun fire. While reading what follows, feel free to insert such imagery as: pulsing vibratory earth strobe, concussive sun sky knife fight, and the wind water war opera within me.

I leapt off the boat and into the lake.

As wildly heroic as this act was regarded at the time, the truth was, my entire body was aflame with poison ivy by then, and I'd have done anything to dose the blaze. What's more, I had to get out of that boat or kiss sanity goodbye for good. I'd had enough of being held captive by the jaws of nature aboard that toothless craft. The sight of that friendly dot of rock fleeing fast away from us forever was beyond unbearable. It was time to go.

I jumped into the lake but didn't for a second try to find and save Teddy. I collided with the elements and all at once all was chaos. The lake was liquid mayhem, and I was overwhelmed by its bland hostility, its dull determination to chew and swallow me whole. I instantly conceded defeat. There was no up or down, no lake or sky—it was all a single exploding entity. Resistance was futile. The boat and island were gone and I was alone with the wind and water, my face kept barely afloat in the maelstrom by my life jacket. The water felt soupy warm and weirdly welcoming. Luckily, the reptile portion of my brain jumped into the vacant driver's seat and seized control. It had me thrashing toward where it reckoned the island should be, working against where the wind and waves would have me go, now in slow motion. The wind and waves were winning easily, but a total fluke intervened to save my life. I felt something scrape along the skin of my inner thigh. Something artificial, something not of the lake, something glowing bright white. Thanks again to my reptile brain for recognizing it as the line from the boat and seizing a hold of it with both claws before it slipped away.

So I was saved. It took a crazed, superhuman effort—here the acid actually came in quite handy—but miraculously, I was back onboard the *Sex Toy Too*, delirious and shocked, puking lake water. Harry was frantic with relief, crying and laughing as he pulled me over the side and into the boat, astonished that I'd made it out alive. "What would I do if I lost you crazy boy?" he kept saying. "How could I live then? I prayed to God for His help. I prayed to God for you bastard crazy boy."

The wind and waves whisked us away from Teddy and the island. I lay on the floor, rehearsing the news of his death in my heart.

Just before dusk a couple of Native fishermen passed near enough to spot our distress. You know how Harry has this thing about Indians, so he was delighted by that turn of events—two First Nations guys in their long skinny aluminium outboard, coming to our rescue. I couldn't believe the chances they took to tow us to shore. The water was almost knee deep in their boat when they pulled us into the dock at their reserve. From there, Harry sorted us a ride back to the cottage in the Chief's Chevy Caprice.

The weather changed by the time we got back to Thomas's. The wind died and the air cooled. We ate barbequed kabobs, had a big campfire on the beach, and then we went indoors and played Parcheesi. The whole time I was treated like a hero for my selfless attempt to rescue Teddy. Harry toasted my courage with multiple high balls, Donna supplied cooing and calamine lotion for my poison ivy, and Thomas introduced me to the teachings of L. Ron Hubbard, having decided that I had the stuff to become a successful Scientologist. Lucky for me, Thomas was such an arrogant self-absorbed dick that his personal belief system held zero appeal. As a teen, I was a sincere seeker of Truth, reading widely and wildly in search of a painless and sexually rewarding path to Enlightenment. So it was a real close call. Had Thomas been a more appealing spokesmodel for the cult, I might well be a Scientologist today. Instead of sitting in a jail cell, facing a murder charge.

I didn't enjoy the night's celebration of me as much as I might, mostly because I thought Teddy was dead. I'd not seen a glimpse of him after he'd gone into the lake. I was secretly deeply ashamed that I'd made no actual effort to save him. Harry kept telling me not to worry, that he'd seen him scrambling onto the island, but I wasn't convinced. And if he had survived, why weren't we setting out to rescue him immediately?

"Tomorrow we find him," Harry said. "Now is too late, is too dark. Is no problem for him to be one night on the lake."

"He'll freeze his ass off out there," I said. "He could fricking die."

"Yes sure maybe but probably no," Harry said. "I think

is good for him to be alone for one night. This is like Indians do with the young men in the tribe. Like spirit quest.
Maybe tonight Teddy will find his spirit animal."

Yeah, like fuck, I thought. He's dead, and it's all my fault.

Plus I knew why Harry was so sanguine about leaving
the dead or alive Teddy out there over night. Right after
Thomas had drained the battery trying to restart the boat
motor, Harry stuck a finger in the gas tank and got a taste of
what was wrong. Thomas figured "some fucking wagon
burner" must have put sugar in his tank, but Harry
reckoned otherwise.

"Don't be talking such shit about Indians always,
Thomas," Harry scolded. "This is a thing only idiot white
boy would do."

I couldn't sleep that night.

The next day, Harry took his time about fetching the
idiot white boy stranded on the island. He woke up late and
hung over and eased his way through a big breakfast with
the help of several Bloody Caesars. Then he had to make a
bunch of calls about borrowing or renting a boat since the
hull of Thomas's boat was cracked. Then there was lunch.
More phone calls were made; more Bloody Caesars were
drunk. Eventually, a boat was found, but it was at a marina
an hour's drive away. "Let's just alert the coast guard," I
urged at one point, "they might have a helicopter."

Harry roared with laughter at the suggestion. "Not for
spirit quest, no helicopters is allowed."

It was late afternoon by the time Harry and I finally
found the island in the borrowed boat. It was an altogether
different day out on the bay—drizzly calm and gloomy cool,
with a low dense canopy of clouds—and the island looked
like an altogether different place. We slowed and circled

around it twice. There was no sign of Teddy, and I figured we had the wrong place. Or else I'd been right and Teddy was dead. Then I caught sight of a semi-naked stick figure squatting in a tree, and my gut skipped a beat. Teddy had his t-shirt wrapped around his head like a turban, and even from a distance I could see that he'd streaked his face and body with muck in tribal-like markings. He was staring blankly straight ahead, taking no notice of our arrival. I figured he'd gone mad.

"Teddy's spirit animal must be cormorant," Harry joked.

This in reference to the hundreds of long greasy black torpedo shaped birds that blotched the island like a living stain. The only place they weren't was on the part of the tree where Teddy sat. The island was an age-old nesting place, layered deep in generations of cormorant filth—bird shit, bits of shell, fish remnants, broken baby bird bodies. It smelled like the flooded rotted basement of a morgue, and you couldn't put your foot down anywhere without stepping in something soft and slimy, or sharp and crunchy. The stench stung my eyes like tear gas. It was a hostile, other-worldly place. Stupid-eyed mother cormorants approached aggressively as I tied the boat up and stepped ashore. Teddy must have had to fight them off throughout the twenty-four hours plus of his stay.

I coaxed the embattled young brave out of the tree, through the mob of birds and onto the boat, and we made our way back to Thomas's cottage. Harry said nothing about the soda pop flavour in the gas tank; Teddy said nothing about being abandoned on an island in the middle of Georgian Bay overnight. Such is the way of the Chups. Teddy spent the rest of the day in the shower.

That then was the memory coursing through my brain as I lay thinly sleeping at the back of the boat early that Saturday morning on Red Snake Lake. In addition to a memory, it had all the familiar components of a dream—the standard cameo appearance of my brother Douglas for example, as always happy and smiling, this time offering Donna a drink from the miniature vial of Mountain Dew he pulled from his pocket, for which she scolded and spanked him and sent him to bed—because it was as much dream as memory. But it was something more than either dream or memory, and here is why it might interest you T.

Father. Son. Boat. Lake. Island. These are the basic elements of the story. Now they were being reconfigured for another chapter in the family Chup saga. And once again, there I was, the sorry witness to their sordid mess. It turns out that my dreaming memory had also been a divination of sorts.

A shift in sound and motion awoke me. The engine went to a whisper as the boat slowed and settled in the water, the waves from its wake lapping against the hull. We were coming in for a landing. I lay there with eyes shut, savouring the ringing quiet as the engine was cut and the boat drifted in and nudged the dock. The soulful sounds of northern lake country arose all around—songbirds and lapping wake waves on a creaking dock—and would have soothed me back to sleep were it not for the less than soothing sounds of Teddy and Harry.

"Leave the fucking beer in the boat," Harry said.

"Aye aye cap'n," Teddy said.

I opened my eyes to see Teddy stepping onto the dock, a silver green tin of beer sparking in his hand as Harry tied up the boat. Morning had arrived with conviction. Already above the treetops, a cheery yellow sun in a cloudless blue sky was promising another smoking hot day. It took me a moment to realize that we weren't back at the cottage. The dock was new and smelled of fresh cut wood, and the vegetation on the shore was thick and wild. I sat up and stretched.

"Drop your cock and pull up your sock," Harry said to me. "Come see my little island."

There was nothing little about it. The island was massive, at least fifty acres, dense with old growth trees as stolid and magnificent as ancient temples, all laced in vines and creepers, with a lush green moss carpeting the rock strewn ground. Dazzled, stumbling off the dock and onto the trail, the slanted sunlight filtering gold dust through the deep green foliage, I felt as if I'd awoken in a fantasy book. I wouldn't have been surprised to see a unicorn dart by. It was a wonder just to set foot in such a place.

"Holy shit Harry," I said. "This is yours?"

"This is mine," Harry answered. "Purchased last winter."

"Dude," I said. "Holy shit."

It struck me as absurd that a person could actually buy and own a piece of the planet such as this. Not just the money—a couple of million easy—but that it could be property at all, subject to the crude machinations of commerce, of banks and interest rates, voicemail and bidding wars, as though it were just a thing, like my mom's condo, which, coincidentally, she'd also bought last winter. Which is probably why I thought of it at the time. My mom's pride and joy condo, the first property she's ever

owned, with its one closet sized bedroom, cramped kitchenette, and single good feature being the eleventh floor
balcony view of semi-truck rollovers on the 401 exit ramp to
Black Creek—there's an entity easily understood as property,
something humans might exchange for money. Harry's
island was in a different realm. It was like purchasing a
piece of creation itself, as though one could put a down
payment on a ring of Saturn.

"The sign goes here," Harry said, pointing to two tall
wooden posts a little way up from the dock.

"Sign for what?" I asked.

"I will tell you what," Harry said. "Sign for Harry's
Paradise Island of Promises. Or I don't know, something
like that, I am deciding still. Harry's Heaven maybe. You are
the writer here. You tell me."

We were walking on a trail newly cut by a bulldozer,
uprooted tree stumps and rolled over rocks on either side,
and underfoot the hard-packed tracks smelled of mud.
Harry was leading the way. I was hanging back with Teddy,
who was faking an amiable alertness and whimsical
bemusement, grinning and sipping his beer. For a
moment I considered telling him that I'd struck a deal
with Harry, signal the good word with a whisper and a
wink. But I decided against it. I couldn't trust his
response, given his condition. Best to keep it close for
now, I figured, put in a little more time playing nice with
Harry till he officially signed off, and then skip back to
town with you later that afternoon. There'd be plenty of
time to let Teddy in on it.

Just then I became aware of something heavy in my
shorts pocket. I reached in and came up with the freaking
Hitler gun. I'd completely forgotten about it. For a laugh, I

held it up at the back of Harry's head, as though we were marching him into the forest for execution. This busted Teddy up. He made a lunge for the gun, and snatched it out of my hand. He pointed it at his head and pulled the trigger. Then he pointed it at my head and pulled the trigger. Then we tussled for it briefly, and I knocked the tallboy out of Teddy's hand. He spun round to pick it up before it all spilled. I didn't want Harry to see the gun.

"So what you building here Harry?" I asked, to make Teddy quit with the gunplay.

We'd followed the bulldozer's tracks until we arrived at the quiet yellow Cat culprit itself, at rest in the clearing it had smashed into the forest, alongside its big buddy, the Skidder, and several neat stacks of fresh cut logs they'd collaborated on. The sweaty work smell of the machinery hung like a pleasant greasy fart in the fresh morning air.

"Here will go the dining hall and centre for arts and crafts," Harry said. "I'll show you the drawings when we get back."

"Yeah? What's the plan Harry?" I asked.

"Boys," Harry said, turning to face us, opening his arms wide, squinting a beatific gaze skyward and then all round, "this is for a camp I am making. Is a place for the children to come in the summer for holiday. For the Harry Chup Children Foundation."

"Wait. I don't get it," Teddy said, taking out a cigarette, patting his pockets for a light. "Hairy children or Harry Children?"

I got it. I got it instantly. We were touring the Island of Teddy's Lost Inheritance.

While Harry elaborated on his plan, Teddy pulled faces, nodding and smiling with an expression of madcap delight, as though in imitation of the very children Harry had in mind as visitors to the island.

"I am making this a camp place for the special children to come in the summer for holiday. I want it for all kinds of children—the mental retard children, or with cancer, or in wheelchairs—whatever race and religion, for me it doesn't matter. I want this to be a beautiful resting place for these kind of special kids to come and relax in outdoors to mix in with nature. Here they can do everything what the normal children can do. Swimming. Fishing. Hunting. Sailing in special boats. There will be trails for wheelchairs. I want to make this place like a heaven for the special children."

I won't pretend to speak on behalf of the world's Special Children, but it sounded more like hell to me. A couple of weeks in such a place would serve mainly to remind special kids of their specialness, an awareness boot camp for the tragically afflicted. But that's beside the point. The place wasn't getting made for kids anyway. The intended beneficiary of Harry's generosity was, of course, Harry himself. The gleam in Harry's eye wasn't from his vision of an island paradise alive with happy handicapped and terminally ill children weaving baskets and singing camp songs. Its source was Harry's vision of his own posthumous recognition as a selfless philanthropist and all-round Great Guy. In death, Harry aspired to be seen as everything he hadn't been in life, via the Harry Chup Children Foundation.

"Wow," I said. "What a beautiful thing Harry. Kids will love it up here."

"Fuck yeah Dad," Teddy said, before draining his Heineken and firing it into the bush. "Righteous."

Harry stared and soured and was about to say something

but changed his mind. I think he wanted to maintain his fine mood, relishing the sense of power and mastery he got just from being there, standing in the clearing with the machines that he'd contracted to clear it, describing what He was going to do with His island. He wasn't about to let Teddy trivialize events by littering just to piss Him off.

"Best thing of all," Harry said, "around here is all Crown land, nothing but wilderness. For miles is completely untouched. Nice and peaceful, beautiful place for children to visit from city. Is like Garden of Eden."

I underestimated Teddy. I thought he might descend into a bitter sulk at this point, mutter something cryptic, stumble off into the bush, maybe return to the boat and sit there brooding and boozing till he finally fell down. But that would have made it easy for Harry. That would have been giving Harry what he wanted. Instead Teddy gave him a surprise, something to think about—namely, his pledge of support and even worse, his passionate commitment to become involved. Essentially what Teddy gave him was the realization that he wasn't going away, that even if Harry died, Teddy would still be around, doing his best to fuck with the big man's Legacy.

"Suggestion," Teddy said. "Keep it simple. Harry Chup Island. I like it just plain simple, Harry Chup Island. A sanctuary of love. Dad? Count me in. Father? I am officially down with the plan. Totally. Fucking. Down. It's brilliant, this. Listen. How can I help?"

"You? You. Nothing you can do for help. It's actually project doesn't need help," Harry said. "I am talking with the Y, also Kiwanis. Some organization like this will run the program. They know what they are doing. I will just build and let them do it. They are the expert in field."

"Yeah but here's what I'm thinking. How about this? I could make a film," Teddy said. "I'll shoot a documentary, right here, starting now. Let the motherfucking world know."

Harry grunted and grimaced. He couldn't even look at Teddy, as though regarding his son's parking lot brawl bashed face as a calculated insult to him.

"We could bring a couple of special kids up here right now," Teddy said. "While it's still being built, right? Get a couple of Down syndrome kids and a kid getting chemo. First we see them up visiting, consulting with you on the project at various stages. Then we bring them back when it's all finished. It would be so fucking poignant man, especially if the kid with cancer dies, right after ironically visiting heaven. The retarded kids freaking out in grief. Like, whoa. Heavy shit."

Short of vowing to detonate a dirty bomb on the island, nothing Teddy could have said would have been more alarming to Harry. The mere suggestion of Teddy bringing his artistic vision to bear on this place turned Harry purple.

"Is all incredible stupid ideas," Harry said. "Honestly Teddy, listen to you. Best to keep the mouth closed when only the garbage comes out."

"Wait. Not so fast Dad. Let's get a third opinion, a tiebreaker. What does our writer think?"

"Something to think about. I dunno," I said.

"Yes sure," Harry said. "Something to think about. Sure. Teddy up here, taking his drugs, doing one of his stupid fuck shit so-called art films. With children. Yes. Is something to think about. Something for police to think about."

"Not only that," Teddy added, "listen, once the camp's up and running? I could come up and do theatre with the kids. Do Shakespeare. King fucking Lear or some shit, and film the whole thing. Or hey you know what? I could teach them film production. Yeah. I was special ed myself. I was always special ed. I feel those kids man."

"So, yes sure, you can come up here and feel kids. Good yes. Maybe also you can teach kids to take drugs, how to sell them, and how it's like going to jail. Around campfire you can tell them scary stories about what is like to waking up in detox in psych hospital from drug overdose."

Their cross-purpose conversation continued. Teddy provoking Harry with lurid film ideas, pissing all over his parade; Harry jabbing away at Teddy with a pointed recap history of his substance abuse, incarceration, and mental health setbacks, on a seek and destroy mission for any last particle of self-worth Teddy might have had left.

Thankfully, a bear arrived to change the subject.

I'd stepped away from the talk to take a leak when I saw it. It was a smallish bear, jet black and wet, fresh from his morning bath. The bear was foraging around the edge of the clearing, clawing at the ground for grubs or something. It was aware of us but didn't seem to care, probably too young to realize that creatures like us might kill it just because.

"Hey," I said. "Shut up."

Harry and Teddy went quiet and the three of us stood there watching the bear, mesmerized. The bear made me think of a young Elvis Presley. It must have been its gleaming black fur, its robust sexy energy and lusty swagger, its native confidence and naive nonchalance. Mostly though it made me feel bad. The bear's vigour and innocence, the authenticity of its purpose, the basic healthy wholesomeness of the bear—in short, everything about the bear—was the opposite of us, the three human interlopers in the wild, with our sordid wants and sleazy agendas, still loaded on the filth we'd been polluting ourselves with the night before. The bear was so good and pure, and we were so bad and toxic. I wanted to be the bear. Failing that, I wanted to go to bed and dream of being the bear. It wore me out just watching that bear go about its business. Watching the bear in action made me dizzy with moral fatigue.

"Hey bro, got a light?" Teddy asked the bear, walking straight at it, a bent cigarette in his mouth.

"Jesus Crimeny," Harry said.

The bear glanced at Teddy but continued doing his thing, clawing the ground, grunting and huffing, not wanting to give up his good grubbing spot. Teddy got within a few feet of the bear before it scrambled away. It bolted with a sulky suddenness, hardly making a sound as it melted into the forest. Teddy followed. I could hear him crashing through the underbrush, talking to the bear in Spanish accent, "Yo mang, wait up, les go downtown mang. We can split a cab yo."

"Fuck," Harry spat. "Hopefully bear will kill him. Save me all the trouble."

Teddy had fractured Harry's good morning mood. He muttered about some work he wanted to check on and stalked off on a bulldozed trail that led away from the clearing. I stood there by myself for a moment, thankful for this respite from the Chups, but sadly missing the bear.

What would the bear do now? The answer came to me and I headed back to the dock, stripped naked and jumped into the lake.

Here is what I'd been wanting most. Whatever else I might have hoped to achieve over the weekend, a swim in the lake was the one dead certain thing. The bear had come along to remind me. So when the opportunity arrived, I seized it

with gusto. A bit too much gusto. The water was cool with
welcome warm patches, and I stroked and kicked and paddled
as fast and far away from the island as I could, pausing to dive
with eyes open wide, down the green sunbeam shafts to the
cold, dark depths below, till my lungs burned and I'd look up
at the dancing silvery surface mirroring the blue sky above,
and claw my way back up to the air. Like this, alternating deep
dives with clumsy swim strokes, I got away from the island
without once looking back.

I thought of you T. I was naked in the cold water, and
you were across the lake, naked in our warm bed. So I got a
boner. I credit the bear spirit for that because it was cold out
there deep in the early morning lake, and I believe that only
a bear could spring a boner in such conditions. It was a
miracle. The miraculous bear boner made me think yet
more about you and so, clutching hold of it, I turned to look
back at the island and the boat at the dock, with a notion of
hastening now to the cottage to find you, warm and
fragrant, drowsy naked in our warm bed, where I would
greet you good morning and share with you all the magic of
my miracle spirit of the cold lake bear boner.

Looking back from out in the lake the island seemed
much smaller than I'd thought, and the boat was barely
visible. Then I realized that it wasn't so much that the island
was small, but that I was far away from it. Real fucking far.

It wasn't like I was going to drown out there, but it did
take a long time and every last bit of strength I had to swim
back to the dock. I'm a terrible swimmer, a sinker by nature.
That magic bear boner didn't help matters much. By the
time I finally dragged it and me out of the water, it was all I
could do to get dressed and board the boat. Neither Chup
was about, so I went below deck to the compact lounge area

wedged into the V of the bow, like a plush white leatherette vagina, set and lit as though for a porn shoot, and helped myself to a couple of bracing shots of vodka from the mini-bar and would have jerked off too but it was so warm and dark down there that I curled up on the sofa and spun straight to sleep.

Sometime later, I became aware of the engine's steady thrum and the boat's rhythmic skip across the water. We were moving at a wicked fast clip. For a moment, an image of the bear driving the boat came to mind while I slept below. But I searched the image and realized it was false. It wasn't the bear driving the boat. It was Teddy. And somehow—the boat's senseless speed?—I knew he was alone at the helm. Neither the bear nor Harry were on board.

And where were you T? Still asleep in our warm bed.

And where are you now T?

I only ask because there's a lonely boy bear with a boner, lost in a dark forest, badly missing you.

Love,

e.

Dear T,

Since I've got nothing better to do today (we're on lockdown
due to a violent three-way dispute involving a dark family
secret, a purloined sock, and some fecal matter—please don't
ask), I spent the morning perusing my collection of press
clippings about the case. That's a bit of an exaggeration. There
aren't that many press clippings to peruse since there's no
trial to report on yet. It takes me ten minutes to peruse them
thoroughly. And then I peruse them again. And again. And
again. And so on. All in effort to fill this empty lockdown day
in jail. Once I got them all perused and arrayed on my bunk
in chronological order ("Impressive fucking work there
Dillinger," said Manfred, admiringly, "make a good school
project.") I was struck by how the narrative unfolds via
headlines that clock the progress of the police investigation. I
read them over and tried to imagine what a disinterested
observer might make of the story. Then I read them again and
tried to imagine what an interested T might make of the story.

The *Star*'s first headline is this taste-tempting teaser, if
you have a taste for this sort of thing: Mystery Surrounds
Businessman's Death (body found in trunk of car).

The *Sun*, unable to resist the illuminating allure of alliteration, opens with: Door Man Dead in Driveway (cops close to collaring culprits).

By the next day, Harry's status grows considerably, and the story itself grows legs. We're on the front page but below the fold of the God Almighty *Globe and Mail*: Wealthy Entrepreneur 'Brutally Murdered,' Police Say (unidentified trio being questioned).

The *Star* also ups Harry's status that day: Millionaire Murdered (police say charges 'imminent').

The *Sun*, with its lowbrow populist instincts, runs a cloying, sentimental and misinformation-packed profile of Harry Chup, headlined: Dynamic, Generous and Full of Love and Life (best pal laments loss of 'greatest guy in the world') in which Harry's "best pal" and lawyer describes his as yet unidentified assailants as "evil lowlife scum," and laments both the loss of his best pal and client Harry, and the unavailability of death by hanging as legal remedy for the perpetrators.

The next day, all the papers go with a variation on the *Star*'s blunt and succinct: Two Held in Chup Murder (controversial artist son and friend charged; police remain close-lipped).

Harry would have been ecstatic by the *Post*'s description of him that day as "the reigning tsar of the automatic garage door industry." Less than ecstatic was my mom, who arose from a sleepless muggy Tuesday night to an even muggier smog alert Wednesday morning to find her son's mug shot featured on TV and in all three daily papers, looking tussled and tossed, wearing a stunned stupid cotton-mouthed pleading no-contest smirk, as though I'd been pinched for exposing myself in a schoolyard. It's the kind of thing that could give a mother a brain tumour. And if she does get a brain tumour, I'll tell you who's to blame. The guy whose luridly bruised mug is beside mine, gazing cool and level and unsurprised straight at you, with an expression that seems to say: Mission Accomplished.

Teddy freaking Chup.

The thing is this T. All the time I've known him, ever since age thirteen, Teddy's been on a relentless quest to get caught and punished. And I've been right by his side for much of it, more than half my lifetime, riding shotgun on the project.

Indulge me this memory.

It was the summer before grade nine, and my mom and I had just moved into a basement apartment in the suicidal new subdivision of Royal Oak Manors, on the wrong side of the tracks and in the shadow of a nearby strip-mall Money Mart. A short distance yet a world away, across the train tracks, past the hydro lines, and beyond the stubble field, the big fat cat houses quietly purred on manicured lawns. On our side of the tracks, with its mix of struggling South Asian newcomers and fifth generation flop-sweat survivors, people lived lives of noisy desperation in cardboard apartment blocks and styrofoam townhouses. I spent my final days of summer holiday alone in this bleak and friendless neighbourhood, mostly kicking along the railway tracks, hoping to find a bag of valuables that might perchance have dropped from a passing train, wishing I had a girlfriend. Or a pet even. Most of all, I wanted my brother Douglas back. It had been three months since the cold wet Sunday night when he'd lost his life jumping off a roof on a dare, right before my eyes, and I couldn't rid myself of the conviction that if I just kept walking around talking to him, he'd show up and everything could go back to normal.

Instead, Teddy Chup showed up.

One day I strayed to the other side of the tracks and under the hydro lines, across the stubble field, over the dirt sound berm, climbed the rust-streaked steel wall, and dropped into Camelot Estates, where I encountered Teddy Chup. Actually it was his dog I first encountered, a big lively lovable golden lab retriever named Boo. The dog bounded over to me, leaping and licking, circling all around me with a big dumb happy dog smile. He was well groomed and well fed and wore a collar, but I instantly decided that the dog must be lost, probably abandoned, and that I would therefore take him home. It was my lucky day. This was even better than finding a bag of valuables. I'd fallen in love.

Of course I called the dog Buddy, and together we roamed around behind the big houses in a narrow strip of old farm forest that the developers had neglected to destroy. It was a humid hot pregnant with rain type of day, and the dog was panting heavily, so I worried that he might die of thirst. I considered sneaking into a backyard to get him a drink from a swimming pool or a garden hose, but the high wooden fences enclosing the sprawling yards made that unlikely. I decided that I might as well take Buddy home. He was probably hungry too. I could thaw out some wieners in the microwave for the both of us.

The problem was there was just no possible way to get the dog over the wall by the railway tracks. I tried to pick him up, but he didn't like that very much—I'd had little hands-on experience with dogs—and even if I could lift him over, how was I to climb the wall at the same time? There was nothing else to do but head for the nearest level crossing.

"Come on Buddy," I said, "I know a way out of here."

"Okay!" the dog replied, with a bright-eyed slobbery smile and his entire body tail-wagging with joy as we set off together, madly in love.

But then, just as suddenly, our love affair was over.

"Hey! Boo!" someone called.

It was a kid on a chrome BMX bike, emerging from out of the trees.

"Here Boo! Come on boy!"

Without a hint of hesitation, the dog left my side and shot over to the kid on the bike. The kid dropped the bike and wrestled around with the dog, a bit too roughly I thought, saying, "Yes Boo, that a boy Boo, good Boo, where you been Boo?" and so on.

Then the kid got back on the bike and stood on the pedals to power his way over to me, hanging heartbroken by the wall.

"Hey. Punk. Trying to steal my dog or what?" the kid asked, skidding to a stop and flinging his bike aside.

"Yeah right. I thought it was lost."

"Yeah right."

"Like I'm going to steal a dog."

"Like you weren't. I seen you taking him. You were trying to get him over the thing. Fucking dog thief."

Meet Teddy Chup, age thirteen. Try to picture him then. He was dewy soft and princely pale and still wore a layer of baby fat, his eyes the colour of caramel candy, with long lashes and a glamour puss mouth. I remember thinking that he had a girl's face, pretty but cruel, and that there was something crazy in his looks, like he believed he saw things others couldn't, the truth behind it all, certain that he alone knew what was happening. He looked at me with an appraising gaze, an uncanny confidence, as though he had the power to see right through me. I'd never been looked at like that before. He wasn't actually angry. It was more like he was amused by my impudence, as if I were some dirty peasant who'd wandered onto his manor to poach animals. He exuded a sense of entitlement that I instantly associated with easy money. In short, everything about this kid made me want to kick the living shit out of him. I would have too, but I didn't want to disappoint the dog.

"Take your freaking dog and go fuck yourself. I don't want him."

Unable to understand English, the dog was oblivious to the animosity between Teddy and me. He was bouncing all around us, happier than ever, since he now had two fun friends to play with. I didn't respond. He wasn't my Buddy anymore. He was this kid's Boo, and so I had no right touch him. I avoided even looking at him.

Teddy mimicked me in a thick mock retard voice— "'Take your freaking dog go fuck yourself I don't want him.' Fucking loser."

I didn't reply to the taunt, waiting to see if he had anything to add, something that would leave me no choice but to merc him. Instead he said something weird, something that confirmed my impression that he was, as my mom would say, touched.

"You should watch yourself around here kid. This whole area's under surveillance you know," Teddy said, revealing to me for the first time his lifelong obsession with surveillance and all matters pertaining to the things people do when they think no one is watching. He'd no doubt been watching me the entire time I'd been with Boo.

"Really? Wow. Well, Merry Christmas, ya freak."

Teddy laughed.

Then he picked up his gleaming BMX bike and cycled off, with his beautiful golden dog Boo bounding along at his side, the two of them heading for one of those palatial homes beyond the trees. Fat globs of rain began plopping all around, falling straight down from a windless sky. I thought to myself, yes, the kid was right—I was a fucking loser—as I scrambled up and over the wall, climbed the dirt berm, crossed the stubble field and under the hydro lines, ran across the train tracks, and arrived at our basement apartment soaked to the skin. There I ate KD and wieners for lunch, and then spent the afternoon watching (non-cable) TV until my mom arrived home from her job as a temp secretary. She passed the evening lying on the couch in the dark, imploring her migraine with whispered requests, while I wandered around outside, talking to Douglas in the steamy drizzle.

A week or so later I found myself in the same grade nine homeroom as Teddy, at Valley View Central Collegiate, a sinister bunker of a building that looked more like a desert military fortification than a school. There was no valley and certainly no view, since the school had gun turrets for windows and, what was worse, all the kids there seemed to have been bonded together in some secret ceremony at birth, during which they'd vowed to exclude any and all outsiders from the clan forevermore. I won't describe how it feels to be the designated lone weirdo hitter in teen world since that experience has been extensively and sensitively rendered elsewhere by real experts. I also won't describe Teddy's steady escalating sly mean mockery of me other than to say that the gist of his jibes was that I stole dogs to eat for food and always wore the same pair of pants, only part of which was true. Nor will I tell you how I obsessed over him, and loathed and craved his attention with a love-hate ache that made me want to murder him. The inevitable punch-up occurred on an early fall Friday afternoon when we were hanging around the track, waiting to get into the change rooms after phys ed class. The funny thing is, I remember nothing of the actual fight—it's a dizzy dusty blur—except that our gym teacher, the porky Mr. Cullen, seemed to really enjoy it. I suspect he was some kind of pervert connoisseur of teen boy brawls.

That fight changed everything.

Instead of being punished, Teddy and I were obliged to engage in a process of peer mediation. It was a new model of resolving conflicts, and Valley View was the self-proclaimed world leader in this progressive innovation. The process involved an exchange of letters and a series of meetings mediated by a pair of earnest, high self-esteem grade twelve students, and facilitated by a grey pony-tailed guidance counsellor drifting toward retirement, during which we'd read each other's letters aloud.

In case you didn't know this, grade nine boys are the greatest comedians on earth. This is because their urge to subvert and sabotage for comedic purposes knows no bounds. I remember later that year we successfully reinterpreted the play version of the *Diary of Anne Frank* as a situation comedy, with the late Chris Farley starring as Mister Dussel, thereby bringing our rookie English teacher, the lovely Miss Underbridge, to tears of frustration.

I'd do anything to see those letters again. It'd be like discovering the Dead Sea Scrolls of Comedy.

My first letter was medium dry. I took full responsibility for the conflict, declaring that I was both sole instigator and ultimate victor in the brawl, whereas Teddy was the shy type who perhaps had difficulty sharing his feelings. I promised

that if Teddy ever said mean things to me again, I would buy
him a bag of chips and take him bowling. Teddy's letter read
like a police blotter written by a demented six-year-old—
short and terse, with improvised grammar and almost entirely incoherent. It ended with something like, "I, Theodore
A. Chup, hereby state for the record those facts of the case
and swear to all parties involved such unbeknownst activities will never occur on the part of my person ever again So
Help Me God."

We both sat grinning at the floor in the silence that
followed the reading of our letters. The two teen UN special
envoys took turns probing us for more.

"How did it make you feel when you read Teddy's
letter?" asked the pretty and poised Eurasian girl.

"Good?"

"Define 'good,'" said the bland blond boy debating team
captain.

"Like, not bad?"

It went on like this until the pony-tailed guidance
counsellor roused himself from his midmorning torpor to
intervene. We were told that this wouldn't do, that we weren't
being sincere or honest, and that we'd be compelled to
continue with the process until we both came clean. We were
instructed to go away and write better letters, starting at the
beginning from when we first met, describe it all in detail, and
share our honest feelings about everything that happened.

Teddy was fuming resentful about having to write
another letter, and I pretended to be pissed too, but in truth
I couldn't wait to get to work on my follow-up missive.

It was a comedic masterpiece. As per the guidance
counsellor's instructions, I began with how I first met Teddy,
and I shared my feelings about everything—"For breakfast I

ate Coco Puffs naked. I felt happy." I depicted my encounter
with Teddy's dog as a harrowing wilderness adventure saga,
with me risking life and limb to save the disoriented dog
from being struck by a Go Train in a torrential rainstorm,
and Teddy as a helpless sobbing waif, howling in the wind
for his lost buddy Boo. Reading it aloud, Teddy convulsed
with laughter at the best bits. It was the first time I'd
experienced the power of my written words to move another
person. I was thrilled by his response; I wanted more. But
before Teddy had even finished reading my letter, the
guidance counsellor threw in the towel. We had utterly
perverted the conflict resolution process. The tables were not
just turned, they were flipped upside down and peed on with
grade nine boy pee. We had resolved our conflict by creating
an entirely new conflict—a conflict with our ostensible
conflict resolvers. We both got suspended for two days, not
for fighting, but for our unwillingness to engage in the
conflict resolution process seriously. From that point on we
were friends. So I guess the process really does work.

To say we were friends doesn't quite cover it. It was more
like a romance, intense and excruciating, the kind of thing
where others are rendered invisible and a new language is
spoken, a pidgin meant to exclude outsiders and confirm be-
longing. There were other guys in on it too, but I was fiercely
protective of my addiction to Teddy. He was serious fun to
hang with. He had the magnetic charm of the truly dangerous, capable of doing anything, fearless of consequence. It
was an attitude I aspired to emulate. It made the world a
place of sky-blue possibilities, a place where reality was what
you got away with. I longed to inhabit such a world. Since my
home life was constrained by cash flow woes and my mom's
quiet crash nervous breakdown, I ended up practically living

at Teddy's, where money was no worry and things were wide-open chaotic and fun, cluttered with brand name consumer items still bearing price tags, and rollicking with action and adventure and drama. Drama in spades. A disagreement at a family gathering might end with Harry flipping a hot bar-beque into the pool. Or Harry might disappear for days at a time, and then arrive home with a shiny new ATV for Teddy, or a violent tirade, probably both, one swiftly following the other, and then another puppy.

In the course of things I learned all about Teddy Chup. One thing I learned early on was that he was hardwired for crime, the consummate buzz junky. It amazed me the lengths he'd go to find a thrill, at ever escalating stakes. There always had to be an element of theatre involved. We couldn't just flee a restaurant without paying. The entire serving staff at Red Lobster would first have to bring a cake and sing him Happy Birthday, and only then would we slip out the emergency fire door. He had a Ronald Reagan mask, and access to both his mom's abandoned wardrobe and his dad's extensive gun collection. So why not rob a gas bar with a vintage handgun on a hot July night, disguised as an ex-president in a black cocktail dress to foil surveillance? We made good our getaway on BMX bikes, flying down a trail in the ravine. That one got on "CityPulse Tonight." As much as these exploits worried me, I always had to stick it out to see where things went. What worried me most was my mom. How would my mom cope if I got caught? I feared it would push her even deeper into her dark corner, from where she might never emerge. Teddy had no such worries. Teddy had no worries about anything. And the thing is, we never got caught.

With all our hanging-out together, all our daring-do and combat camaraderie, I came to believe that I alone knew

Teddy. And in a way that was true. There were many things
about Teddy that only I knew. One thing I knew, for example—although actually Harry knew too, since he was the one
to discover it. I was there when that happened, the summer
we were fourteen. Harry, drunk as a lord at one of his Thurs-
day backyard barbeques for company staff and clients, play-
fully grabbed a hold of Teddy with the intention of wrestling
him into the pool fully clothed. Teddy struggled loose, tearing his shirt open in the fun. All at once and at first inexplicably, their play fight became a fight fight. Harry exploded in
rage. Teddy spun away from a ringing slap to the head, his
torn open shirt revealing the shimmering mauve camisole
beneath, and bolted out of the yard. I remember the look on
Teddy's face—shocked humiliation and fury, yes, but cold
calm acceptance too. So his secret was out: big fucking deal.

I don't remember thinking anything much about it. It
was just another thing about Teddy. It didn't even surprise
me. Nothing Teddy did could surprise me. I don't even
remember talking to him about it afterwards, other than
him insisting that he wasn't gay, which I already knew.
Actually he was glad I'd found out because we instantly
came to an unspoken understanding, which he, of course,
worked to his advantage. This understanding meant that
when we were at a house party or something, I might have
to run interference while Teddy set off on a bedroom safari
to rifle through dresser drawers, hunting for big game
trophy undergarments. He couldn't help it, so I had to help
him with it. I also understood that whenever we pulled a
break-and-enter, Teddy would linger longer inside to emerge
later, pockets stuffed with lingerie, while I hung outside in
the lane, holding the goods and desperate to flee, barely able
to breathe.

I understood. I understood all about Teddy Chup. And because I understood, I felt for him.

What I failed to understand was that none of what I felt was reciprocated, that Teddy is incapable of authentic fellow feelings for his fellow humans, myself included. It was like I was playing a board game and paying out in cash, whereas Teddy only ever used play money.

I didn't know this until it was too late. I didn't know this until I was put in jail, falsely fingered for murder by Teddy. I think I still don't know this since I still don't hate him, even now. I can't explain. I can only tell.

I can tell you that upon awaking later that Saturday morning aboard the boat at Red Snake Lake, my first thought was: Where is Teddy? Not, where are you? Or even, where am I? Where is Teddy was what I wanted to know. I woke up below deck, stuck to the sticky white leatherette sofa, soaked in sweat, the air broiling hot with that new boat smell. My mouth tasted like old ass and a pain pulsed behind my left eye. I popped up on deck to be greeted by a sunshine sucker punch so severe it could have knocked me flat. I covered my left eye with my left hand and surveyed the scene with my right eye. To my disappointment, we weren't back at the cottage. We were docked at the bright and busy Swear Blind Bay Marina, and I was alone onboard, afloat in fuel fumes, the boat's chrome trim sparking in the sun, the white plastic parts and padding glowing hot.

Certainly I wasn't the first person ever to walk the sagging wooden plank floor of the General Store at the Swear Blind Bay Marina carting a hangover. But that's how it felt. Like I was different. Not a different type of person, but an altogether different species, a shifty shaky species, sweaty and furtive, stinking of drink, incapable of language. All the Caucasian cottage folk bustling about there that morning appeared in tip-top form, happily embarking on their sunny Saturday summer's day of fun recreational activities, loading up on snacks and gas. The buzz of breezy conversation filled the store as polite people exchanged pleasantries with an ease and assurance that I could only marvel at. If called upon, I would not have been able to produce a single affable banality. Thankfully, the happily holidaying homosapiens were inclined to grant me an extra wide berth that sunny Saturday morn.

It took all of my focus to accomplish the multi-stage task of selecting from the various colours of Gatorade available in the cooler, locating a litre of chocolate milk in the dairy section, exchanging currency for these items at the counter and exiting the store with my purchases.

Outside I walked with a stiff limp. I felt eggshell fragile, with that global sort of self-awareness hangover that provides one with a golden opportunity for some searching reflection. But I didn't interest me much. I found a quietly spinning shaded glade to hide under a tree near the dock where I drank the blue Gatorade and puked, and then drank the chocolate milk and didn't puke. After which my head knocked the hard ground under the tree and I slept. I dreamt I was trying to flag a cab downtown in a snowstorm with Harry and the bear. We made the bear duck behind a bus shelter and smoke a cigarette until the cab pulled over, lest he scare it off. Douglas came from out of nowhere and jumped into the front seat, smiling.

"Let's rock," I heard a voice say from outside my head and felt a toe tap tap my foot.

I opened one eye and looked straight up and into the booze-blotched, coke-crazed face of Teddy Chup. His nose had purpled to twice its regulation size, and both eyes were black bruise ringed, cartoon raccoon style. The orange tinted cycling glasses framed the damage like crime scene police tape.

"Whoa, look at you. You got a broken nose son."

Teddy tested his nose with a tentative touch.

"No, it's fine. It's healing up fine."

"Want to see a doc?"

"No time for that. Let's go."

I sat up. "Where you been? Where's Harry?"

"What?"

"Where you been?"

"Had to see a man about a dog."

"You're fucking kidding. Here?"

I shouldn't have been surprised that Teddy managed to score in a quaint lakefront resort town in cottage country on a sunny summer Saturday morning. It's his specialty. You could send him into Vatican City and within an hour he'd be smoking rock and hooking up a tug job at the only Vietnamese massage parlour in town.

"Where's Harry?" I asked again as we boarded the boat.

"Who Harry? Harry who? Yo, check this shit my nigga."

We went below and Teddy cut a couple of lines on the mini-bar. It would have made no sense not to toot up at that point. Likewise, there was nothing to be gained in refusing the vodka and Clamato Teddy mixed us up for breakfast.

"Friend, that there is some filthy snay," I said, worrying my nose. "Where'd you get it?"

"Local hoser. It's not bad. For local."

"Shit's badly compromised. Fucker stepped on it with Comet or some shit."

"Works fine. Keep trying. Don't be a baby."

I braved another brutal line, shuddering it down, feeling it find its way into my hollow head and guts, shaking me to an abrupt and jagged wakefulness, and then we carried our drinks up on deck, untied the lines, and slipped out of the marina, Teddy confident at the wheel, adhering to his own version of the rules of the sea. He gunned it when we got clear of the multi craft cluttered marina area and into open water. The boat sat up and fairly flew, wobbling wildly when Teddy got sloppy with the wheel, over-correcting before regaining the groove. The lake was a lush tropical green, the sky a heaven sent infinite blue, and I felt much better now. It felt fine to be perched up high on deck, flying in a fast boat across the lake on a fine sunny day. I had that sense of open-ended exhilaration that I used to get when hanging with Teddy, free to do anything since all things are possible. Or okay, it could just be the drugs. I was high again and meant to stay that way. It was a delicate high, as frail as an arthritic dowager, and would require constant care and maintenance. Coming down now was too horrific to contemplate. I'd learned my lesson at the marina.

Teddy modulated to a cruising speed and instructed me to find some tunes. From Harry's impressive collection of *Very Best of* CDs, I selected the *Very Best of George Jones*. We welcomed George's smooth country baritone aboard, and he regaled us with cornpone tales of sweet hurt and boozy regret. Which reminded me: What about Harry?

"We'll get him tomorrow," Teddy said, "once he's finished his spirit quest. All he needs is one night of solitary wilderness, a little Harry time. Give him a week out there, he'd be a full-on fucking shaman."

"Let's don't be stupid. We shall go now and collect him forthwith. Do it now."

"No. We shan't. Not today," Teddy said. "I find him. Unpleasant. He makes me. Unhappy."

"Teddy. Think. Centre. Focus. Fuck. What are we doing here, anyway? What did we come here for? The whole thing is to pitch him our thing. This here? This here fucking off with his boat? This could piss him off so much he might not want to even talk to us no more."

."He doesn't want talk to me no more irregardless. I'll tell you what, Harry messes my mind something terrible. You don't even know."

"Get over it. You're a big boy now. Move on. Burn that motherfucking bridge."

"I am burning that motherfucking bridge. I'm on that motherfucking bridge and I'm burning it from both ends. See, this here's a dad thing, so you don't understand. You're the lucky fucker: sans dad. You never had the big bad dad disaster fucking your life. Being a dick. With carrot and stick. Making you sick."

"Cuz my daddy's slick Rick."

"Only done that one trick."

"Then he don't stick."

"Outta town he done flick."

"Dropped like a brick."

"Lit like a wick."

"Yes ras, jus' cool den, seen? Hol' up on de rhyming son, before me mum get implicated in da scheme."

"Face fucking facts," Teddy said, "your dad, whatever he was, he did the righteous thing. Didn't hang around to make a mess. He was gone. Adios amigos, farewell. You never had to deal with his bad dad shit. Brother, you were born free."

We broke into song, two and a half lusty verses of "Born Free," rekindling my headache.

I could see Teddy's point though, especially in the context of Harry. But absence makes the heart grow strange, leaving its dad-sized hole. Having never met the man, as a kid I used to make myself mad with speculation. So many gripping fantasy scenarios of discovery and reunion I dreamed up and acted out. All pure conjecture since I'm uncertain even of the circumstances involved. All I know is my mom was sixteen and living in Gander, Newfoundland, near the airbase where her dad was itinerant pastor. The man in question (let's call him "Dad?") was with the U.S. Air Force. And that's it. That's all I know. However, my mean drunk Uncle Rae once while staying with us, mocked my mom about her "Newfie honeymoon in the back seat, parked at the sports bar after the Leafs game. Leafs lost two-nothing I believe," thereby plunging her into a helpless mute tearful rage, so clearly there was some truth there. Right around then I stopped asking her about "Dad?" and learned to stop bothering myself about it too. I still don't ever bother about it or him. And by the by, if my mom found out I ever told any of this to you T, she'd be devastated. She'd hate the thought of you thinking any less of her T. So if it ever does come up, just go with that story I told you before about the high school sweetheart exchange student killed in a tragic car wreck, okay?

"Come now boy. For real. Go fetch Harry," I said. "I'll do the talking. It's all on me, the boat thing."

"He knows you'd never do no such thing. You love the man Harry. He knows that."

"He thinks that. All the more reason. Go. Now. Know the way skipper?"

"'Course." And then after a moment, "Alright. You win. Let's go get Daddy."

Teddy steered the boat in a wide lazy circle, which he traipsed around twice before choosing a direction, probably on a whim. Half an hour later we were hopelessly lost in the crazy maze of semi-suburbanized points and bays and cul-de-sacs, although Teddy kept insisting that he knew where we were, and that Harry's island was always just around the next corner. I don't think he was even trying. Not that I was especially concerned after a while. We got to conversing about our film, as though it were already a shiny polished masterpiece, complete and in the can. Everything was going super good. How could it not? We had the beautiful day well in hand, a lux boat at our command, plenty of booze and blow onboard, and our brilliant life-altering film project to delight and astound. What a dazzling day for we two monsters of creation, potent young Gods of the Arts, on the cusp of true greatness, basking in the sunshiny glamour. The dominant mood was one of savoury self-congratulation, combined with a serious sense of satisfying superiority over the mere mortal mediocrities all around us, with their base amusements, their lakefront cottages and pricey watercraft, trite distractions from the vacuity of their tiny lives. It's hard not to feel gigantic when you're one of those rare big sparking souls, a crafty necromancer with the magic to conjure something out of nothing.

Naturally, as Art Gods will do in their leisure, we talked aesthetics. Teddy tends to define his art by what it isn't. It's not this, it's not that—not didactic, not referential, not ironic, not ambiguous—none of that. What is it then? Teddy never commits. But if you listen long enough, you will eventually hear him say that it isn't the complete opposite of whatever he might have said it isn't previously. If it's not instinctive or visceral at one point, it will soon enough not be calculated or knowing. If it's not accessible or narrative at one point, it will soon enough not be wilfully obscure or audience-hostile. Above all, it's not art about art. But it's also not anti-art about art. This was all very interesting. Until we bottomed out in swamp.

Here was a buzz killer. The boat got hung up on the muck at the shallow end of what had appeared to be the mouth of a wide river, but then suddenly revealed itself as a dead end bog. We hadn't been paying much attention. Instead of backing out as I suggested, Teddy tried to turn her around, thus planting the boat way in the weeds. He worked the throttle hard, back and forth, trying to dislodge the stranded craft, which only sank us deeper into the quagmire, churning the water a bloody caramel colour, the surface festooned with swamp debris.

"Reminds me of the Cordoba," I said.

"Fuck bitch move," Teddy said, beet-red face soaked in sweat, hammering the throttle. The boat stuck still.

Do you remember how much it snowed last winter? I do. That's why this event brought to mind Teddy's terrible Chrysler Cordoba, that monstrous brown seventies relic Teddy came rolling to town in from the West Coast in a tragic-comic attempt to impress Harry. Those cold black and white winter nights I'd be out making the rounds with Teddy, pretending to be his silent enforcer during some fraught business transaction in some hellish, thumping club, my only tangible function being to push the car out of the snow whenever it got stuck. Which is basically whenever it snowed, the car being such a low wide heavy bald summer tires rear-wheel drive piece of shit. We'd be exiting some sketchy club scene or other and the Cordoba would get stuck and I'd have to leap out and push and rock the ugly sluggish chocolate brown sled from behind, catching a full frontal spray of crappy slush before the big ugly bastard would finally bust loose from a minor snow rut. Then I'd jump back into the car, with its cracked cream-coloured Corinthian leather seats and the heater screaming like a cat in heat but delivering zero warmth, and our magical misery tour would resume.

Would you call it ironic that I then found myself stripped to boxers waist deep in a soupy swamp on a hot summer day, trying to push the stuck Sea Ray boat while Teddy punished the throttle? Or is that just a fucked up coincidence? Or is fucked up coincidence the true definition of irony? I've never been entirely clear on that.

"Try rocking it," Teddy said.

"Yeah right."

Bare feet seeking purchase in the ooze, I pushed and pushed, but to no avail. The white plastic shell of the hull was hard and unyielding. It was like trying to push a freezer or a house. Or a boat stuck in a swamp. It was not to be budged, let alone rocked. But Teddy would die trying or run out of gas, whichever came first. He ran out of gas.

Since neither of us had functioning phones, it took a passing teen jet skier to come to our rescue. Eventually, one of the older Badger boys from the Badger family owned and operated Swear Blind Bay Marina arrived in a mega-powered service boat to get us unstuck. Then he gave us enough fuel to get back to the marina and tank up fully. The whole deal cost about the same as a return flight to Buenos Aries.

"Cash or card?" asked Grandpa Badger after we got all sorted out, and after every possible joke about off-roading by boat had been thoroughly enjoyed. Lucky for us, Harry was well known and warmly regarded by the Badgers, and his account there was in fine working order. Teddy and I were less warmly regarded. In fact we were regarded warily, like infectious lepers. I sensed that the smirks rippling through three generations of Badgers implied that we'd gotten the boat stuck due to homosexuality. Teddy's wrecked face was met with blunt curiosity.

"What happened to you?" asked every Badger, point-blank. "Long story," Teddy would answer. "I'll bet," the Badgers would then say, as if they already knew the story and found it revolting.

We headed directly back to the cottage from the marina. Teddy said he could easily find the island to collect Harry if we used the cottage as our point of departure. The boat sounded funny to me.

"Does the boat sound funny to you?" I asked.

"Yeah. It does. You're right. It doesn't steer right either. All to be expected."

"This is not good," I said. "Harry won't like us very much if he we fucked up his boat."

"Fuck him. What's he got? Three, four boats? Two here, at least two in Florida. Whoa. Fuck. Feel that?" Teddy asked, while letting go of the wheel. "It's drifting starboard."

"I believe that's port."

"Check. Port."

These matters were of little concern to me now. You were my only concern now. The folly on the lake had made me snap-to. What in hell was I doing leaving you alone for so long? Throughout the long tedious ordeal of getting the boat unstuck and refuelled, I was moaning and groaning with grinding teeth, recalling my promise that I'd be joining

you in bed shortly, anticipating a fifteen minute max
nightcap with the Chups. That was about ten hours ago.
Events had conspired to keep me from you. I didn't know
what to expect when we got back, but the more I reviewed
the situation, the more I worried. Worry became panic.
Maybe you'd left already to find your own way home? Panic
became paranoia. Maybe you'd use this fresh fuck-up as the
rationale to dump me for good? Paranoia became a line of
blow. Maybe this was the event that would deliver you back
into the soft pale arms and cookie crumbed bookish bed of
Byron? A line of blow became redoubled paranoia, plus
anguished despair. Which led to another line of blow.

We arrived at the cottage solemn and war torn, yet
swaggering triumphant, as though congratulations were in
order. You cannot imagine my surprise and delight at
finding both you and Harry there—you sitting at the kitchen
table, flipping through the "Style" section of the Saturday
Globe, sipping coffee and chatting pleasantly, while Harry
whipped up a rancher's brunch.

"So ho! Here comes pirates I told you about. Bastards
stole my boat," Harry said.

"It was all his doing," Teddy said. "Don't look at me."

"We couldn't find you Harry. We had to get Teddy in to
see a doctor," I said. "Look at him. Then we ran out of gas."

"Nothing in reserve tank?" Harry asked.

"The what?" I asked.

"Ice. I need ice," Teddy said.

He pulled a bag of frozen blueberries from the freezer,
which he held to his face, head tilted back, eyes shut.
"Doctor said to ice it."

"Yes, good idea to ice it. Take extra special care of that nose, please," Harry said, thrashing eggs. "You need that nose for putting shit in your head. So your head can keep full with shit."

I hadn't taken my eyes off you once since the moment of our arrival. I was in urgent need of your attention T, some small hint of reassurance that all was okey-dokey. What's more, you were clad in summer hiking garb—cut-offs, knee socks and Nikes—which, to my way of thinking at the time, suggested a hike followed by alfresco lovemaking deep and dark in the warm woods, directly after brunch.

Finally you darted me a glance, black pencilled slant blue-chip eyes quick in appraisal. "Having a nice time?" you asked, with eyebrow arched and a sideways knowing smile before returning to the "Style" section. I admired the poetic geometry of your hair, head, face and neck, its internal rhyme scheme, the way the angled bangs quoted your jaw line.

"Splendid. You?"

"Mmhh-hmm," you answered. "Lovely."

"So how'd you get back Harry? We went back and couldn't find you. We searched the whole island," I said, the whole time searching you.

"Did you? Indeed. Well, what do you think? First I had a sleep in my little hammock out there. Then I phone a friend, Dr. Blank, on cellular phone, said help help, I am shanghaied by pair of dirty shit ass pirates. He came and got me. From his building site he came. Showed me new place he is building. Five thousand square feet. Unbelievable. Will look like casino."

"You know what that means, don't you?" Teddy said from beneath the bag of frozen blueberries. "That makes Dr. Blank your official spirit animal."

Harry directed him a look that Teddy didn't catch, a look of bland, frank hate.

"I need coffee. And a shower," I said.

And another line, I might have added. But why now document every instance of doing that? From here on in, you can safely assume that unless I'm depicted otherwise engaged in some activity or conversation, I'm offstage behind the curtain, tooting up. I'm not proud of that. I'm just saying. It's sickening in fact, retrospectively, when I think of all the blow that got blown and the state it blew me to. Piggy, piggy, piggy. Would that I could step off the pigcycle. But I couldn't.

I stretched out on the bed in our room for a moment, finding there the residual sweet and sour sleep smell of you, and closed my eyes to explore the possibility of a brief restorative nap, some way to stop this spinning thing, if only for a moment. Or perhaps you might come and join me to help? Please. But no, neither happened, so I hit the shower, snuck a quick line with Teddy, and then the both of us were back in the kitchen, where brunch was wrapping up.

This piggish overindulgence in blow made me indulge deeply in my every thought and feeling, while at the same time warping the very processes that produced these thoughts and feelings. I'd ramped into a mood T, wild with want of you. Why hadn't you come check in when I was in our room? It seemed like days since I'd seen you last. Didn't I deserve a chance to clear accounts? I craved benediction, a little sugar even. But you weren't giving me much of anything.

Instead, lounging over brunch dishes, you ignored me while telling Harry of challenging times on the old family farm, all due to the perversity of our economic fundamentals, whereby a jumbo pail of popcorn at the multiplex costs about the same as an entire silo of corn at the farm gate. Your dad, you explained, had been forced to diversify, intensify, extensify, exploding the operation into a million-acre frankenfood factory, supplemented by a modern industrial hog death-camp annex. Yet still he was steadily going broke. Harry listened actively, knowingly. I listened too. But you know me. All this farm talk was making me sexy. I took to daydreaming as a means of distracting myself from my hot impatience to be with you, just we two, for a moment of mutually beneficial healing.

I daydreamed of us visiting your family farm, let's say right around next harvest. Your severe second-generation Ukrainian farm folk parents would be distant and taciturn at first, taking their time to warm to the dark city stranger arrived in their midst. But eventually I'd win them over with my quiet manners and the sincere respect I show them and their simple rustic lifestyle choices. I saw myself operating a tractor or something in an endless field of wheat, toiling right alongside your father and brothers, bringing in the harvest with that legendary Prairie sunset providing a suitably filmic backdrop. You, in calico dress baking pies, barefoot in the kitchen, with skin flour dusted and white cotton panties, anxiously awaiting my return from the field. Your entire family would be impressed by my capacity for work, and amazed by my ability to so swiftly master the myriad skills of farming. And by my lusty appetite for pie. Having gained their esteem, I'd suggest to your dad that he go organic, which he does, reluctantly at first. He makes a fortune off the idea and the farm is saved. A barn dance is held in my honour.

"You're all invited to a barn dance," I suddenly announced, interrupting your farm report.

"Jesus," you said. "What the hell."

"Nothing. It's just. We really should really oughta have a barn dance."

"Yes," you agreed. "That'd be nice. Did you just have a stroke or something?"

"Listen here girl. Let's get married and have a barn dance. Before it's too late."

"Never too late for a barn dance," Teddy said.

"Eat," Harry said. "What's wrong with you? Eat. Food."

I forked at my food and forced down a cold and salty soggy bacon slice, the colour and texture of chewed bubble gum.

"Oh well," you said, standing, stretching and sighing, "guess that's that. Looks like time to saddle up and go."

"Hey? What?" Harry asked. "Where you going?"

"Yeah, afraid I gotta get back to the city Harry. You know how it is—shit to do. But thanks for brunch. That was great. Make the pirates do dishes."

"Forget it," Harry said. "Is too hot now for going. What shit to do?"

I took your wrist as you passed and held you there, checking your pulse. With a wink of eye, a click of tongue and a snap of cell phone, you slipped from my grip and headed for our room. Good god girl, no wonder you make me mental.

"What's she doing? Dives, go make her stay," Harry said.

"Baby please don't go," Teddy sang.

I scrambled to intercept. You were in our ensuite bathroom having a pee when I entered.

"Baby please don't go," I sang.

"Fuck are you wasted," you said, deftly wiping, standing and flushing.

"Somewhat. Perhaps I shouldn't drive."

"I'll drive."

"Why? What's the panic?"

"You know. I got so much shit to do. I told you. Anyway, it's too weird here. Honestly. Let's go. Before it gets way weird."

"I see dead people?"

"Exactly. Dead dickheads. You don't even know how mad Harry is at you guys."

"Come on babe, seriously, why not stay for a bit? I can handle Harry. Let's hang out, have a swim, play board games. Relax. Enjoy. Life's long, summer's short."

"Too bad, so sad, gotta go, get out of my way."

I blocked your escape, filling the door with myself. You tried to slip under my arm, but I held firm.

"Speaking of which, those are summer shorts, aren't they?"

You went to bite my arm so I took your face in hand.

"Give us a little kiss then," I said, helping myself to your mouth.

"I will hit you."

"What exactly is calico anyways?"

"You did have a stroke."

"Just wondering."

"Get out of my way."

"Not till you say you'll stay."

You reared back to kick, but I saw that coming and caught your foot.

"What have we here?" I asked.

"Grrrrrrr," you said.

"Can I explain why we need to stay?"

"So you and Teddy can double-date your inner demons?"

"That's good. I'm going to use that. You're good."

"Shut up. Let go my foot."

"Listen T-bird, I'm sorry about that last night. That was ridiculous. I'm sorry."

"I knew that would happen. That's what happens. You two disappear. Move."

"No. Listen."

"I'm going to scream."

"Don't. Okay?"

You screamed.

"T for fuck's sake. Would you just listen?"

"Why did we even come here? This is so stupid I can't even believe it."

"That's what I want to talk to you about. If you could just listen. Fuck."

"What? Fuck. Okay. Listening."

I then, for the first time, disclosed to you the plan to extract money from Harry to make a film. You listened in noncommittal silence, hand on hip in a pretence of patience. Your forced cool forced me to say more than I might.

"In conclusion, I got to talk to Harry."

"You had all night."

"Right, and I made progress. Now all's I got to do is close the deal."

"You said you were done doing shit with Teddy. You said he's mentally ill."

"A little. Somewhat. So what? This is different."

"Different from? Different from like, driving around all night in his car? Dealing drugs? Getting shot at? Fucking strippers?"

"T, please. Come on. That never... I didn't... whatever. Yeah, different from that."

"You said you were afraid of him."

"What? No I didn't."

"Terrified, you said."

"I exaggerate. I hyperbolize."

"You know what? Ever since he showed up it gets worse and worse. Now this."

"Now what?"

"This stupid fuckery. Making a film with that lunatic. Please."

"T, this is a serious big chance for me. Serious."

"Probably you haven't noticed this, but Teddy's fucked. Like, you know, seriously fucked?"

"Whatever. Thing is he's done amazing shit. Just 'cause you don't get it."

"It's not that. Look at him. Don't you see? Run away. Run far away."

"He'll be okay, once he's working. He just needs something to focus on. He's done brilliant shit. He could do a wicked film."

"Oh my god, *Secret Santa Two?*"

"Or even I could just do it without him. Harry wants to invest. He told me."

"Yeah? How much?"

"A couple hundred thousand, for starters."

"He'd actually give you that? He said that?"

"Yes, to me, not to Teddy. And I could easily find other partners. Daniel and those guys. Or even those Montreal assholes, Sean and what's his face—John—if that's your worry."

"This is insane. It's all so... I don't know... freaking stupid."

"No it isn't. Why?"

"I don't know. It's just... that's a lot of money."

"Not to make a film it isn't. And it's nothing to Harry. Harry's loaded."

"Actually, you know what? Let's just go. I really got to go. This is stupid."

"This is not stupid. Stop saying stupid. This is what I want to do. This is what I have to do. It's not fucking stupid."

"Don't yell at me."

"I'm not."

"Jesus."

"It's important."

"You're scary, all jaggedy and shit."

"I'm just. This is it. It's real."

"Is it?"

"Fucking A."

"Jesus. You."

"It's totally fucking real. This is real."

"Is it? Okay. Fuck. Whatever. How long?"

"To what?"

"Do we have to stay."

"I don't know. Not long. I don't know."

"Look at you. Holy crap."

"I'm cool."

"No you're not. Okay. Go talk to Harry."

"Okay."

"Look at me. You can't even look me in the eye."

"Yes I can."

"No you can't. Try. See? Brother. Okay, go talk to Harry. Find out what's what."

"Okay."

"Then come talk to me."

"Okay."

"I'm going to go down to the dock and read. Do dishes, okay? Be normal."

"Okay."

"You gotta chill. No more blow."

"Okay."

"I'm packing still. And don't go so mental on me."

"I'm not."

"Be sweet."

"I am."

"No more blow. Do you got any more?"

"No."

The kitchen was vacant. Only the brunch debris remained. You were right about doing dishes. It was exactly the thing to take the edge off, positively therapeutic. I managed to escape from myself for a bit merely by being useful, loading the dishwasher, scrubbing pans, wiping the table, counters and stovetop, deeds demanding little thought but distracting enough to be meditative. I could have cleaned the whole cottage, washed floors and all, it felt that good to be preoccupied.

Harry entered smoking a cigarette, the business section under his arm, having just completed his bathroom business.

"So, she's staying?"

"Yeah, well, I'm working on it."

"Good."

"Where's Teddy at?" I asked.

"Who knows?"

I'd find that out later.

"Anyway," Harry said, "is good he's not here now. Is good because I need to talk with you some more about this movie business. Listen to me, I'm sure in movie business is same like all other business. This much I know—the man who walks into room with big swinging dick is eventual winner. Everyone else is go-home loser."

"Yeah. Suppose so."

"And so," Harry continued, wagging a finger at me, "you must be with full confidence for this. Sure of what you are doing. You hear me? Fuck them all. Fuck anybody. Tell them what you want, and don't take no. No means yes please. You understand me?"

"Yeah. I hear that."

"Other main thing for you here is—very important—you can't be doing any kind of business with Teddy. I tell you this again. Teddy is heading straight back for jail or to mental hospital or who knows what. To hell maybe. It's not good, I know, but nothing you can do to help it. Nothing I can do to help it. And you don't deserve it. You don't deserve his hell. You think you do because you are his friend, but you don't. I know. I know him, and I know you."

"Yeah," I sighed, "you might be right there Harry."

"Of course I'm right. I know. I know you. That's why now I am talking to you like this, like you are my son. Because I know you. I know you like a son. Like a good son."

This was the kind of thing Harry used to say to me when I was a kid. I never had anything to say in response. I still didn't. There was a brief silence. Then he instructed me to write something up for his lawyer to look over—keep it simple, a brief description of the project would do, with a basic budget and timeline. He was meeting with his lawyer on Monday and he'd show it to him then.

"Now I have to check some calls and have my nap. Show me later."

"Cool Harry."

I needed a workspace, a place where I could do this without encountering Teddy. That's how I found myself stretched out on the front seat of Harry's Buick Electra. I'd spotted the keys on the kitchen counter and figured the car would be the ideal place to hunker down and hide while crafting my proposal.

Luckily, the car was parked in the shade, so it was warm inside but not cooking. I lowered the windows to catch a cooling cross breeze. It was nice and roomy and super clean in there, with tawny plush brocade bench seats and the sickly sweet scent of ersatz pine. It had the space and ambience of a three-star motel lobby, the perfect place for paperwork. It took me only two drafts to get my shit lined up. I'd ask Harry later if I could polish it on his laptop. I'm pretty good at this kind of thing.

"Nice car Mister."

I looked up and there you were. You'd slipped up unseen and stood a demure distance away, coquettish and coy with coltish legs, one finger coiling a pinky blond lock of hair.

"You like it?"

"Sure is big. Shiny too."

"Care for a ride Miss?"

"Don't know about that. Mister."

"Sure you do. Get in. Car won't bite."

"Well, I don't know."

"Say, what's your name?"

"Candy."

"Candy. Well I'll be."

"What's yours?"

"Tyrone."

"Tyrone. Car sure is big. Tyrone."

"Yeah, gots more than enough room in here. It's nice. Here, come see girl."

I sat up and reached over to nudge the passenger door open. You looked all around to make sure no one was about before slinking past the big stunned-face chrome front grill and slipping inside. You curled like a cat against the door, leaving three yards of Buick between us. It afforded me a fine view of you and I leaned back to look. Such a perfect package you present T. Everything the right size and shape, feel and heft. It's funny how subtle the combination has to be, how just right or else it's all just wrong. It's funny too how large your presence, for one so small. You filled the car with you.

"Never been in such a great big car before. Tyrone."

"Guess there's a first time for everything. Candy."

"Guess so."

"First time's the time you don't forget."

"How do you mean?"

"Well Candy, let me show you a little something something."

Every touch was like the first touch. I know you so very well T. I know all about your hows, wheres and whens. But I touched tentatively, as though I'd never touched you before and wasn't certain how, a calculated clumsiness, getting things right as though by chance, an insistent knowing force concealed by a shy, urgent ineptness, clumsy with buttons and belt, shirt and shorts. My hands and mouth searched your face and mouth, hair and neck, to your small breasts flat tummy smooth thighs, keen for knee and calf and ankle, then off with shoes and socks for feet, because I keen for them most all the time. I tasted you too, fake inexpertly, shorts partway down and panties sideways up, like I'd never tasted you before, as this was your first time being with a big man in

a big Buick, and you're a superstar high school gymnast
lapsed Catholic Girl Scout barnyard ballerina runaway stray
farm girl hitchhiker turning tricks at a truck-stop. All of this
in the overheated hothouse of my mind, which is where these
things happen. What was in your mind? A different narrative
no doubt. So it could be I'm a preacher or teacher or escaped
slave bad boy with a big boner in a stolen Buick. Then all that
fades and it's simply you and us I'm into. Loving you T. The
car's vast interior landscape held restrictions while providing
opportunities, position wise. With fist firm on dashboard and
toe tucked in door handle, the warm brocade grazing skin, I
went in slow and you sobbed and shook and shuddered and
then turned over so it was from behind with all my weight on
you and my hand around your slim throat choking because
you want that—to be caught and held and thus released—
which you did again, and soon so did I.

The end.

"You okay?" I asked.

"Oh my god. I think I just lost sight in one eye. Give us
a sec here."

Okay T, as you know, none of the above actually happened.
It should have, but it didn't. You never did come visit me in
the Electra. That was all merely in my mind. I mean, it has
happened for real, plenty of times, almost exactly as quoted
above, those strangers-when-we-mate scenarios you dig so
large, but not that time. Never in the Buick Electra. Sadly.
And since when it does happen, much of it happens in the
mind, I figure it's fair game for me to write down what
happened in my mind at the time. Plus, after all, I am in jail
here. I have only my mind.

All that actually happened is that I finished my paper-work and then I guess I pleasured myself, with the above happening in my mind. Then I picked my nose and tried to fall asleep. I only realized last night when I was writing this—the extended dance mix rough draft version, the one I'm keeping here with me—that I did this in the car, by myself. An intriguing array of my DNA was thus deposited about the car's interior. All this I'd forgotten about until last night, at the end of a long lockdown day in jail, scribbling in my cell. The things is, I must have told Banning and Marcucci about a hundred times that I'd not driven that car, or even sat in the front seat. Now I realize that the Crown has abundant forensics to put me behind the wheel. Here's how I fear they'll play this in court. They'll put Harry's cadaver in the trunk and me in the driver's seat—evidently while picking my nose and masturbating—against my insistence that I'd never even once sat behind the wheel. Exposing me as a dirty liar. How is my mom supposed to cope with this portion of the trial? Where exactly is she sup-posed to look while expert testimony on this portion of the Crown's case is being presented and cross-examined? Will the Electra's front seat be ushered into the courtroom and subjected to black light? Will projected slides of my stray pubic hairs be a topic of contention?

After I'd finished being with myself in the car and was attempting to have a nap and actually succeeding in doing so, I came to suddenly, groggy and soggy with sweat (yet more DNA) to Teddy hammering the door.

"Give me the gun," Teddy demanded.

"The what?"

"The fucking Hitler gun. Harry thinks I stole it. Give it up."

That gun. Whatever happened to that stupid fucking gun? I checked my pockets, the floor of the car, in the crease of the seat. It wasn't there. It might have fallen out of my pocket when I'd flopped on the bed in the cottage. Or maybe when I'd flopped on the grass at the marina. Or maybe when I'd flopped below deck on the boat. With all the flopping about I'd been doing, it could have been almost anywhere. I couldn't even remember the last time I'd seen the gun.

"You had it last," I said to Teddy.

"No. I didn't. You did. Fucknuts. Come on, let's go find it. Harry's totally freaking. He's in the cottage, freaking out."

I have to end this letter here, with Harry freaking in the cottage instead of with Candy and Tyrone, getting freaky in the Buick. If you had come to visit me in the car, things might have gone differently.

Here's what else could have happened, but didn't, in the Electra. After we were all done lovemaking, you could have said, "Don't get mad, but I packed up your shit and threw it in the Pony. Let's just go. No need to stick around. Call Harry when you get back why don't you? No point staying now. Come on, let's scat."

"Yeah. You're right kit-kat. You're always right. Let's get gone."

Then we could have driven away together, home to the city.

But you didn't come and so we didn't go. And now here I am. Not that I would have gone anyway. Still, it's sad fun to pretend that way, isn't it?

Love,

e.

Dear T,

Well then Manfred's done. He went for a third bail hearing and didn't come back. I'm going to miss Manfred. A good if troubled man. That's what happens around here. They come and they go. Probably the better part of the population has turned over three times since I got here. It's hard to take, to keep seeing guys coming and going, when you know you're not going to be going anywhere anytime soon. Guys arrive still alive with the life outside, as though torn from a dream, but that soon fades when they wake up to the realization that they're ass-deep in jail. I well remember the feeling. Like a fish pulled from the lake, flopping on the dock, till I finally just lay there, wide-eyed and gasping the strange air. Nick says I'm probably looking at two years in here, maybe more, and is always quick to remind me of the "silver lining"—time done here counts twice against an eventual sentence. I'm always quick to remind him that I'm not anticipating an eventual sentence, that I am Innocent and, moreover, shit doesn't have a "silver lining." Shit's just shit. Time is just time. My time in this shit.

     Currently my time is spent in a cell meant for two with

three other guys—two bad ass actors from the domestic
stage (neither have much to say for themselves, but I'd bet
on it; they've got that sulking hard done by bewilderment
mixed with dimwit fear and rage of the household monster
caught and caged) and a forty-something schizophrenic
squeegee kid from Quebec who won't stop yelping and
babbling, laughing and crying. Manfred used to make him
shut up by getting right in his face and singing Led
Zeppelin tunes in fake French, with breath so rancid it had
stopping power, even for the psychotic. Been a long time,
been a long time. Now there's nothing to make the guy stop.
The two deadbeat dads are useless.

Manfred's absence makes me miss you all the more T.
I'd been using him to help fill the void, distract me from
you. We talked for a million hours about everything—
culture, politics, history, law, sports, ancestry, cuisine—but
now he's gone and there's no one else I want to talk to so
I'm left with you alone. And you're not talking T.

T-bird girl, I'll be in here so long I'm dreading the day I
wake up to the realization that I've forgotten how you look,
that I can't bring your image to mind. Such a nightmare
that day will be. For instance, what will I do when I can no
longer conjure you up from last Halloween? I don't want to
ever forget how you looked that splendid, spectacularly
stupid night, that night of tricks and treats.

Remember how warm it was that night? It was a weird wet
warmth, amping up the reckless festive energy of the
evening's festivities on that, the night of the living dolts.
Unseasonable heat has an unreasonable impact on we, the
people of the North, in climates cold and dark, casting a

spell, making us feel like sailors granted a bonus shore leave
to go whoring in a tropical port town. But I wasn't feeling it
just yet. For one thing, I've always hated being in costume,
and even more so being around others in costume, the way
it confuses by concealing and revealing, the way everyone
has to tell everyone else what they're supposed to be. For
another thing, I was toying with the idea of going to see you,
and I felt sick with the thrill of it.

I was at a Halloween party at Connie's, mulling things
over on the back deck with a mug of mulled wine, when it
struck me that my anxiety at being in costume stems from a
half-remembered childhood trauma involving a bunny
costume, a winter carnival, a skating race, and my mean
Uncle Rae. The only reason I was even at that party and in
that costume was because I was waiting for the drugs to kick
in, killing time while deciding whether or not to go see you.
Actually, I wasn't deciding anything. It had already been
decided. I was going to go, alright. That much was certain.
Turning the idea over in my mind while pretending to
ponder the program was just my way of convincing myself
that this was a reasonable course of action. When it wasn't.

It had been weeks since our peace summit at the Saigon
Palace wherein we'd agreed not to see each other ever again.
A strict radio silence policy had been put in place, and a
sensible no-fly zone established. Since then, I'd been more
or less true to our agreement. I'd just about mastered my
urge to lurk about where I hoped you'd pass by, just to watch
you walk the walk I could spot at a hundred yards: All barn
cat élan in motion—shoulders square and head up,
economical but for that bit of a snap in the strut, the way a
sweet petite girl warns off would-be weirdoes with certainty
of stride. As per our agreement, the emails had stopped too.

I'd written loads, but never clicked Send. Prose poems left to
die on the hard drive. I did, however, bombard you with
telepathic messages. (Did any get through?) I also sleuthed
out events on your social calendar, through casual inquiry,
and so I knew where you'd be partying that Halloween night.
I even knew you'd be a bird, a magpie of course. I also knew
I'd be going to see you. That it was well outside my control.

Love is a drug. So is ecstasy. The latter clicked on so it
was time to go.

Before leaving Connie's party I went upstairs to take a
leak. The kids were in the TV room, back from trick or
treating, so I popped in to check the scene. This was more
like it. Halloween belongs to kids, or ought to and used to,
before the big scary grownups barged in to steal the fun.
Ideally, the adult population should be at home in civilian
dress, guzzling highballs and distributing discount sweets,
instead of out there, clumsily costumed and causing con-
fusing. A movie crackled on the flat screen like a fire in the
hearth—*Spiderman*—and Connie's sister's two kids and five
or six of their friends were sprawled about in a chaos of
candy wrappers and costume parts, comparing hauls and
working treat trades. It was like visiting the winning
dressing room after the big game. The kids were relaxed in
victory with faces flush, costumes loose and capes off,
masks and weapons tossed aside, tired but exhilarated.

A Ninja Turtle turned to look at me as I slipped in
behind the couch.

"Boo," I said.

"Oooh I'm so scared. Not."

"Dude. Got any Rollos?"

"Yeah. No."

"Listen Donatello, shouldn't you be out there terrorizing

the neighbourhood by now? Same goes for all you guys. You should turn this crap off and get busy throwing eggs at cars and shit."

"I'm Michelangelo, doofus, goofus."

The kids roared at this bit of cheek. But I noticed a pirate sharing a meaningful glance with a helmet-less Darth Vader sitting across from him in a beanbag chair, their eyes glowing with possibility, galvanized by this call to tradition from the mysterious masked elder. The logistics would be tricky though. How to get to the fridge for eggs with all those other, more responsible elders crowding the kitchen? I was about to suggest that they might also consider setting garbage on fire, but thought better of the idea. The oldest kid there was probably about nine. I'd have to provide them with the matches myself, which would have been terribly irresponsible.

See? I'll make a super dad some day, despite what you say.

"Well folks," I said, "gotta go. I'm off on an extremely dangerous top-secret love mission tonight. Wish me luck."

Smiling deep in my mask, I trotted downstairs with the kids hooting and laughing after me: "Good luck doofus!... Good luck goofus!... Good luck dorkus... Good luck dinkus poopus!"

It felt good to be out of the crowded confusion of the house. It felt even better to be driving and smoking a cigarette with the windows down on a weirdly warm fall night, my thoughts and feelings all over you.

This was a good and innocent time T. We'd yet to make the leap, you and I, so we were pure potential then. We'd come to the edge and stopped, all for the sake of you. Feeling a oneness with my car, the little Pony so warm and responsive in my hands, like a living thing, I pointed it uptown, finding fourth gear. You were to me then something sweet and delicious that I'd left on the table and walked away from, entirely out of respect for you and the goodness of me. I didn't even want to think about having sex with you then. My fantasies were schoolboy chaste. Sex is bad and dirty, and you were clean and good, and I didn't want to sully you with bad dirty sex. I was that good then. Alone, driving in my car, virtuous to a fault. This is the best time in any relationship. The time before there is one. When I'm good.

A good driver too. The traffic was medium with occasional heavy patches, the pace swift, and I was holding my own in the middle lane—nimble, focused, gracious—so much so I was convinced that other motorists must surely be admiring the studied finesse of my driving style.

Gone were my feelings of vexed embarrassment by the costumed party scene, replaced by a warm surging sense of companionship with the happy fun-seekers teaming the city streets. We are all one after all. I felt connected with every single being out there rocking the big city, and the blinking lights of jets drifting lazily across the black night sky above connected me with all of humanity, in cities big and small, right round the globe. The whole world was at party. I honked a friendly honk at a gaggle of masqueraders flagging a cab. "Fuck you!" came the response, a sobering reminder of which city I was in.

After travelling up the Allen expressway and tooling about on the 400 series for no reason whatsoever, I doubled back and plunged downtown on Mount Pleasant, enjoying the way in which the pleasant four-lane street curved and dipped as it flowed down toward the lake, through neighbour-hoods thick with trees and money, the Valley of Options in the Kingdom of Lexus.

But just off Davenport, while stopped at a light, I was

rudely jolted from my reverie. There was a crunchy splashing sudden bang-bang-bang against the car door, and a gooey warm wet on my dangling forearm. Eggs. Some bastard little shits were pelting me with eggs. The light changed and I sped away from the ambush, but not before taking two more hits, including a partial to my masked head.

That decided it. Here was the sign I'd been waiting for. It was time to go see you.

There was no place to park. It used to be nice and vacant down at King and Dufferin, an inner-city wilderness frontier of empty warehouses and abandoned factories. Now it's dense with condos and trendoids and no place to park. That didn't trouble me none. I'd been experimenting with a new approach to parking. I called it Stopping. I'd circle once in search of a convenient legal place to park, and since that's never available, I'd bring the car as near as possible to my target destination, stop and get out. Leave the hazard lights flashing. At that point, so far so good—I'd been ticketed plenty, but never towed.

So I stopped and got out and walked straight into that hot-as-an-oven former appliance factory, where I was instantly smacked upside the head by the brittle sonic crunch of the London soul the DJ was spinning. It was an exclusive, invite-only event, strictly for fashion and design types, the costumes extravagantly well realized, so I didn't pause in the crowded foyer, where two dome-headed heavies were providing muscle for three slutty nurses collecting passes ("Hey! Thing! Yellow Man!") but instead greeted someone I pretended to know, and strode directly for the bar. One of the door boys came after me, but I eluded him by changing directions and melting deep into the teeming dark and swirling lights. I knew eventually I'd get spotted and tossed—I was pretty distinctively costumed—but I wasn't planning on staying long anyway.

What was I planning?

I was planning to hang coolly at the bar, slamming vodka shots while clocking the scene. I'd watch for the sweetest little magpie in the house. Then, when I found her, I'd ply her with drinks, jokes and drugs, and carry her off in the Pony.

It was only after I actually did spot you that the blatant wrongness of this plan struck me full force. This was an abduction fantasy, a lurid and potentially criminal act, and a grotesque contravention of the Saigon Palace Accord. It was bad and I was good. The initial sighting of the magpie was partial and brief, a mere flash of feather, but it was enough to make me feel bad, sick even—sweaty palms, blurred vision, the whole deal. I could have puked. I turned back to the bar and ordered one for the road. It was time to go.

But go where?

I couldn't stand the thought of going home by myself to hang out with me. Returning to Connie's was also out of the question since I'll admit I'd cruelly ditched D there in her cat costume and now she'd be wildly pissed. Plus if I left now and changed my mind, getting back in might not prove so easy. It was time to rewind and reconsider. I had to reframe the caper as a light hearted prank, comedic and non-life-threatening. Make it fun. If I could catch your eye, you'd get the joke, have a laugh, and then I'd go—mission accomplished. All I really wanted anyway was to see you, just once, up close. And since I was in disguise, I figured I could get close without revealing my secret identity. Then, when the time was right, I would. Or maybe I wouldn't. Maybe I'd just see you and go, no harm done. You'd be none the wiser. How would you know it was me? After all, you'd never seen me before in a canary yellow tuxedo and Walmart werewolf mask.

I went for a stroll around the space, a lupine recognizance of the terrain, looking to pick up your scent. For the first time that night I was feeling the persona of my costume. I was werewolf, foul and fetid, my pain and appetite all too horribly real, anxious lest I be spotted and set upon by an axe-wielding, torch-lit mob.

There were a whole lot of sexed-up bird costumes about, and I didn't have my glasses, but I instantly knew it was you. That walk you walk T. You were with a throng of friends, moving into open space, about to dance. This was meant to be a big fun night for you. Meet Cake was playing later and you'd cut her hair and designed her CD cover. I watched you, ringed by beaming best friends flashing cellphones. Was Lord Byron there? I couldn't tell. There was a bearded tooth fairy, a Rasta Einstein, some kind of medieval trailer trash wizard or something, and what I guessed was meant to be a human iPod. Was that Byron? I was checking for that soul patch he fancies. The guy looked too trim to be him. Anyway mostly I was checking you, wishing I'd brought my glasses.

Sweet bloody baby Jesus on the cross, how you looked that night T. The theme was black and white with feathered wings of wire. A black hooded cape came to a beak over your head and flowed to the floor in the form of white streaked tail feathers, under which a black slip revealed garter and stockings with holes suggestive of the sweet and hidden holes beyond—so much for my chaste schoolboy day-dreaming days; this moment marked the official end of that era—your oval face painted ivory white, lips and eyes outlined in high-drama black, and tiny green glass jewels twinkling over your shapely Slavic cheekbones and arching over your eyebrows. The thought of you going home like that to give it up for Byron came like a sudden-death lightning strike of jealous nausea. And holy cow girl, could you dance.

How could I resist the urge to hit the floor with my own bad thing? Mister Selector was spinning a thumping Afro-Brazilian jungle mix, underlined by a deep thumping kick that kicked me straight at the fray. At first I roamed the perimeter with canine cunning, a tortured werewolf on the prowl, skittish yet bold and feral, making love to the crowd, edging ever close to you. You were getting busy with Einstein, flanked by the iPod and a kitchen appliance of some sort, and I danced into view.

Then the werewolf succeeded in getting the magpie's attention. He thought he saw her smile, then laugh. Perhaps she found his costume amusing—such an obvious last-second thing, the yellow tuxedo lifted just last week, in fact, from the wardrobe department on a movie-of-the-week set— or maybe she appreciated his moves, so sincere and committed to the groove. There was something else about the werewolf, but the magpie couldn't quite put her finger on what. When the Rasta Einstein busted a funky duck spin, the werewolf seized the opening to move right in on the magpie. He danced and she laughed. Then she caught a glimpse of the eyes beneath the mask, glowing hot and holding her fixed in his wolfy gaze. The shock of recognition hit the tiny bird from the inside out, as though a bomb had exploded deep within, leaving her hollow and still. She stopped dancing and stood stunned, staring up at the big scary werewolf.

Here was something the werewolf had not anticipated. The magpie was crying. Her fine featured face contorted in pain. The werewolf had made the small bird sad, not happy. She was blinking real tears. Those tears would mar the perfect details of her makeup. Mortified, the werewolf wheeled and fled like a drunk driver from a hit-and-run.

It was panic time. I'd fucked up large and knew it. There was still one slim hope of salvaging the situation. If I could make a clean getaway, I'd go straight home, rinse off, dry out, cook up an alibi and deny everything.

You weren't about to let that happen. You must have tracked the steaming beast as it crashed through the crowd and headed for the can. There I peed and puked (goddamn mulled wine—heartburn in a mug) washed my face, and slipped back into my mask, now drenched with sweat. Quick, to the Pony.

But not so fast. You were waiting for me by the can door, arms crossed, wings in disarray.

"You're a bastard," you said, loud over the music.

"What?" I said, making my way to the exit.

"You're a fucking bastard," you said louder, keeping pace with me.

"Right. Bye for now."

"Admit it. You're a total fucking bastard."

"I am a total fucking bastard."

We neared the exit. I stopped.

"Look," I said.

"Why're you picking on me? Take that thing off already."

"Look. I."

I felt a thick finger prod beneath my left shoulder blade. It belonged to one of the bouncer boys from the door.

"Out," he barked, close to my ear.

The finger stayed in my back. I could sense the force behind it, the certainty of swift, professionally administered

violence for non-compliance. The finger pointed me to
the exit.

"He's on the list," you said, "he's okay."

"No I'm not."

"Out."

"Get your hands off him."

"Just a word here."

"Sir? Listen to me. Walk. Out. Now."

I walked.

"Would you take your hands off him? Please? He's on
the fucking list."

Things got messy in the foyer. Others got involved. The
list was looked for. The bouncer boy's grip on my shoulder,
rock solid certain, me trying to edge out with it, keen to go,
you clinging to my tuxedo jacket. It was a variation on the
Mexican standoff, so naturally a guy in a sombrero stepped
up to help sort it out. Then you, a bit crazy drunk, I suddenly
realized, smacked hard the hand of the bouncer on my
shoulder. He took exception, making a move to subdue you.
Both sets of your claws went for his face. I put myself
between you and him. There was a skirmish, screaming and
yelling, the eyeholes in my mask went sideways, smearing
my view of events, and then both door enforcers, targeting
me as the source of all the bother, brutally bum-rushed me
out the double doors and would have slammed me to the
pavement for good measure had I not pushed off and spun
around to face them, ready to run, adjusting my mask to see
you come out after us and fly at the bouncers, just as mad as
a magpie could be. Two nurses tried to hold you back, with
the help of an Asian Amy Winehouse and a giant cupcake or
something, thereby wrecking your wings.

What mollified matters was the weather. Now we saw

what the weird warmth had been about. It was the prelude
to a violent change of season. A bitter cold wind spritzed
the street with icy rain droplets. It might be snowing by
morning. Had I remembered to roll up the Pony windows?
Everyone halted to behold Old Man Winter crashing in
through the door left open by the capricious warmth.
Groups of smokers huddled on the street, tightly shivering,
now distracted by the commotion. I slipped away and
almost made good my escape as the others involved in the
fracas darted back inside to flee the cold. Except for you.

The Pony's hazard lights were meekly throbbing—
would it start?—and yes, the windows were down and I had
won yet another award for excellence in parking.

"You got a ticket. What are your emergencies on for?"

"It was an emergency."

"What's all that shit?"

"All what shit? Oh. Eggs."

"Okay. What is wrong with you anyways?"

"Plenty."

"You know what take that fucking thing off already."

I removed my mask and dropped it to the pavement.

"Surprise. It's me, Peter Parker."

You seized me by the lapels.

"What's the big idea?"

"Nothing. Go party. I'm leaving. It was just a joke."

"Nice joke. I don't get it."

"I wanted to see you is all."

"You said."

"I lied. So what? It was worth it. Look at you, so
beautiful kid, no shit."

"No I'm not. I fucking hate when you say that. Why're
you playing me?"

"I'm not. Go inside. The rain's going to wreck your face."

"Why don't you pick on someone your own size? You're just doing this to me."

"You're just doing this to you. Go inside. Forget it. It was a joke."

"Ha ha."

"Don't cry. Please. Christ sakes. Go in."

"I can't."

"Why?"

"It's all fucked up. I'm an idiot."

"No. What do you mean?"

"I messed up. Where you going?"

"I don't know. Home. I don't know. Go back in."

"How's D?"

"I don't know. We split up."

"Oh dear. Not again. Poor D."

"Go back in. Please? I'm gone."

"Can't. Okay. Whatever. See you around."

"Where you going?"

"I gotta get some air."

You swung away with a wobble and walked into the wind, wings drooping as you went, dragging your tail feathers in the wet. I went with you, my arm around you.

"Don't be nuts. It's fucking freezing. Go back in. Listen. It's Meet Cake."

Muffled synth punk came pulsing through the brick wall to our right. It sounded like a mad girl screaming at a stuck video game console. The crowd roared its approval.

"I can't."

"Why?"

"I messed up. We had a big fight. Byron left all pissed. Then you. Then that."

"Oh gee."

"I'm an idiot."

"No you're not. Stop."

You stopped. We collided. I could have crushed your fine bird bones to powder. Your hair and face and neck and smell; my mouth and hands and arms, and well—me all over all of you. I plucked your wings and held them in my hands.

"We said. You promised. We're supposed to not."

"I'm sorry. I can't help it."

"You're not even trying."

"I'm going to start trying. Starting now."

"I'm just a little white girl," you sang, even more drunk than I'd thought.

To tell you the truth T, I did want to go then, to leave you there. From off in the distance came the sound of a freight train rolling by, nice and slow, rocking and swaying with steel wheels squealing and long low horn moaning. I had a sudden urge to dash off and hop that train, to flee this town for good. My work here was done. But it was too late. You'd upped the ante. You'd turned this into a very big deal. I was forced to respond in kind, in recognition of the bigness of the deal. When what I really wanted was to go. I wanted to be good still. But it was too late for that.

I managed to get the Pony started and warmed while you went inside to grab your things. Then we went for a drive, not saying much, knowing now where this was headed. Next stop Cherry Beach, where big bad werewolves and naughty little magpies go when they decide it's time to knock boots.

The Pony was caked in snow when we left before dawn.

Love,

e.

Dear T,

I misled you about Manfred's mullet. It's more a rat-tail than
a mullet, the hairstyle often favoured by middle-aged balding
guys who desperately don't want to appear middle-aged and
balding. And rats. They like it too. I wish I could tell you this
in advance of your meeting him, so that when you do, you're
not disappointed by the fact that he doesn't have what could
be officially deemed a mullet, but instead lamely rocks a
greasy red rat-tail. I worry that you'll wonder what else I've
written here is untrue, just because I misled about Manfred's
mullet. I swear T, that was the only liberty I've taken with the
truth, and did so purely for literary reasons, a detail contrived
to convey character. Not that it matters now since I guess
you'll be getting to know Manfred personally sometime over
the next year or so as the Crown ramps up for my trial. I'm
not sure how this works exactly, but I imagine the Crown likes
to take its Star Witnesses out for relaxing luncheons after
intense morning-long How to Testify seminars. Some place
nice. Or perhaps to the Keg. There, you and Manfred will have
the opportunity to meet and mix informally. Maybe your old
pals Banning and Marcucci will swing by too, special surprise

guests, and treat everyone to a celebratory round of mojitos.
It'd be a lovely little team building exercise. Go Team Rat.

Nick was characteristically blunt this morning when he
informed me that Manfred was an informer.

"Are you fucking stupid or something?" he asked before
I'd even sat down. "What I tell you about talking to guys in
here?"

"Nothing Nick. You don't tell me dick."

"No? Guess maybe I just assumed you had the smarts to
know that already. Listen to me. That fuckhead Manfred?
Your big bro? He'd snitch on his own grandmother if he
thought it'd shave an afternoon off his sentence. Jesus
Christ guy. Wake up already. Look around. You're in jail."

The rest of the conversation is pretty much a blur.
Shock does that. I felt myself slipping into a deep dark hole.
The more Nick spoke, the deeper I slipped, with the details
of my demise being called down after me as I descended,
deep, deep into a jail hole, a hole within a hole, out of which
I might never emerge.

So Manfred was wired the whole time. Meaning that
even though he'd have zero credibility with a jury—"Evil
piece of shit like him? I'll eat him for lunch on the stand,"
said Nick, mixing metaphors—it's my own recorded voice
that will ring out loud and clear in the courtroom,
confessing to crimes I did not commit. In shameless detail,
boasting even, as members of the jury peer through reading
glasses to follow the bouncing ball on their written transcripts. That I said these things only to protect myself by
making a favourable impression on Manfred will be, as Nick
sees it, "a tough sell, given that word in here is you two were
getting along like a pair of long-lost brothers, talking
philosophy and whatnot, chilling, doing crosswords. Tell

you the truth, some guys thought you two had a, you know, a what do you call it, a thing."

"A what?"

"You know. It happens."

"What the fuck. Who said that?

"Clowns. Clients. Whatever. Don't worry about it. I'm just saying."

"I don't feel so good Nick. I think I might barf."

"Serious? Not again, okay? Not in here."

What hits worst of all in all of this is that it's going to ADD TIME to my TIME in pre-trial custody. This sensational new evidence will delay Disclosure significantly. And even after that, Nick is going to request additional TIME to peruse the evidence himself.

T, can you see what I'm up against now? I mean, in addition to the cops and Crown, an abundance of compelling physical evidence, the courts, jail, Teddy, you, and now Manfred and his covert recordings of my false confessions? Can you picture the gut-wrecking despair, the sickening sense of powerlessness, the sour taste of self-loathing seasoned with guilt, anger, regret and anguish I'm currently experiencing?

No. You can't. It's an emotional cocktail you will surely never have to drink of, with a twist of endless empty rattling around boredom in a cage. To put it plainly, I would very much like to curl up in the fetal position, shit my pants and die.

After ass dragging back to the range in a daze, I made three resolutions:

One: A Vow of Silence.

Two: Write Only What's Relevant.

Three: Don't Stop till I'm Done.

So here goes.

The Hitler gun was looked for. In the Electra, the Pony, around the grounds, and all through the cottage. It was nowhere to be found.

Harry was in his mezzanine-floor office in the cottage, barking business down the phone.

"Teddy?" he bellowed from his lair when he heard us rummaging around the rooms below. "You got it? Bring to me here. Now. Or do I call police?"

I didn't want to have to face Harry until we had that gun in hand. He'd been philosophically detached or at least drunkenly indifferent about its disappearance last night in the dark on the deck. But now, semi-sober in the daylight, he'd wound himself into a rage about the thing, having deduced that Teddy was ripping him off. I suspected likewise.

"Just a sec there Daddy-o," Teddy sang back to him, and then, wagging a finger at me and grinning, enjoying this way too much, "Come on now. Funny's funny, but fuck guy, enough already. Hand it over."

"I don't got it. Must be on the boat."

"I looked."

"Then you got it."

"No. I don't. You do."

"Swear to god."

"Right. Let's go scour that boat again," Teddy said, by which he meant it was high time we board the boat and toot up.

Down at the dock you were sunning yourself with your dark novel on the boathouse roof deck. You came to the railing to look down at us searching the boat.

"What's up?" you asked.

"Can't find it," I answered.

"Can't find what?"

I pantomimed shooting a pistol while forming a moustache with my forefinger.

"Do you got it?" Teddy asked up at you, squinting.

"Yes Ted. It's right here," you said, showing him your middle finger.

Teddy and I huddled to take stock of the situation, reviewing the night before and the morning after, retracing where we'd been and what we'd done. We theorized that it was either at the marina, where I'd napped under the tree, or by the dock on the island, where I'd stripped to go swimming in the lake. Or, most likely, Teddy had it the whole time and was holding it to provoke a performance from Harry.

"When it turns out you had it the whole time," I told Teddy, "I will be forced to kill you. You realize that right?"

"Ditto."

I looked up at you. "We're going to go look for it. Come for the ride?"

"Forget it. Who cares? We got to go E. Let's just go already."

"Can't babe. Not till we find it. Harry's freaking out. He's talking about calling the cops."

"Jesus fuck you know what? Which one of you assholes has got it? For real."

We were both squinting up at you, hands cupped over our eyes.

"Seriously," you said.

I knew then you knew what I knew: Teddy had it. But I had to play along with him T. I had to get it from him to give back to Harry, otherwise I'd never sort my deal.

"We'll be right back," I said.

"Yeah right," you said.

We decided to go to the marina first since it was closer, and also because we'd probably never find that island without Harry. And also because there's a licensed liquor lounge at the marina whereas there isn't one on the island. I selected the *Very Best of Barry White* for the ride.

There was a mammoth fleet of watercraft clogging the marina, so no space to dock. I wanted to stop and get out, just drop anchor and swim for it. The whole boat show thing was beginning to bore me mad by then. It'd felt like fun boating that morning, but now it was straight up vexing. Being stuck in a parking-lot boat jam reminded me of how much I fucking hate boats. I've almost never been on a boat when I'm not thinking about when I can get off the boat. It must be something in the blood, the trauma of history, a sad souvenir from the middle passage.

"Let my people go," I said.

Paying no attention to nautical protocol, Teddy abruptly manoeuvred around the wrong side of a gigantic mauve and white cruiser that was vying for a just-vacated slip on the dock. Their boat was much bigger than our boat—long high and wide, with swooping shark inspired lines. And since recreational boats are essentially ego flotation devices for rich white twats, the skipper of the offended cruiser took it personally. He gave us a double blast of his twin air horns. Teddy returned fire, our horn smaller, more plaintive than aggressive.

We'd already had one mishap at sea and I wasn't keen on another, especially at the Swear Blind Bay Marina, where we'd established a reputation for unsafe boating practices among the presiding Badger family that very morning.

"Teddy," I said, "let the baby have his bottle."

"Chips ahoy there Captain Morgan!" Teddy called, waving at the jowly frowning senior at the helm of the cruiser, three times our size and not three feet away, "Sorry about that there Dad. Didn't spot you on the radar."

Barry White was moaning for it right now as a wake wave rolled us mere inches from colliding with their cruiser. Heads popped up on the deck above, looking down at us in alarm. I suppose we may have looked somewhat alarming too, me in pale pink plaid Kanga fedora and oil-slick tinted aviators, chewing on the foot-long Cuban cigar I'd found onboard; Teddy styling his FBI's Most Wanted skinny white guy tattooed ex-con chic, now with added boot-bruised face, recklessly piloting our boat within touching distance of their cruiser, close enough that we could leap up with rope and grappling hooks to commandeer the craft had we the equipment and desire. We simply didn't present like proper marina people.

"Aprez vous," Teddy called, gesturing up to the crusty cruiser captain.

The affronted mini yacht with ego bruised patriarch, the party mood of his onboard progeny now spoiled, pulled ahead and docked. The rear of the vessel revealed its name: *Looks Like We Made It*. I returned a warm smiling wave to their icy inquiring frowns as the gang disembarked and trooped past us on the dock.

Proof positive that Teddy had the gun came when he didn't even bother to pass near the tree where I'd napped, but instead led us directly into the Badger Den and ordered up a round of boilermakers. But when I pointed this out, he took umbrage.

"I would never lie to you about anything brother," Teddy said. "Never have. Never will. Goes against code. Hurts just to hear it."

"Whatever. Where in fuck is it then?"

"You tell me."

"Will that be all gentlemen?" asked the Badger barkeep. She was pear-shaped and pushing sixty, with frost tipped hair and frosty little blue eyes, dressed in sporty blue stretch shorts and an appliqué vest, likely home crafted, over a knee length "I'd Rather Be Trick Skiing" t-shirt. She'd also rather we pay up and leave.

"I believe we'd like to do that all over again please," Teddy said.

"Not for me thanks. Just water please. Or okay, better make it a screwdriver."

"Into the trick skiing, eh?" Teddy said. "That's exactly how I received my injuries. Dangerous sport, especially at night."

"Unless you got a full moon it is," she said, playing along. "You should really get that looked at hon. That beak of yours looks something frightful."

"Physician, heal thyself. Worry not kind madam, I am currently in third year medicine at the University of Haiti."

"Are you? Well, isn't that something. Anywho, you sure you need anymore to drink today-doctor? Which one of youse is operating the boat this afternoon?"

"Neither-neither. Drove the car here."

"So let's see. You drive the boat in the bush and the car in the lake. Makes life interesting, I suppose."

"Yeah well, you know how it goes—kicks just keep getting harder to find," Teddy said with a chuckle. "No we're just funning you ma'am, we're waiting for my dad. He's the one operating the boat today. And this'll be on his account, by the by. I can sign for it. Chup, Harry."

"I know. I remember you. I remember you from when you were a kid—you used to come here."

"Fondly?"

"Oh. Mixed."

Teddy downed his chaser and went to the can to toot up. Not for the first time did I sit in amazement at his appetite and stamina. How does he do it? *Why* does he do it may be the more critical question. But how does he do it is the more interesting one, in a human marvel, Believe It or Not kind of a way. I know you think I have a "problem" T, but the truth is I don't have the strength to cultivate a genuine problem. It's more like a harmful hobby than a serious problem with me. I'm far too fragile to push it over the mountain pass into the Valley of Problem. It takes a four in the morning determination to push on like Teddy, to keep up the frequency, pace and quantity required, knowing that you'll just have to start it all up over the next day. That's a full-time job. I can only do light recreational, at best on an every-other-day basis. I jam out when things approach serious.

I was more than ready to jam out at the Badger Den. My screwdriver sat sweating and unmolested. I badly wanted to leave, sort out the Harry thing, and hit the highway home with you. Being briefly by myself in the Badger Den made me even more anxious to go. A floor to ceiling window presented a view of a small exterior deck and the busy dock below. The sunny sky rinsed the lounge with light. The glazed wood of the bar and furnishings glowed like chrome, and the a/c was set on Arctic, cold enough to give me the shakes, sitting there waiting for Teddy. The place felt afloat in an icy blue sky. Aside from the barkeep, there was only one other person there, the day too fine to be squandered indoors. Ball cap over bed head, bearded and oafish, an extra-large man was munching Fritos with his rye and Coke, sitting at the bar watching golf on a whispering flat screen TV, four inches of fat hairy ass crack yours to discover. Tiger Woods smoothly drained a preposterous putt. The man reacted—"son of a bitch"—but I couldn't tell if that meant dismay or delight.

Teddy emerged from the can and ambled over to make friends with the lonesome stranger at the bar. They talked golf. This had to be nixed immediately. The next thing you know, Teddy would haul the big bearded fat man aboard the boat to go bang golf balls off the boathouse deck back at the cottage. I beckoned him to our table with an insistent wave.

"Let's get out of here already."

"Good news. My nose works better than ever."

"Excellent. Well, let's hit it."

"Wait. Come say hello to Tim. Tim's from Barrie. Did you know he actually owns and operates a fleet of tow trucks?"

"Really? Fascinating. Listen, fuck Barrie, fuck Tim, let's go."

"You fuck Barrie and Tim. I'll just watch."

"Right. I'm gone."

"Relax. Sit down. We're on holiday."

"I just want to get this thing done and go."

"Well, same here."

"Well, let's do it then."

"Well, can I at least finish my lil' drinky poo? Jeez, chill guy."

We moved out onto the deck where I could resume work on my cigar. It tasted like shit, but I couldn't stop smoking the thing. I told myself I was trying to cultivate an appreciation, but it was more like trying to solve a mystery: How do people find pleasure in these vile slow burn stink bombs? Are they pretending? I was.

The narrow deck was exposed to a searing hot all seeing sun, the tables set in a row along the railing with but a small

ratty umbrella for shade. Sweat poured into my eyes. Then
Teddy went sideways, flipped, crashed and burned.

It started with a cocaine quick march retrospective of
his art career, hung on a tale I'd heard before.

"Best thing that ever happened to me was going to jail.
'Cause see, in contemporary cultural production, mostly
what matters is the persona, the image. The work? The
actual work you do? Please—let's don't be stupid. Generally
counts for dick, only causes confusion and disappointment.
See, when I got back on the street, I was already a name,
already an up and coming curiosity 'cause of the string-art
prison escape plans I'd done inside. So when I started making serious work? The kind of thing I couldn't do in the jug?
Shit was greeted with open arms. Everyone wanted to come
see. Not the work. Me. They wanted to watch me fuck up.
Which of course totally fucked me up. Totally. I was like, are
you folks feeling desirous of a fuck-up? Well then, please,
come, watch and enjoy. Take a seat. Here's a hanky. It didn't
matter what I did, no matter how bloody-minded boring
banal devoid of premise conceptually suspect retarded, or
just straight-up steaming shit bad it was. I did this commis-
sioned installation once where all's I had was like a couple of
scrap two-by-fours and a freeze dried cow's head wrapped in
cellophane, sitting on the gallery floor, with a tire swing
made out of barbed wire, all backlit in blue, and the "I
Dream of Jeannie" theme music playing loud with a laugh
track. I called it "How the West Was One." Fuck knows why.
Obviously there was no toehold there, no concern regarding
audience discourse with or interrogation of these elements.
But there you go. Made me queasy just looking at it. At the
opening 'course I got fucking totally loaded, winging cheese
at this art fag critic who was like, my number one fan. Then

I got into an argument with this giant asshole curator from Belgium. About Belgian complacency. Fucker was about seven feet tall. I mean it, dude was a freak. We came to blows, slaps actually, head slaps. Ends up I get tossed, exiled from my own opening. Fuck yeah, good times. The best part is the critic wrote this thing in *ArtFront*, calling it, quote, an incisive, simmering, non-narrative epic, fucking unquote. And then—but get this—the Belgian giant brings the thing to Brussels to show. The point being, that's how it was snapping with me all the time out there. That's why I had to flee Funcouver. That and the fucking rain, especially the fucking rain. I couldn't take the rain. I'd a gone to LA, but I couldn't cross the border. On account of my dirty sheet. No thanks to you buckaroo. Jail fucking ruined me by the way."

"Bummer."

Which raises the painfully poignant possibility that, were the West Coast not quite so wet, none of this would have happened. But for the Lower Mainland rain, there might have been no Teddy coming to town in the leaky smoking Cordoba, hunting me down to reclaim our sunken comradeship and salvage ancient debts. We'd had little contact after he'd done his stretch. I knew he'd broken big in Art World, but I didn't realize how big until the night of his opening at Dirt Lab. Big buzz, big crowd. *Secret Santa* had made him a minor celebrity. That and his highly touted toxicity since, as Teddy well knew, everyone enjoys the instructive spectacle of another's self-destruction.

The Dirt Lab show was the first time you'd met Teddy. You instantly appraised him as an "asshole" and his artwork as "hateful and obvious, which would be no problem except for it's also total crap." I've never told you this, but I'm pretty sure it was Teddy who tumbled through your bag that night,

when it went briefly lost and found. How else could he have
known where to send those sinister thank-you flowers?

I remember I was looking for you to leave when Teddy
took me aside.

"I need you to do me a solid tomorrow."

"I don't know Teddy. Tomorrow's not good."

"Yeah like fuck. I'll swing by around noon. Anyways,
let's flee this place. This art sucks shit. And vice versa. Plus
your friends are all fags."

"And vice versa."

You'd already gone by then—our stinging chance
encounter with D earlier on had made you miserable,
followed by Teddy and his disturbing art, and then the yet
more disturbing missing bag thing—so I was forced to leave
without you. And with Teddy.

That's how I ended up running around partying all
night with Teddy and his soon to be ex-girlfriend, the odious
Tabba. That's also how I ended up riding out to a Mississauga
motel with him the next day, where he met with a Trinida-
dian chap called Fry Pan. Turned out Teddy had a shit load of
blow to deal. How much, I don't know. But it was plenty. So
much so that he needed to establish contacts, acquire clear-
ances, negotiate an understanding regarding turf and the
like. Watching Teddy work his deal, I realized that this
wasn't about money. Partly of course it was about having a
steady supply for personal. But mainly it was an art production, a performance piece. For this performance, Teddy had
styled himself as a wily and virile East Euro gangster, à la
Grand Theft Auto—goatee and close cropped hair, black
leather car coat, black watchman cap, combat boots, and, for
some reason, purple parachute pants. He took to speaking in
a casually Jamaican idiom with a vaguely Russian accent,

and to calling everyone "boss" or "chief," blatant verbal signifiers of having done time, and thus a likely snitch to avoid more of the same. It's a miracle he never got clipped. And what's a performance without an audience? That's where I came in. That was my job.

Mostly my job involved riding in the car. I remember flying back downtown on the QEW, the Cordoba hogging up the fast lane, pondering my new job. I didn't have a job at the time. The local film industry had just been flattened by the shifting winds of currency exchange rates, gone like it was never there. Suddenly there were no more orange cones or white cube vans needing to be moved around. The two-script deal I had with those two bold face lying filmbiz fuckstick fraudsters you met in Montreal, Sean and John, just got cratered. My mom came to the rescue with the number of a friend of hers in the telemarketing industry, and the suggestion that she and I get our realtor's licences together, and resume practising Transcendental Meditation. And also take up yoga. It looked like it was back on the bike courier saddle time for me again. Thus this new job could not have come at a more opportune moment. A career in car riding—I could handle that.

At first I thought it'd be all fun and free money. But it wasn't. For one thing, there wasn't a single second riding around in the Cordoba that I wasn't gripped by a grim certainty we were about to get pulled over and taken down. The wagging tailpipe, the expired B.C. tags, the parachute pants—any one of these might have been deemed Probable Cause for a Stop and Search. Plus I hardly ever understood what was happening, unable to follow the tune of Teddy's ever-shifting arrangements with an array of ever-shifty sleazebags. So much greedy paranoia, so much desperate idiocy, and all the while, the possibility for a sudden explosion of berserk violence lurked like a silent partner at each and every transaction. And that's just downtown. Can you guess what it was like in the moneyed suburbs? Richmond fucking Hill, for example? The whole play was mad stressful, the nights seemingly endless. Teddy was sloppy with inventory, and his payment collection method often involved the honour system, plus we got robbed twice. Thus all told I probably made about five dollars an hour. I'd have been more relaxed and done better working the night shift at a 7-Eleven.

Luckily, since you and I weren't officially living together yet, you knew little if any of this. Until that night I came crashing into your tiny but perfectly cosy Annex attic flat after the Parkdale bike chase robbery and shooting incident, and shared some of it with you. The next morning you dumped me for the second of three times. That thing finished me off with Teddy too, for good, I'd vowed. If only.

It was also in the Cordoba at nights that our idea to make a film was conceived, born and raised. Teddy said it was time for him to bring it up a notch, art career-wise, and claimed that he was poised to shoot a major motion picture. I had major misgivings. But you know how desperate I've been to get something done with my writing, and Teddy can be pretty persuasive. And the fact is, he's never once not done exactly what he said he was going to do. Teddy always finds a way to get it done. Always. He loved *Galvanizer 2067*, and couldn't stop talking about it. Soon, that was all we talked about.

"That was destiny, that," Teddy reminisced on the deck at the Swear Blind Bay Marina. "I show up in town, bad needful of a project, and you've got what's wanted, just sitting in your sock drawer. Fucking ace case script. The fates arranged all. We were always meant to blow up big together son, from

the get-go, since the world began. Cordoba Productions was
birthed. Cheers."

"Cheers. Speaking of which, let's bounce."

"'Cause at the end of the day, all that matters is the
work. It's what you leave behind that counts. What I leave
behind is gonna cripple their tiny minds. Wondering what
in fuck that was all about. See, that's exactly what all of them
skinny rich white boy art-school haircut fucks don't get.
They don't get art's a crime. Art's a fucking war crime. It
ain't no lark in the park. But you get that my brother. That's
why I wanted you on my float, to join the hit parade. You
know the costs entailed, the collateral damage, the killing of
innocents."

"Wait—you're a skinny rich white boy fuck who went to
art school with a haircut. So what?"

"Yeah, but I never graduated. Plus I don't take this shit
serious."

"Oh. I see."

Teddy rambled on, contradicting himself with every
other drag on his cigarette, while I sat there quietly trying to
crack the mystery of the Cuban cigar. But then I became
aware of a controversy in the Badger Den. Grandpa Badger
was there, talking to the barkeep. While they talked, they
turned to look at us. Tim, the tow truck man from Barrie,
talked and turned to look too.

"Oh-oh. Looks like there's trouble brewing in the
Badger Den," I said. "I believe it concerns us. Teddy, we best
dip. Like, now."

Too late. Grandpa Badger came out on the deck. Neat
and trim, in sharp creased khaki pants and short sleeve
plaid shirt, he flipped the dark clip-on lenses down over his
steel-frame glasses as he approached, tapping a cellphone

against his thigh, a busy man on a busy day. I wondered
how much he'd gross on a busy day like this. I wondered if
anyone's ever robbed a marina.

"Teddy?"

"Sir!"

"How you boys doing?"

"Super. How you today?"

I noticed that he was wearing old school label
skateboard shoes. Maybe a grandson got them for him as a
joke. Or maybe he saw them on sale at Giant Tiger and
thought they looked practical.

"Busy. So tell me. I heard you boys had a little problem
down at the dock."

"No," said Teddy, "no problem down at the dock. There
wasn't a problem. Why? Was there a problem? I don't recall
a problem."

"Well, problem is I heard you pretty near hit another
boat. So I'm told. And now here you are, you're sitting here
drinking, and I don't think you just started just now, did
you? So, yeah, I'd have to say that's a problem."

"I'm not quite clear on this. Do you mean to say—wait—
what exactly is the problem? Can you spell it out for us?"

"I just did."

"No. No you didn't. It starts with *p*, then *r*, come on, you
can do it."

"So now you're only making the problem worse, aren't
you? I thought there might be a problem when you boys
came in here this morning, after you run aground out at
Hanson's. Well, just now I phoned your dad Harry. Told him
we had a problem."

"What? Well now, holy fuck. Now that *is* a problem.
What in fuck you do that for?"

"Well, no, now settle down, not really. There's no problem now. Harry says tell you to sit tight and he's crossing over. So problem solved, eh? Care to give him a call?"

He held his phone out for Teddy to take. Teddy looked at it appalled, as though he'd been invited to pick up a turd. "Yeah, you kidding me? Fuck that."

Grandpa Badger started, unable to fathom Teddy.

"It's all an evil ugly fucking lie I tell you. This is an outrage. Just 'cause some heinous old fucksack doesn't know how to drive his big cunting boat doesn't mean that it's our fault. He almost hit us is what happened there, the gnarly old bitch."

"Young man, you best watch your mouth."

"Teddy. Serious. Chill."

"Mr. Badger, I demand the opportunity to confront these accusations. I want you to mediate the dispute Mr. Badger. I want a full and fair fucking investigation, an inquisition, like a trial, right here in the Badger Den. This here is my attorney, Mr. Beaver, he'll be acting as my representative in the matter. Where is that ancient cock-sucking mariner anyway? Is he hereabouts? I'd like a word with Captain Highliner."

"I asked you to watch your mouth."

"Listen now, I don't blame you Mr. Badger. I know it's not your fault. Any piece of shit can float in here and tie up. Start making accusations. Charter rights my ass."

"Teddy, please, chill, shut up."

"You don't stop with the shenanigans," warned Mr. Badger, "I'll have the OPP come round."

"Shenanigans? You call this shenanigans? Show you some shenanigans."

Teddy slumped across the table and buried his face in his hands, laughing or crying I couldn't tell. Mr. Badger grimaced and shook his head, aghast.

"Beautiful day," I said.

"Is it? Been too busy to notice."

I should have been thinking about how we might escape this unpleasant scene. Instead I found myself thinking about how I might bring the conversation around to the topic of the marina operation. Do much business in cash? I wanted to ask. By then I'd come to totally resent the smug and busy Badger family and their busy money-sucking marina. I figured the way to go would be to hit it at dusk, in animal masks, with a flight plan into the bush where you await us with a canoe. Then we'd paddle quietly out on the lake and go fishing. Our base of operation would be a dumpy cottage motel by the highway, with creaky steel frame beds, where we'd celebrate after the big job with C.C. and seven.

"I'll bet," I said. "Busy day for you Badgers."

"Yep," he said, still staring at Teddy. "That it is. Listen, I want you to mind your friend here till Harry gets across. Harry's a friend and I don't want to have to—"

A crackle and hiss came from the walkie-talkie on his belt. "Mike?" He took it out and turned away—"Yep?"—and left to get on with his busy day. I envied him his busyness. I would have like to be busy too. Instead of sitting around getting trashed, witnessing Teddy's airborne disintegration.

I guess what tipped Teddy into a tailspin was the news of Harry's imminent arrival. He'd been riding the razor's edge for who knows how long, so that's all it took. He was reduced to a sloppy gibbering mess, helpless in anticipation of Harry's rage. I too could sense Harry on the way, speeding across the lake in his antique wooden Chris Craft outboard, perched up on the seatback, face clamped tight and toilet brush hair fringe flying. He'd be coming flat-out. But it took a moment to realize how badly Teddy was taking it. He folded in front of me, muttering and sobbing, holding his head in his hands. I could barely hear him, but what I did make out sounded pretty bad. He hadn't slept in years. He was tired now. Too tired to do it anymore. This was it, the end of the road. No point in carrying on. He was a hopeless waste. His was a hopeless case. It was fated to end like this. All his efforts unappreciated, meanings misconstrued, love unrequited, shenanigans thwarted. Such were the sentiments he repeated, amid strangled sobs and helpless hiccups.

"You know what?" I said, trying to cheer him up, "We should tilt this fucking marina. We could do this place proper. Want to know how?"

Teddy didn't respond. How was I ever going to get him out of there? It'd be like trying to move a mud puddle. From where I sat I could see the golf on the tv behind the bar inside the Badger Den. That gave me something to do while waiting for Teddy to bottom-out. I felt bad for him, but what else could I do? I watched golf through two commercial breaks. Then I'd had enough. I crushed my cigar and tossed my drink back.

"Got any meds back at the cottage? Harry must have all kinds of shit," I said, putting a firm but gentle hand on Teddy's shoulder. "Dude, you should try to have a snooze or something."

"Snooze eh? Right on. Not fucking likely," Teddy said, looking up at me, bloodshot eyes beseeching. "What do you think? I'm on pharmaceuticals X, Y and Z. Nothing works. Fuck me man, I am the last Cat in the Hat. Let's kneel and pray brother. That's our only hope now. Together. Come. Pray with me brother. We're hideous men, you and me. Please. Join me in prayer."

"Teddy. What? Fuck no. Don't."

Ignoring my pleas, Teddy slid off the chair and went to his knees, praying silently at the table with eyes closed and head bowed. The other patrons on the deck had been pretending we weren't there the entire time, but they couldn't resist gawking at Teddy in prayer. That was it. I had to get him out of there. What I foresaw happening next was Teddy attempting to lead the whole congregation in prayer, followed by a sermon and some song, just as the OPP arrived in full swat team gear.

"Listen man, you got to buck up. Let's get on the boat, do a bump, and fuck off out here before Harry comes. Come on son, pull it together. We got to go."

To my surprise, I managed to coax Teddy up off his knees, and we slipped down the outer stairs and headed for the dock. The folks on the deck were so relieved to see us go I thought they might burst into applause.

Teddy rallied on the boat. More than rallied. He exhilarated. This was actually the most alarming part of the entire episode. A suddenly joyous Teddy is a scary dangerous Teddy. If he'd merely regained some composure and calmed down a little, it would have been fine. What I didn't like was his phoenix-like recovery and exaltation. It smacked of utter lunacy. Plus he had this conviction about him, as though relieved to have arrived at a momentous decision. I worried about what that decision might be. What made it all the worse was how he kept saying that I was the only one in the world who'd ever understood and believed in him, neither of which was, strictly speaking, true. We hugged still.

I put on the *Very Best of Dusty Springfield* for sanity's sake, and we eased out of the marina. All the coke I'd just done met up with all the coke I'd already done. At first the new coke and the old coke greeted each other warily, like a pair of dirty perverts meeting by chance in the park after dark, both up to no good. Then a horrific conflagration occurred. I'd only done those additional lines to be sporting and supportive of my friend Teddy. I instantly regretted that decision. I should have chipped off a little chip, just enough to maintain the delicate equilibrium I'd been working. Instead, I'd foolishly done a face full. The inside of my head felt stripped and singed as though by a forest fire, leaving only the smouldering stumps and burnt dry stick limbs rattling in the sunny breeze. My heart was a small bony fist trying to punch its way out of my chest, and a thing was lodged at the back of my throat, a mucousy wad of sandpaper that refused to be spat or swallowed. A steady throbbing buzz droned in my ears, like a malfunctioning electric transformer about to explode. My face froze, and I became serious and resolute, grim and hard. If only a small local war would break out so that I'd have a purpose to match my mood, an outlet to vent the urgent surge within. I could have taken out an enemy mortar battery single-handedly: I'm going in, Sarge.

Midway across the lake, Harry flew by in the other direction. Teddy didn't see him, but Harry saw us. I looked back to see Harry swing around and come about to follow us in.

"Here comes Harry," I said. "Step on it."

Like a hyper-alert commando scanning a perilous shoreline, I looked for and spotted you up on the boathouse deck well before we got to the dock. It occurred to me that you'd be near finished with your dark novel by then, and thus solved the mystery at its core: Was the improbably handsome, super-fit new boyfriend merely a pedophile, encouraging the recovering alcoholic single mom to go vegan while surreptitiously grooming her ten-year-old son for sexual exploitation? I always meant to ask you about that.

I tied up the boat and went directly to check in with you. Teddy took off too, striding across the dock and scrambling up the steep steps to the cottage.

"So?" you asked, plucking pink iPod buds from your ears. "Find it?"

"What? No. Afraid Teddy's cracked," I said, roaming around the sun-bleached deck while you lay on the lounger, under the partial shadow of a big beach umbrella.

"Is he? Oh dear," you said, sitting up, setting your book aside and putting on your sunglasses. "Anyways, fuck it, let's get out of here."

"Okay. In a sec."

Harry arrived and I went to the railing to watch him dock. He glanced up and I saluted him. He gave no sign of acknowledgement, looking straight through me, and then trotted up the stairs to the cottage.

"Seriously," you said, "we got to go."

"Wait."

"For?"

"Just. To make sure."

"Make sure of what?"

I would have elaborated, but for the moment my jaw was wielded tight. Until my facial apparatus loosened up a bit, I was limited to bursts of language, spare words spat through gritted teeth. I was so freaking buzzed T. I needed to step it down, gain control and containment, before engaging in meaningful dialogue. Plus I had this disorienting sense of being on a stage with you on the boathouse roof deck, as though viewed from above, with some angry prehistoric god frowning front row centre. You had all your things with you—book and magazines, music and phone, sunglasses, sketchbook, refreshments, bag, and change of clothes—and this struck me as deeply distressing and unbearably sad. I forced a halt to my pacing and pressed myself hard to the railing, like a brute dumb racehorse kicking at its stall, and rolled a jaundiced eye over the fun leisure activities underway in the sparkling bay. A bunch of kids were goofing around on the diving platform while a big clear plastic inflatable frog chair floated away, forgotten.

"Die fuck," I muttered at a jet skier, passionately jet skiing.

"What?" you asked. "What's that?"

"Nothing."

"You alright?" You peered over your sunglasses at me.

"Yeah. You?"

"I'm good. But. Go pack. Okay?"

"I have to. First. Okay. Just. Be back in a sec."

"Oh no. Oh no you don't Mister."

"But."

"But what?"

But I had to find out what was up with the Chups, see why Harry hadn't returned my greeting, discover what Teddy's worrisome resolve on the boat had meant, locate the Hitler gun, and ascertain if the deal had any life left. In short, I had to see where exactly in hell this whole entire play was going to go.

But I couldn't tell you any of this.

Instead, after I finally worked my mouth loose, I unloosed my anxiety about all of it on you. Why wouldn't you give me a little time to sort shit out? Why weren't you being supportive of my schemes and dreams? Why did you always doubt me? Why are you always trying to ditch me? Why couldn't you be in my corner for a change? Why can't you just for once be like I need you to be? Why won't that fuck on the Jet Ski fuck off already?

"Why don't you shut up already?" you interrupted.

"Don't you get it? I am scared as shit here and I want to go home. Something's going to happen. You've gone mental or something. We got to go guy, holy fuck."

"I can't," I said. "You can go, but I can't."

"Why?"

"I just can't."

"Baby. What is wrong with you? What happened?"

"Nothing. I think. I'm just a little tired is all. Plus I'm worried about Teddy."

"I'm worried about you. Are you crying?"

"No. I wish."

"Look at me."

I couldn't look at you. All I could do was hang on the railing, with forehead pressed on forearm, now feeling the caress of your hand on my back. Then I did turn to look at you.

"Can vegans drink vodka?" I asked.

"What?" you said, suppressing a sniffle. "I guess. Why not?"

"I mean. It's just potatoes."

"They can drink anything, except for milk. It's all about animals."

"Yeah right of course. There's no booze made with animal by-products, is there?"

"No," you said, lifting your sunglasses to clear a tear with a single elegant sweep of left thumb knuckle. "I don't know."

"Bacon beer. You should give that idea to your dad."

"You're fucking nuts."

"Barbeque pork rum. Smoky delicious."

You sobbed and sighed and then laughed.

"White wine chicken coolers," I said. "Sweet and sour."

"Look how high you are. Holy doodle."

"Salty rib-eye rye whisky."

"Gak. I've always hated the word 'salty.' I don't know why."

"Really? I hate lots of words. The word 'whilst,' for example."

"Is there any left for anyone else? Or is it strictly for private?"

"Oh it's for private alright. It's on the boat. Very strict. Oh so private."

It's safe to say we fucked on the Sea Ray
Of a sudden standing, barefoot below deck
Whilst peeping out a porthole at the bay
Sunshine summer taste of salty neck

After all of that, we went for a dip in the lake. I wanted to be frisky and frolicsome, but I didn't feel much like playing. My head spun dizzily on the water. It felt light as a balloon, like it could catch a breeze and get blown clear across the lake. Sex hadn't helped me as much as it might have. Far from it. In fact it weakened me, rendering me needy and vulnerable, dull and soft, without a hot clue of what to do. All at once I was flooded with worry. I took my big dizzy worried balloon head out of the lake and onto the boat, where I perched it on the swivelling pilot's seat so that it could sit and worry while watching you swim across the bay and far away. I tried to cry, but couldn't. What worried me most was how easy it'd been to talk you into staying. I'd framed it up as an issue of simple loyalty since I know you're loyal to a fault, incapable of turning on those you've let get close, no matter what. That's why, while most everyone wants to get close, you're hesitant, even hard about who's allowed in, since once

in, they're in deep. I was in. And I was calling you on that.
But how could you have possibly fallen for a line of such
blatant bullshit? It made me a bit mad at you T. I mean, what
might happen to a good small girl like you out in the big bad
world? In far off Florence, Italy, for instance?

In addition to playing the loyalty card, I'd also directed
your attention to the happy face sticker I'd slapped on the
caper. I wanted you to see the fun inherent. Nothing scary
about it, your witchy peasant portents notwithstanding.
Scamming dough off of Harry was a super fun game to play,
and you could play too. Teddy was out of the game, so that
left just you and me on the field of play with Harry. And so,
you got in the game. You'd gotten high, had sex, and gone
for a swim. See? Already the game was filled with fun. For
my part, the fact that I'd made you cry, got you high, and
then conned and had my way with you left me feeling bad
about me and worried about you. Plus of course I knew you
were right T. It was way past time to go. You are always right
about everything you.

"Why study design anyways?" I asked. "Design what?
What's to design? Look around—it's done. Like, I've never
once walked into a room I didn't think was meant to be that
way, found object, perfect as is."

"That's pathetic. You're retarded."

You'd returned from your swim and lay stretched out,
soaking sun on the tanning deck at the stern of the boat,
forearm over face, shielding your eyes, murmuring in a lazy
hot summer day way. I was interrogating you from on high
in my perch on the swivelling pilot's seat. Memorizing your
tummy moles like a treasure map. Inspecting your coral
coloured toenails. Sizing up your tasty overbite upper lip.
Hypnotizing myself on your crop-circle tat.

"Design won't save the world. That's all just fat magazine propaganda. Might as well study plumbing in Italy."

"Nothing will save the world. Not even Italian plumbing."

"You already got your degree."

"Yeah I need another one. A better one."

"Why? You get lots of work."

"Yeah right. Like three fucking jobs. Too bad I don't want any of them."

"Why not?"

"Just 'cause. Just 'cause I don't want to do someone's drawings for them, or cut someone's hair, or wait someone's table. Don't want to be a servant all my life."

"So, well, what do you want to do then?"

"Oh my god."

"Sorry, sorry. So sorry."

"Brother. Anyways. I'm not going anywhere unless I get that grant."

"Well, fingers crossed."

"Got that right."

"Oh baby baby it's a wild world. It's hard to get by just upon a smile girl."

"Stop it."

It must be your diminutive size that makes me ache with this protective instinct for you. That would also explain the overwhelming force of my attraction. Your petite portability calls to my core hunter-gatherer. You'd be easy to carry off from a raid. Sure there'd be mad biting, clawing and kicking, but I'd no doubt dig that, striding into the dark woods with you over my shoulder, your clan's wrecked campfire casting shadows in the trees. The rest of my brief hunter-gatherer existence would be devoted to protecting you from the likes of me.

All too soon it was time to go see what was shaking in the
cottage. But in keeping with the protective theme, I didn't
want you to come until I'd ensured that nothing unseemly
was happening up there.

"I should go check in with my producer, Dr. Faustus.
See if he's ready to sign the cheque. Plus I need some reefer,
take the edge off. Think it's in the car?"

"You mean Mephisto. You're the Faustus."

"Oh yeah right. Mephistopheles."

"I want to go water-skiing," you said. "Can we at least go
water-skiing? I want to do just one like, normal cottage type
activity, since I think we are at a freaking cottage, right?"

"Yeah, no problem. We could do that. We'd need a third
though. A spotter. I'll go see if Beelzebub's doing anything."

"Oh god. Right. No, forget it. Honestly, I can't take
those guys. Especially when they're together. I can't take
ugly."

"I like how you pronounce it 'ekspecially'—is that a rural
Manitoba Ukrainian thing? It sounds more like Jamaican."

"I'm especially wondering how you plan to get money
off of Harry without Teddy in on it."

"Be innocent of the knowledge dearest chuck, till thou
applaud the deed," I said in my surprisingly authentic
Jamaican accent.

"Thank you William. Now pray, whilst thou fuck off?
Seriously though. How?"

"Dunno for true," I continued in Jamaican. "Me hava go
an fine out."

"Harry is so hating on Teddy. You wouldn't believe the
things he told me about him. Did you know this? You know

what I probably shouldn't even tell you this. When he was a kid, Teddy used to cross-dress?"

"Him jus' a use to?"

"Really? Jeez. Really? That's the only nice thing I've ever heard about him. Honestly, why is he such an asshole?"

"Da boy jus' a likle insecure."

"Don't be gone long, okay? I can't be alone here anymore."

"Jus' cool den seen? Me jus' go and gather some sensi and check what about de Chup family."

I'll tell you what was shaking in the cottage: me. The place was perfectly still and apparently empty, cool and quiet. I hadn't readied myself for it. I'd just blithely blustered in. Instantly I became alert to a dark malignant energy, an ethereal yet powerful sense of dread permeating the place like a vapour. Every empty room, every object and piece of furniture was animated by this sinister immanence, with a soundtrack provided by the hiss of central air, that sour septic tank smell stronger than ever.

"Teddy? Harry?" I called, the tinny sound of my voice echoing tremulously in my lake water ear.

I tread softly on sandalled feet, checking Harry's mezzanine office and trying the locked door of his den until I became aware of sounds coming from one of the unused bedrooms. I came to the door and listened. There was a clicking of keyboard keys, the sound of recorded voices and music, too low to make out. I suspected pornography usage.

I tapped on the door. "Harry? Teddy?"

"Yes. Come," Teddy answered.

"What's doing?"

I pushed the door open and my eyes landed on the

bright blue screen of Teddy's laptop, the only light in the gloom of the closed curtain room.

"Yo dude. Got some good stuff here. Loads of crap, but some gold too. Enter. Peek and freak."

He was kneeling on the floor at a coffee table, with laptop, cables and cameras neatly organized in front of him, a long ash cigarette smouldering in a big cut-glass ashtray on one side, a can of Grape Crush on the other.

I took two steps in for a better angle on the laptop. At first what I saw I could not process. I saw you, me, Teddy, Harry. But where? The angle and colour. It looked like in-store surveillance footage. Then I got it. Teddy was clicking through scenes captured on cameras he'd hidden around the cottage—mostly in the kitchen, some in the living room and back deck, jumping from one scene to the next, pausing to catch a line of dialogue here, a bit of action there. I felt sick or, as some would say, violated. It was bizarre and shocking to see and hear us the night before, the morning after, and then that very afternoon—talking, walking, laughing, drinking, smoking, eating, standing, tooting—like an out of body recap of recent events, the unedited dailies for the three second biopic they spin for you at death's door.

"Check this shit," Teddy said, calm, focused and eerily cold sober. An image from the night before of you and me necking by the kitchen counter filled the screen. Teddy tweaked the volume. There were rumbling loud sucking sounds and a soft sigh, backed by the big band swing music from the patio.

"Aw," Teddy said.

"Wait. What the fuck?"

"Or. How's about?"

The three of us are in the kitchen when Harry enters,

clad in black Speedo and carrying a power saw, humming "Imagine." "Where is extension?" Harry asks.

Teddy laughed. "What? Vintage Harry action."

"What are you doing?"

"Doing art child. Art bitch never quits. Never no down time."

I heard a power tool light up. It took me a second to realize that it was real-time Harry from outside the cottage, and not on-screen Harry from inside the laptop. Here was a definitive Chup moment—at once sad, sick, comedic, chilling, and utterly inexplicable to the uninitiated. Instead of having a showdown over the issues and grievances that had accumulated over the past day and night and lifetime as normal folk might do, Harry and Teddy had avoided each other and gone straight to work on their respective projects.

"So like the whole time you've been taping shit? Taping us?"

"Looks that way, don't it?" Teddy said, never taking his eyes of the screen or his hands off the keyboard.

"Teddy, that is entirely fucked up."

"Last Weekend with Harry."

"You crossed the line."

"How so?"

"I don't want to be in your weak-ass art project. That's not what I came here for."

"I know. You came here to suck off my old dad for money."

"Yeah. Whose idea was that?"

"How should I know? I'm not even in on it. Want to see?"

Teddy dialled up the scene of Harry and me talking about working the deal without Teddy's involvement. Harry and I are facing each other in the kitchen, in identical arms crossed postures, talking business.

"That's acting asshole. That's me, acting."

"And the Oscar goes to. Look how cute."

"Right. And why did I have to do that? 'Cause of you, you dickweed. All you've done all weekend is go all out to fuck things up, pissing Harry off, wrecking everything. Okay, the fucking Hitler gun? Give it up already."

"Me give it up? Please. You're funny."

"You think I got it? Why would I do that?"

"'Cause you're a skeezy thieving weasel. Same reason you wrote him up that deal memo thing—no mention of me or Cordoba or nothing, it's all just you and Harry."

"Wait. You went into my stuff? Teddy that—"

"It was in the car. It was sitting in the car. There it was. I just picked it up."

"Okay. Teddy? That was a prop. What you saw in the kitchen was acting, what you found in the car is a prop. Why do you always got to mess shit up? Why are you always such a fucktard?"

"Blow me."

"Wait. There a camera in our bedroom?"

Teddy tsk-tsked me, tapping at his laptop. Things could explode with a single poorly chosen word. Then Teddy made several poor word choices, and chose to deliver them in Ebonics.

"Nigga please. This here piece is called Last Weekend with Harry, not Last Weekend with Skanky."

I started at nigga and lost it at skanky, not realizing what I'd done until I felt the sensation in my foot, a stinging frosty burn. I saw a wrecked camera on the floor under the ding in the wall where it'd hit. Before a thought had time to form, I must've kicked the coffee table, catching it on the corner for maximum launch, sending everything flying, the laptop, ashtray, pop can and cameras, sprayed around the room. Teddy stayed where he was, on his knees, his head lolling, holding his arms up like a spent boxer, whinging and waiting for the knockout blow. It was such a revolting, submissive posture. It was the worst thing he could have done. It was infuriating. I'd seen him assume that very stance as a kid with Harry. He was clearly begging for it so I took one step back and three steps forward and hit him once hard on the side of the head with my fist, and down he went. I went to hit him again, but the coffee table was in the way. I had to hit something, kill something, anything. I opted to kill the coffee table, going at it with both feet until I'd battered it to death. Teddy winced with every crunching kick and stomp.

I left Teddy turtled on the floor and went to the can in our bedroom. I washed my face in the sink. My hand hurt and foot throbbed. I learned later I'd broken my toe. That slate black hardwood coffee table was like a piece of iron. I must've been cracked to kick it. I couldn't stop shaking. What to do now? I didn't want to tell you about the hidden cameras. I didn't want to tell you what I'd just done. I didn't want to tell you any of this. But I had to tell you something. And I couldn't think of what that something should be.

Then it all came clear. I'd go see if Teddy was okay and try to make it right with him. I'd tell him I was sorry. I'd talk him into riding back to the city with us. We'd hug when I dropped him off. Then I'd avoid him for the rest of my life. I'd persuade you to let me come to Italy with you. We'd make plans together. I'd work, even bike courier, save every penny, whilst studying Italian.

With all of these disparate fantasy fragments coming

together in my mind, I emerged to see Teddy lumbering out
of the bedroom and wheeling down the hall, looking like
he'd just sprang up late for work with a bleeding nose.

"Teddy man, sorry about that. That was. I just lost it."

"No. It's cool. No worries."

He brushed by me. He was carrying something, something big and black, holding it stiff-armed down at his side.

"What's that?" I asked.

"Nothing. Colt .45."

He was past me and into the kitchen, walking faster
now, and as I turned to follow him, he was already out the
back door and onto the patio. I called his name and came
after him, getting out on the patio in time to see him
crossing the lawn toward the garage. Harry was just
outside the open door of the double garage, head down
over a screaming belt sander, unaware of Teddy's approach.
The sign for his island he'd been working on leaned
against the garage wall. It struck me that he probably
hadn't misspelled the word as "Paradice" intentionally. I
limped after Teddy, calling him once, wanting to intervene
but hesitant too, for obvious reasons. I bet getting shot
with a Colt .45 hurts like a bastard. I was twenty paces back
when Harry looked up and saw Teddy. The sander went
silent and the chorus of "Volare" could be heard from a
portable radio. I called Teddy again. Harry looked at me as
Teddy stepped beside him, bringing the gun up in his
hand so that it was pointing straight up between them.
"Look Dad I found the—" said Teddy. "That's the—" said
Harry. There was a split second of confused grappling,
followed by a sharp metallic click-click and a bang so loud
it rocked me like a boulder. Harry dropped straight and
stiff to his knees, and then instantly sprang back up. We all

three stood there shocked still, the sound of that cannon-
loud explosion ringing in my ears, "Volare" faint in the
background.

It took me a moment to realize that no one got shot.
Or so I thought. Harry went hurrying past me on his way
to the cottage, in long loping, Groucho Marx–like strides,
holding his jaw as though nursing a toothache. He had a
miffed expression on his face. Must have popped an
eardrum I figured. I didn't know till Nick told me later that
Harry had in fact received a gunshot wound to the head. I
reckoned that receiving a gunshot wound point-blank to
the head from a Colt .45 would make hurrying to the
cottage with a miffed expression on his face impossible.
He'd probably not even have a face to make a miffed
expression with. What happened was the bullet travelled
into the garage and pinballed around, pinging off the
inside of the open steel door, panging off the brick back
wall, ponging off the concrete floor, before ripping back
out and into the soft tissue between Harry's skull and
neck, right where the last remnants of his hair resided like
a grimy grey curtain.

Nick explained it this way: "The ballistics for an event
like this are beyond conventional modelling. All bets are off
once a bullet exits a gun and commences encountering hard
surfaces, like the inside of that garage, which must have
been built like a bunker."

"But how could he take a bullet and just walk away?" I
asked.

"Actually it wasn't a complete bullet. More like a shard,
about the size of a ball bearing at point of entry. And thing is,
it's not the entry that does the damage. It's the exit. Ever seen
that Zapruder tape of the JFK assassination? That's what you

call an exit wound. You can take a bullet in the head and survive. I mean it might reconfigure your personality, probably give you a fuck of headache, but you could live. And Harry was one tough old buzzard, too crazy to die. Until you, he, you know, he died."

So Harry got to live. For a bit.

With Harry gone, I was left alone with Teddy and a loaded gun.

"Teddy," I gently said, "what in fuck?"

"Oops," Teddy said.

"Here. Give."

He looked down at the gun in surprise, as though he just realized he had it. "I didn't know it was loaded. I was going to clean it."

"Yeah? Here. Give," I said again, reaching out for it.

He looked at the gun, hesitated, and then handed it to me. "Harry's going to be pissed when he sees that table. What you did to it."

"Yeah. Sorry about that. You look tired man. You should maybe have a snooze."

"Yeah you're right. I'm gassed."

"What was that?" you asked when I got back down to the dock.

"What was what?"

"What was what? Those fucking gunshots?"

"Oh. Yeah. I don't know. Harry must've had a tool malfunction or something."

"Yeah bullshit. I grew up on a farm eh. I know what a fucking gun sounds like."

"Or maybe. I think the neighbour shoots crows."

"What? What an asshole. Who would do that? I love crows."

"Yeah who doesn't? I guess they get in his bird feeders or something."

"That freaked me right out. I thought for sure you got shot. I just sat here, waiting. It was so quiet. That second shot I almost peed my pants. I didn't know what to do. My phone's dead. I wanted to go up, but there's no way. I thought I was next."

"Yeah you're funny. The third Bad Thing."

"The what? Oh. Yeah. The third and fourth Bad Thing. Jesus Murphy."

"Damn girl, you're sweet. Will you marry me?"

"Shut up. Which neighbour?"

"What? The guy over there. Harry said."

"What an asshole."

"Yeah, no kidding."

"Shit! What'd you do to your foot? Jeez guy, look at your toe. What happened?"

"Fricking, stubbed it on a rock. Hurts like a mother."

"Baby."

"Quick, let's go for a swim."

"Are you crying? Look at me."

"Blinding pain is all."

"Baby."

"After I'll start up the barbeque. Chups are having nap time."

"Thank god. Yeah, okay. Are you alright? You look sort of. White."

"No I'm cool. I just want to have a swim."

I'd planned to write this straight through to the end, but I'm afraid I have to leave us in the lake. It's not a bad place to be, all things considered, in the lake. I'm too tired to swim back to the dock now. I'd rather stay in the lake with you anyway.

Love,

e.

Dear T,

I've got to make this quick. I'm making my kick for the
finish line now. I meet with Nick in a couple of hours. I
need to finish here and be done with this, hand it over to
Nick for safekeeping. The very last of my Hilroy notebooks
to you T.

Right after the gun incident or accident or attempted
murder or attempted suicide or attempted murder-suicide
or whatever that was—and I'll tell you honestly I do not
know what Teddy's intentions were or even if he had
anything specific in mind, since it looked entirely improvised, as though wanting to allow for a wide array of
atrocious possible outcomes—I walked him back to the
cottage and steered him into his bedroom. Teddy toppled
crossways on the bed, eyes shut, breathing heavily, clinging
to the mattress like a life raft. I asked him if needed
anything to sleep.

"No, I'm good."

A bracing blast of gunshot inches from his face seemed

to act like a powerful sleep-inducing narcotic on Teddy. Had I known, I might have tried it earlier. He curled up, twitched, grunted, groaned, and then snored, tumbling into sleep. I waited till I was sure he was unconscious. Watching him sleep, I sensed the trap I was in now. There was no way I could leave him alone at the lake with Harry, not after that. Whatever that was. Nor could I tell you about that. You'd say, okay cool, let's go. And I couldn't go. What if something happened? Wouldn't it sort of be all my fault?

Now for the truth about the second gunshot.

I went to the bedroom where Teddy had been uploading his footage. I tidied up, piled the cameras together, put the laptop in its bag, and shoved everything by the door, ready to go. I leaned the broken table against the wall. There was nothing to be done about the cigarette scorch on the carpet.

On the way out of the cottage I took a detour past Harry's den. Harry was reclining on his red leather La-Z-Boy, cradling a high ball on his stomach, an unlit cigarette in his mouth.

"Alright then Harry?" I asked. "Bit of a close shave there eh?"

Harry looked at me with an expression of anxious bewilderment, as though he'd never seen a hominoid before. Must be shock I figured.

"Here," I said, handing him the heavy warm Colt .45. "Might want to lock this thing up. I believe it's loaded."

He looked at the gun but didn't reach to take it. I put it on the table beside him. "I'll just leave it there then, okay Harry?"

He gave me a thumbs-up, splashing drink all over himself.

I was almost at the door and out when I heard the second

gunshot, a boom so loud it shook the bones of the
cottage. I froze, closed my eyes, and concentrated on my
out breath. With my in breath came a complete preview
image of the shambolic horror show I'd have to deal with
now—the ghastly corpse, the cops and EMS crew crowding
the cottage, the arsenal of firearms spread out on the floor
for inventory, Teddy hamming it up, inconsolable—all because Harry had gone ahead and topped himself. (Strange
to say, what also came to mind was my vast backlog of un-
paid parking tickets—would the cops note and run the
expired Pony plates? I'd been dreaming about my parking
tickets.) I limped toward the den on my throbbing foot, anticipating the sight of Harry toppled backwards in the La-Z-
Boy, a smoking hole in his forehead, staring up at the ceiling,
blood and brain bits describing a perfect cone-shaped
splatter pattern behind him. I peeked in, cringing. Harry's
eyes were open, but he hadn't moved so I knew he'd done
it. Then he flashed an impish grin and held his hands up
in mock surrender, like a small boy caught being naughty.
The gun was on the floor beside him, and the only smoking hole was in the shattered head of a trophy caribou on
the wall.

"Not funny Harry. Fuck sakes, what you do that for?"

"This is gun I lost."

I thought so—I knew I'd recognized it. When we were
teens, Teddy had used that very gun for staging gas bar
robberies, target practice by the train-tracks, tormenting
hapless winos and other such youthful escapades. Had he
kept it all these years?

"Yeah? Well shit man, lock it up. Christ Harry. Someone
could get hurt."

"No no. No one ever gets hurt here."

I left him and went down to the lake to tell you that lie about the neighbour shooting crows.

You were like a spooked kitty cat clinging to the boathouse deck. As bad as I felt about me, I felt even worse about you. Most of that day you'd spent down there by yourself, with everything you needed with you, so as to minimize your Chup exposure. You'd been packed and ready to go pretty much from the moment we'd arrived. You always so wanted to avoid all that's stupid and ugly, and yet here I'd brought you to Red Snake Lake for a weekend long forced feeding of both. I felt bad about that T. Especially when I saw how shit-scared you'd been by those gunshots. The look on your face when I came down to the deck—relieved that I hadn't been shot, anxious about who had. I wish I'd thought of a better lie than the crow-shooting neighbour. What a stupid ugly lie.

We went for a swim. It was late in the day and calm in the bay, with no buzzing Jet Skis or screaming kids. Just us two and a lone bachelor loon. We swam toward him and the loon went under. He resurfaced about thirty yards away. We snuck after him, but he dove and disappeared again. We split up and went searching for him in opposite directions. The loon came up beside you, just a few feet away. You talked to the loon and the loon listened. I was too far away to hear what you said or how the loon replied. You edged closer to the loon, so close you could whisper to him. I stayed put, treading water, watching you whisper to the loon. The loon went under and you followed—smooth shoulders squared and the curve of your back flowing down, a spark of setting sun on the round of your small bum, slim calves tight together, followed by feet and toes perfectly

pointed—slipping quick beneath the surface. I sighed and
watched and waited, treading water. It seemed like you two
were down there for hours. You emerged further away, near
the diving platform anchored in the middle of the bay. You
climbed onto the platform and stretched out flat on your
stomach. The loon reappeared, flying now, beating its
stubby wings as it skimmed along just above the surface of
the water, zipping out of the bay. You turned onto your side
in time to see him go. You waved a little wave goodbye.

I swam back to the dock and boarded the Sea Ray, where
I mixed a couple of weak white wine spritzers and rolled up
a fatty.

"What were you guys talking about out there?" I asked,
when you joined me on the boat, the two of us sitting up on
the pilot deck with the *Very Best of Charlie Pride*, my flaming
foot cooling in a bag of ice.

"Top secret. I promised not to tell."

We hung out down there on the boat for what remained
of the day.

I remember reading somewhere that in the era of the
big con, back in the 1920s, whenever a team of con-artists
had a mark on the hook but felt a slight tug of resistance,
they'd make the counterintuitive but brilliant suggestion
that he call home to the wife. They'd advise the mark to let
his wife in on the deal, and canvas her opinion about how to
proceed. Inevitably the little lady would scold the mark for
being such a risk-adverse limp dick, and urge him to double
down his investment for an even more spectacular windfall.

I think that's sort of where you are at T. How else to
account for your newfound zeal for my deal with Harry? All
at once you were full of encouragement and advice. Looking
back on it now, I realize I was more than ready to fold and

flee by then, what with the freaking Chups and all the sordid lunacy I'd witnessed. If you'd only said the word, we'd have been gone. I was probably still in shock from the gunplay, and I was mortified about what might come next. Yet I stayed the course, mostly because I wanted to be onside with you, together like a team, charmed by the sexy mischief dancing in your eyes. I'd seen you look like that before. But don't get me wrong T. I'm not blaming any of this on you. You had no idea about what had transpired because I hadn't told you any of it. Still, it's interesting to note how the prospect of big easy money can short-circuit even your finely tuned instincts.

"Play nice with Harry," you said. "Tell him whatever he wants to hear. Forget about Teddy. Seriously—fuck 'im. Keep him out of it. He'll probably get wrecked as per usual and hopefully just disappear, go smoke his own vomit or whatever. Seriously. Listen. You know what? You should try and get Harry to make out a cheque right away, like tonight, before he changes his mind. Never mind some lame-ass deal memo thingy. Fuck that. Think money. Tell him you need an advance to do another draft. Writers should get paid, yeah?"

"True dat. And don't forget, there's a payday in this for you too T-bird. For real. Line reads: Consulting fee. High five."

"Be smart. Be cool. Okay? Be together."

"Damn. You are one larcenous little bitch. Will you have my baby?"

"Shut up."

We sat chilling on the boat as the fiery orange ball of sun was extinguished in the lake at our feet, and the light went as soft and gauzy pink as a pillow. Then it was time to head up.

We braced ourselves for the Chups with a big bracing line of that dirty blow below deck, cleaning up what remained of the spillage Teddy and I had previously spilled all over the mini-bar, with the *Very Best of Frank Sinatra* taking us to the moon.

On the way up to the cottage, you comically exaggerated your dread of the Chups by clinging to my back, your face buried in my t-shirt. I limped along the stone path laughing, but in fact yours was a fitting response to the circumstances. There was every chance that we'd come upon a scene of appalling carnage, the horrific aftermath of the big finale. In a way, I was kind of hoping for it.

Instead, nearing the cottage, we heard what sounded like a rousing hootenanny happening. Way up high on the expansive deck perched out front overlooking the bay, Teddy was playing guitar and belting out "Roll in My Sweet Baby's Arms" for Harry's pleasure. The Chups were enjoying a musical interlude. We went straight up and hit the deck dancing. Together we danced to the railing in a two-step spin about, with the lush high summer green treetops and dusky blue smooth water bay spinning below us. Harry sat perched on the edge of his chair, clapping and singing along, head bobbing and toe tapping. He didn't know the words, and was making them up as he went along, calling out random sounds and parts of words, in and out of tune.

It wasn't just that Harry didn't know the words to the song, he seemed to be having difficulty with words in general. This became even more apparent when the tune ended and I asked if I should spark the barbeque and get dinner happening.

"It's all the same, in'it?" Harry said. "All the same balls. Just another fucking Chinaman in a Mercedes."

His accent was London, but not very convincing, a sort of bad actor's cockney, and he seemed to be chewing the words as they left his mouth. Oh-oh, I thought—dirty old bastard's already boozed beyond oblivion.

"Harry? You good?" I asked, examining him closely.

"Eh?" he beamed, face flushed with excitement, speaking in this weird mockney-cockney accent. "Yeah I'm great. What could be better? Here with me best lads and their beautiful young lady friend. Perfect, this. Never been better."

I could see something in Harry's eyes, or rather behind his eyes, something he didn't want acknowledged. There was a thing lurking inside him, running around in there playing pranks, like a vandal in the house, tipping furniture, smashing plates, starting small fires. Harry was aware of it, this malicious gremlin making mayhem, and he was doing his best to conceal his distress and subdue the trickster. One can only imagine the bottomless horror he was experiencing.

It was good for a laugh at the time though, at least for Teddy and me. Of course there wouldn't have been any laughs at all had we known there was a shard of bullet in Harry's brain. But since we didn't, it provided welcome comedy. We tacitly concluded that Harry's periodic eruptions of mental disarray were due to an unholy combination of pharmaceuticals and alcohol. And, since for the most part he was able to engage rationally in conversation, chew and swallow food, drink without spilling, and light the correct end of a cigarette, those occasions when he did the opposite were deemed darkly comedic. His accent too was regarded as delightful good fun. Soon we were all talking in London accents and calling each other cunts, it was that infectious.

In addition to some laughs, we also have the shard of bullet in Harry's brain to thank for giving us cause to celebrate. It's no doubt why Teddy succeeded in getting the befuddled Harry to commit to Cordoba Productions' production of *Galvanizer 2067*. Teddy's laptop was open on the table, the deal memo I'd written now transcribed and glowing with promise on the screen, and father and son were getting along swimmingly. I could hardly process this astonishing turn of events, and the ease with which it had fallen together. Here, it seemed, was a perfect example of how Teddy always gets his way. Whatever he says he's going to do, he does. Instantly I forgave him everything. That gunplay episode I dismissed as typical Chup-like tomfoolery, and even his hidden camera art project seemed as nothing to me now. The cameras were no doubt back in place by then, but I didn't care so long as you didn't find out about them. I mean, just think how pissed you'd have been by that.

To block Teddy from unleashing his entire three tune repertoire of hell-raising hillbilly sing-a-longs, I found a rootsy station on the satellite radio while you and I collaborated on the food preparation. You said next to nothing the whole time, hiding deep in your hoodie. Of course I knew you were dismayed T, but I chose to pretend otherwise in the hopes that you'd eventually come to accept what was happening. I knew this was not what you'd had in mind, but to understand my position, please consider two essential facts: My script was to be made into a movie with Harry's money and, secondly, magic filled the air. You should also appreciate that Teddy would have murdered me in my sleep if I'd even joked about doing the film without him. Above all, keep in mind that I'm a total fucking idiot.

Can you remember how nicely The Mighty Diamonds

niced up the place, with the stars above trembling in excitement, as though in concert with events below? Can you remember how sweetly silent and sullen you stayed by my side while I worked the barbeque, grilling steaks the size of truck tires that we hardly even touched once we all sat down to eat? Can I thank you for allowing me to pretend, if only for the moment, that you were by my side forever? Can you ever forgive me T?

As immensely pleasurable as all this was, Harry's condition soon became a concern. I suspected Teddy had been messing with his meds, and I wondered if the deal might be a blank to him in the clear light of morning. I decided I had to nail the thing down right then and there, that night in the dark on the deck.

Teddy was being useful for once, tending to his father's needs, pouring him brim-full pewter goblets of cold white wine, making certain he masticated his meat sufficiently, and smoothing things over whenever a murky crevice showed in his cognitive process. Harry's cellphone kept calling, its caustic "Knock Three Times" ring tone always a shocker, to which he reacted with wonder but never answered until Teddy slipped it from its holster and shut it off. Teddy was high again, but his maniacal edge was gone, and he seemed placid and content, his manner languid. Even his facial wounds looked less livid, more like festive makeup for some exotic Mediterranean masquerade than welts from a near-northern Ontario cottage country kick in the face. He made me laugh.

There was a cocktail party at Dr. Blank's, and Harry was always on the verge of going to attend, before talking as though he'd already been there and back.

"Maybe we should all go to Dr. Blank's," I said. "We could

work the scene for investors. Moneyed crowd there Harry?"

"Bloody hell," you said. "What a terrifying idea."

"Why don't you have a tattoo, then?" Harry asked me.

"Everyone else here do. Why not you, then?"

"Me ma won't let me Harry."

"What a cunt," said Teddy.

"What's all this, then?" Harry asked, pointing at the Chinese script scrolling the underside of Teddy's forearm, from wrist to elbow. "What's it say?"

"Sorry Dad, can't tell. That's only for me to know. Ancient Chinese wisdom, in'it?"

"Can't tell or can't remember?" I asked. "Harry, I believe it says, 'Forget it Jack, this is Chinatown.'"

"Close. You're close," Teddy said. "Tell you the truth, you know what it says? It says, 'Try Our Beef Ball Soup.'"

"Bollocks," I said.

"No shit. In Mandarin. I just liked the way the letters look," Teddy said. "Like I give a fuck what it means. I deplore meaning in all its guises. None of my tattoos mean dick. You think I care about Foghorn Leghorn? Or the Space Shuttle Discovery on my ass? I reject content. I fuck meaning."

"Weather keeps up like this much longer," Harry said, "I'll miss me flight."

"There's no flight to catch Dad, don't worry about it."

"Guess that explains your art," you said, "the whole fuck-meaning thing?"

"Prexactly. I'm talking art here. You can learn."

"Harry," I said, "we should discuss locations. I'm thinking of adding a couple of scenes set in Italy. Any thoughts?"

"Don't care what you say," Harry said, "I'll be buggered if you catch me playing the ponies again. Lost a packet at the track, I did."

"Yeah, you're right Dad. That shit's fixed. How's your wine?"

"Where's that waitress then?" Harry asked. "Lovely tits, yeah?"

"Okay, you know what?" you said. "This is way too much already."

"Let's get him to sign," I said to Teddy. "Go print that thing off."

"Tits, tits, tits," Harry said. "I love lovely tits. Time for a song then my son. All about tits."

"Touch that guitar I'll throw you off the deck I mean it," I said. "Go and find his cheque-book."

"Oh my god," you said. "Wait till morning. Harry, go to bed."

"Speaking of art and meaning," Teddy said to you, "of course you well remember my *Midget in a Bottle* series? Now that—"

"Probably she doesn't," I said. "Let's talk film instead. Perhaps your final and greatest work. Harry, I gotta get you a copy of the script, so we can get your thoughts, any notes you might have."

That got Harry talking about the story. I was amazed how much he'd remembered from what I'd told him the night before. He went straight at it in detail, returning to his favourite element—the love at first sight between the two main characters, and how neither realized the other's identity until after the kidnapping was well underway.

"You know how it goes Harry," I said, "'Whoever loved who loved not at first sight?' To quote the poet."

"Yes, so true, so true," Harry said. "So very true. At what point then, after the kidnapping, do you know it's her, this girl you fall in love with from before?"

"The character?" I asked. "He knows right away, the moment he sees her. But she doesn't know it's him 'cause, remember, he's wearing a mask, right? Except maybe she does know it's him all along, but she doesn't let on. See, that's the tension in the scenario."

"Clever. You are a clever little thing you," Harry said, leering at you. "Admit it, you knew it was him darling, didn't you? All along. You sensed it, at first, that it was him, yeah? And then you knew for sure. You would. You would know. And then you used him, to get that secret formula for your-self, yeah? To cheat your old dad. Am I right?"

There was a pause here while we pondered where Harry was going with this. He sat grinning in triumph, like he'd just whipped you in chess.

"He's no match for you, this one," Harry continued. "You can see right through him, can't you darling? You play him any way you want to get your way, then toss him aside when you're done. That's you, all the way girl."

"Oh my god," you whispered, "he thinks I'm her. He thinks it's real."

Teddy and I glanced at each other across the table perplexed and then fell about laughing. This was too rich not to be savoured. I didn't know what the implications might be for Harry's funding of the project, but at that moment, it was stupid funny. It was fascinating too, listening to Harry talk about this story I'd made up as though it were real. It was like having an idiot savant as a story editor. In fact it helped me to identify a couple of weak bits. Like this bit.

I was hoping you might find it fascinating as well, but you said nothing once we got talking about the script. My little muse you. Then you slipped off to bed, despite my pleas for you to stay up and have some fun. You said you were too tired for any more fun.

Looks like I did it again T. I rambled on too long and wrote too much, trying to get it all down right. So I didn't get to the end or even to the things that matter most. That'll have to wait now. It's time to go meet with Nick. He passed word to me that he's got good news. Short of telling me that I'm free to walk straight out of jail and into the bright and breezy free oxygen in the parking lot, there's nothing he could say that would be truly good news. These days, all I think about all the time are all the things I'm missing out there. They're not the kind of things you probably think I'm missing. Like right now, the thing I'm missing most is a big aimless afternoon spin on my bike, followed by a grilled cheese sandwich. That's all. Just that. With a glass of chocolate milk. Doesn't seem like much of a thing. But believe me, it's very much a thing.

Love,
e.

Dear T,

I'm just back from my meeting with Nick. There's no point in writing the rest of this for you now. You're not in it anymore. Turns out you never were. This was Nick's good news.

Nick figured I'd be thrilled to learn that you weren't testifying against me. It was all a sleazy lie concocted by Banning and Marcucci to smoke me out. You'd given them a nothing statement, two and a half pages long, and that's it. Nothing more. You walked. All the way to Florence, Italy, via Virden, Manitoba—you walked.

I should be thrilled, but I'm not. I'm killed. You killed me T. The thing is, I had you here with me every single second of every dismal dread-filled day in jail, all through all this shit I've been living, you were present, right here with me, my sole reason for pushing on, page after page, writing all this down, all for you. Only to discover I've been alone all along, scribbling away in a void, filling pages for no one, for nothing, calling into an echoless canyon, pleading down a dead phone line. You were just a shadow puppet on a cell wall, shaped by my own hands. I'm wrecked T—I can't tell you how this does me. To discover that I am alone and writing for no one, just like with all the writing I've ever done. And you being so fucking practical, so commonsensical, the way you coolly absented yourself from the scene, leaving me alone in this stew. At least when I thought you were going to testify against me, I had some small hope with you. Now I have no hope of anything with you. I had you in deep T, involved and committed, a compelling little actress with a vital role. Only to learn that you have no role, no stake, no care, and never did. Turns out you packed up and blew out of town first chance you got, leaving Metro Homicide with a contact number should they need further help with their inquiries, a courtesy you didn't extend to my mother.

So that's all there is to tell T. You don't get one single more of my words.

Goodbye,

e.

Dear T,

Okay, so I lied. I can't stop. I put this aside for good, but then everything changed and now I must needs see it through to the end. There are many things I know that you know, and other things I know that you don't know. I need you to know everything T. That's why I needed a proper trial. But that's never going to happen now.

You may or may not know and may not care either way that I'm out on bail.

The wheels fell off the Crown's case when Teddy opted to negotiate terms on a guilty plea, exonerating me of any and all involvement in the death of his father, Harry Chup.

You're probably wondering why Teddy would do this.

Nick thinks it was a simple strategic decision, and that Teddy's busily assembling an insanity showcase in advance of sentencing. Nick told me word is that Teddy sports a desert prophet's beard, and that he's renounced all forms of contemporary art-making as inherently evil, aside from painting and poetry. He's in protective custody and under a suicide watch up in Maple, writing spiritually themed lyric poetry and doing watercolours of obscure religious scenes that are said to be of astonishing, delicate beauty.

Could be it's martyrdom, just like with that thing in B.C., and that Teddy's decided he wants to suffer alone for our sins. That's part of it, I'm sure. But the bigger part only became clear when I watched the tapes he'd made, and saw how he was putting the raw material together, searching for a narrative. Think about that weekend as one big performance art piece, an open-ended improv, with Teddy orchestrating everything, not certain how it would all turn out. I think Teddy came to see it as a great fail. The piece didn't work. After cooling in jail for a while obsessing about it, he disavowed his and all other art. To make the point, I got to walk.

I wish I could go visit Teddy and talk to him about all this, but I can't. It's one of the many conditions imposed on me at my bail hearing. I'm still facing a slew of related charges, and the murder one charge has only been Stayed, meaning that the Crown has a year to mount it again, should additional evidence come to light. Nick says he likes my chances. He says the cops bungled the case from the get-go, with two competing police forces mangling evidence, improperly questioning witnesses, misleading the Crown, and a host of other abuses, including falsifying paperwork to get judicial approval for that jailhouse wiretap rat trap.

You'd be glad to know my mom finally got to wear her pearl-grey Chanel suit in court. Only she got to wear it while hearing her only son being depicted by Crown Council as "a lying, thieving, drug abusing, drug dealing, manipulative, nomadic parasite with extensive criminal associates and in-volvements and, as such, an obvious flight risk." Ironically, the only criminals I've been extensively associated with other than Teddy Chup were the ones I met in jail. As to be-ing a dishonest, calculating, itinerant leech with a substance

abuse problem, just where in fuck did they come up with
the hard data to make such an abysmal character assess-
ment? I'm hoping it wasn't you T. And there's no risk of
flight. I'm here in my mom's condo now, and I don't plan
on flying anywhere anytime soon. I've got nowhere to fly to.

I should be elated by my newfound quasi freedom, but
the truth is it's not been so great. I did three months in
there and it felt like three years when I was doing it, but
now that I'm out it feels like it was three days. In fact, it
feels like I'm still in there. In a way I wish I were. I spend
my time avoiding contact, not returning calls, mostly just
playing Scrabble with my mom after punishing myself on
epic all day long haul bike rides that leave me blurry with
fatigue. I ride with headphones on, strictly drum and bass,
because I can't take song lyrics that sing of others' pain. The
Tour de Trance. No films or fiction, either. The only TV I can
take is "Sponge Bob Square Pants," which I sit watching as
though it were a bleak experimental Swedish suicide drama.
My mom calls this post-traumatic stress disorder and urges
me get counselling and go on meds. I refuse to do either.
Yesterday it was too cold and wet to ride so I stayed indoors
and had a shower instead. An all-day shower. I sleep fifteen
minutes a night, max. I did sneak out once for beers at the
Dog Gone Inn, a risky violation of my bail conditions. I
smoked a billion cigarettes and drank my way into a
swirling vomity blackout. Apparently I also threw a bottle at
the TV to punctuate a point I was trying to make about the
Leafs, and came off a barstool and lay on the floor lamenting
the buds' lack of transition speed in the neutral zone, and
the complete unwillingness of the forwards to go to the net
without the puck. Luckily, I don't remember any of this. I've
been barred for life from the Dog Gone Inn. This is fine by

me since I do not drink, smoke, or take drugs anymore,
which are the only reasons I ever frequented that asshole
bar in the first place.

One other thing I've done since getting out of jail is
review the tapes. I went to Teddy's studio and watched the ten-
plus hours of cottage weekend footage all the way through. I
had to watch, but only once. Once was plenty enough.

That the cops never found this material speaks to their
woeful incompetence. One assumes that the higher powers
always act with utmost professionalism, but the truth is it's
the same lazy ineptness as everywhere else. They'd searched
Teddy's shared studio space, but I guess they didn't know
what they were looking for, knowing nothing about the
secret cottage cams, so that one specific DVD—hidden in
plain sight, marked "New Art Works: Rough Cuts"—
wouldn't have interested them much, especially for a couple
of art connoisseurs like Banning and Marcucci.

Nick warned me that those two dicks are steamed as
shit I scored a get out of jail free card, particularly Marcucci,
because it was in large part his doing. I've seen them
following me on at least three occasions, one time sitting in
a car out front of my mom's condo the entire night. So
when I rode down to Teddy's, I took a circuitous route,
doubling back three times to make sure I wasn't being
followed, before slipping into the lane off Bloor and
Lansdowne and sneaking into Teddy's studio garage.

It's quite sobering to sit alone in a garage all day
watching surveillance footage of yourself. It challenges
one's perception of the self. Turns out I'm not at all who I
thought I was. Turns out I'm basically a striving conniving
hideously crazed coke clown monster. And you? You're a
timid scared little bird, half the time hiding in a hoodie. It's

given me a whole new understanding of myself, you, and the events of that weekend. It's also left me with the haunting sense that I'm under surveillance at all times now. I therefore act accordingly. Maybe that will make me a better person. That and the cognitive therapy provided by "Sponge Bob Square Pants."

One thing I can tell you for certain: I do not want ever to be that person I saw onscreen—the reeling lunatic cornering you in the kitchen as you try to go to bed that Saturday night, urging you to stay up and do a bump.

"Just for the hey of it," I said. "Hey why the hey not?"

"'Cause," you said. "Just 'cause. I'm tired."

Off the screen you go and into bed, while I go off to the deck with a bottle of cognac for a celebratory toast with the Chups.

Back on deck with the cognac, I became aware of a pattern in Harry's behaviour. Whenever any new stimulus was introduced into his milieu, he'd be baffled by the change and knocked into a brief spell of delirium before regaining his grip. It was as though he'd have everything clearly arranged and categorized in his mind, and then one small change would blow it all to bits. The shock of the new I suppose. So when Teddy picked up his guitar and started rocking the deck, Harry said, "Just like being on the telly, this. Like it's all happening again. Over and over again. With all of them dead stars above, repeating it over and over, a million blinking eyes. Feels like being up a tree. On a swing. Out at sea."

Teddy was dropping a freestyle version of "The Wreck of the *Edmund Fitzgerald*," and he swung around to Harry, strumming and slinging rhymes, confronting him with a face full of guitar. Harry stared at the instrument mystified, as though amazed the device was capable of producing such outlandish noise. Teddy shifted into a stream of consciousness ramble of words and yodelling, accompanied by a wild crescendo of guitar shredding. This, I believe, was the stimulus that finally and utterly discombobulated Harry. He reached out, groping with both hands, and placed them on the guitar. Teddy stopped and held the guitar out for him to take.

"Here you go old man," Teddy said, "take us way down south, Delta way. Bring us to the hurt."

Harry held the guitar awkwardly on his lap, facing backwards and wrong-handed. It slipped between his legs and hit the deck with a dull *blang*. He lurched to his feet, seized the guitar with both hands, and proceeded to smash it to splinters. Teddy made a move to retrieve it, but the damage was quickly done so he stepped off and watched while Harry completed the demolition.

"Happy now?" Teddy asked. "That's not what I meant, you fucking fruitcake. Freak Dad. What is wrong with you?"

Teddy circled to my side of the table and poured himself a cognac, watching and wary that Harry might have a go at him now that he'd finished with his guitar. He laughed. "Harry, Harry, Harry," he said in a cockney accent. "Fucking hell Harry. What we going to do about old Harry, then?"

"Oh oh," I said. "Harry?"

Harry stood staring wide-eyed at the bay, as though he could see something terrible coming at him out of the night, holding a chunk of guitar in his hand. A dark patch was expanding rapidly across the crotch region of his lime green golf slacks.

"Ah geez," said Teddy.

The dark patch grew, spreading down both pant legs until it reached his knees. It appeared as though a week's worth of urine was being released all at once. Harry clutched the piece of guitar and stood swaying with his feet slightly apart, knees bent, groaning with relief as he flooded his pants. His mouth twisted distractedly and he looked away with an expression of immense sadness.

Teddy sighed and shook his head. "Lordy, lordy, mercy me."

"Teddy, I want the Walther back," Harry said, his London accent gone. "Where is that fucking Walther? I won't give penny for your shit fuck movie till I get the Walther."

Teddy went over to him, gently took the broken instrument from his hand, and put an arm around his shoulder.

"Dad, listen. We'll find it in the morning. Don't worry about that now. Come on. It's time for bed. You look tired."

More than tired, Harry looked grey, broken, and a thousand years old. He gazed down at his Reeboks shuffling across the deck. Teddy guided him toward the door. I was touched by Teddy's sensitive ministrations to his fragile father. It was a poignant moment. An exclusive moment too, for blood relatives only, because when I stepped over to assist, Teddy pushed me off.

"No, don't bother," Teddy said, as though this were all my fault.

Okay by me, I thought when, hovering near, I realized that Harry had also gone number two. I decided to let Teddy handle the matter on his own since that's what he seemed to want.

When Teddy came back out a few minutes later, he

poured himself a cognac and said, "I'll thank you for not telling little Miss Thing about this. Fucking bitch has been sticking it to Harry all weekend."

"Has not. Shut up. What are you talking about?"

"I know what she's up to."

"What are you talking about?"

"You know too."

"No. I don't. What?"

"Don't always pretend to be such a moron. Burn the witch."

I wasn't certain what Teddy meant by that specifically, but for my part I, too, had become increasingly suspicious of your motives and actions over the course of that day. Why had you so abruptly changed your mind about wanting to go home? Why the sudden zeal for assisting my getting film project funding from Harry? And what exactly had you been talking about with that loon? I had no plausible answer for any of these questions. I did, however, have a Theory. My Theory went something like this: You decided to stay to help me get money off of Harry so that you could get a nice slice for yourself and, more importantly, because it would ensure that I'd be pinned down trying to make a hopelessly doomed piece of shit indie art film with a demented director hell-bent on apocalypse now, while you slipped off to fabulous Italy, never to be seen again. It was all part of a brilliantly devious exit strategy.

Follow the twisted coke-line logic of the above. Thrill at the dark druggie freefall plunge into a scorpion pit of bad faith and defective brainwork. Feel the hot panicky rush of deep-fried paranoia that would make such bleak idiocy shine like brilliant insight. Then try to understand and forgive me my act T. Basically, I was a little off that weekend.

Teddy and I stayed up late on the patio out back, nailing the rest of his bad blow and talking film. Our excitement over the thrilling prospects for the project triggered a frenzy of plan making, prognosticating, and robust line snorting. All in a lather, we talked of scouting locations and scoping talent as soon as we got back to town, and we discussed the finer points of soundtrack, set design, opening titles, and the banging of budding starlets at the Sundance Film Festival.

I was, in effect, inventing a world without you T. You were going away and leaving me and it was time for me to accept that fact and move on with my life. I began by constructing an alternative world, right there on the dark patio. This new world was essentially a hastily built lean-to shack with a false front and no internal floor or frame, wiring or plumbing, held together entirely by bullshit and cocaine. But no matter, because the important thing was it was my shack, and you weren't allowed in. You had no business getting involved in my deal with the Chups in the first place. You were an outsider, an interloper, and you knew nothing of them or me or my art. And how could you possibly comprehend the profound bond between Teddy and me, or the stirring narrative that had forged that bond?

Then the blow was done so it was high time for me to go and share with you the many things on my mind.

You were in bed asleep when I strode into the bedroom, stretched out on top of the covers, and commenced sharing. I shared my thoughts and feelings, lying there fully clothed, sharing away, saying one thing after another, word following word, not knowing if you were awake and hearing any of it, but relentlessly sharing anyway, sentence after sentence, methodically cataloguing my crazed accusations of mendacity, greed, scheming cruelty, and abandonment.

Then came silence, and for a moment I thought you'd slept through the whole thing. Unfortunately, you hadn't.

"It's official," you said quietly. "You are a total fucking asshole. Listen to you. All I've ever done is support you, but you can't see that. I've been trying to save your life here, you stupid fuck. But you know what? I give up. Go away. Go hang with your brother."

I was left lying there, stiff and staring at the ceiling.

In the tense quiet of the dark bedroom, I found myself recalling a conversation we'd had not long after we first met. You said your attraction to me was of concern because, as you put it at the time, "You're like a magnet for all these beautiful, borderline personality psycho bitch retards, so what does that make me?"

"Don't worry about it babe," I'd said, "you're only one of the above."

"Yeah? Which one?"

"Come on girl, don't make me come over there," I said, coming over there. "You little retard you."

I was recalling that conversation because I sensed you were experiencing a crisis of self, lying in bed in the cottage at Red Snake Lake. I sensed that your biggest shock wasn't about me and the appalling shit I'd just spewed, but rather about you and the things that these circumstances said about you. I believe that you were going through a process of internal interrogation, asking yourself: How exactly did I end up lying in bed with this individual? What kind of a person am I that my life has arrived at this juncture?

I hope you've not been too hard on yourself T. It's not your fault. I tricked you. I trick myself in much the same way. Unlike you, however, I'm at a disadvantage in that I can't decide not to lie in bed with me whereas you can and have. Most of all, it's my stupidity I can't forgive. Even an animal knows its own nature. Yet I'm too stupid to know mine. That's how I trick myself.

I was lying in bed with me for a very long time, listening to you fall back asleep and then listening to you sleep. You'd fended off my attempts at talking or touching my way out of the mess I'd made. All I could do was lie there and think about various relative ratio probabilities of my getting to sleep. For example, I calculated that I was as likely to fall asleep as I was to become the next mayor of Montreal. The coke was that dirty, chockfull with unhealthy additives, much like my mind.

The faint sound of distress and breaking glass from outside came as a relief. At least now I could make myself useful. I would step out and quell the disturbance, lest it escalate and wake you.

Teddy was alone on the back stone patio, spinning about and pacing around on broken glass, his laptop open on the table. He was in a bad way.

"How am I supposed to work under these conditions?" he demanded. "My face hurts. Does your face hurt? 'Cause it's killing me."

And then, laughing, he picked up an empty wine bottle and dropped it on the stone patio. "You see that? You see what he did to that guitar? A cultured individual would not do such a thing. This is not a man to be trusted around culture. This is not..."

He'd picked up another bottle, but before he could drop it, I snatched it out of his hand.

"Teddy. Shit guy. Steady on."

"Right. Will do. However, I am afraid we have to make a run."

This was not a just for fun drug run. This was a five-alarm-fire drug run. We took the Pony. The sound of its little engine exploding to life upon ignition—I'd forgotten about the missing muffler—shocked the crap out of me and probably woke up half the cottagers on the bay. There was no choice, though. This was, as I said, an emergency. It was so dark on the highway that I kept working the headlights, thinking they must be off, their sallow beams producing only shadows in my mind. Plus I'd forgotten my glasses.

"Don't call me by my real name," Teddy kept reminding me. "Call me Jordan."

Have you ever driven through a small town with its pleasant Victorian main street and wondered what it would be like to live in one of the apartments above a store? I have. I've always imagined them to be roomy and quaint, with high ceilings and low rent, a little rundown funky, but nice, with friendly, quirky townsfolk neighbours across the hall, and big round white 1950s style appliances in the kitchen. The perfect place to hide out and write that novel I've been threatening.

Teddy's area dealer lived in just such a location. It was right there on Main Street above a store called Doilies n' Driftwood. We came up the fire escape at the back and walked right into the kitchen through a busted screen door.

"Yo Dennis," Teddy called.

This place was not at all what I'd imagined. This place was bleak and filthy, with an acoustic tile dropped ceiling and a loud buzzing avocado fridge. The smell was indescribable. If I had to hazard a guess, I'd say it was the smell of bacon left to boil in a pot of urine overnight. I followed Teddy into the living room where one contributing factor to the smell was asleep on the couch.

"Yo Dennis," Teddy said.

Dennis was flat on his back under a baby blue blanket. His eyes popped open while the rest of him remained perfectly still. Against the wall, a silent flat screen TV presented two girls in bikinis with slow motion tits bouncing as they laughed and splashed on a beach, a 1-800 number scrolling across the bottom. By automatic heterosexual impulse, the attention of all three of us was drawn to the image. We watched it for a few seconds of visual information gathering, a small addition to the vast storehouse of such images that are daily insinuated into the hapless male brain.

"What the fuck?" asked Dennis, his voice like a rusty car door wrenched open.

"I phoned. You didn't answer," Teddy said untruthfully. "Place was open so in we came. Country living, eh? Never no need to lock up 'round here y'all."

"It's always locked. I fell asleep. You're fucking lucky Trooper's locked."

Trooper was another contributing factor to the smell. He was in the room beside the TV, scratching and thumping at the door, whining and keening and groaning. Dennis threw off his blanket, releasing a puff of pulp mill-like gas into the room and revealing a mixed bag of Celtic, Polynesian and wildlife tattoos, shiny red Adidas shorts and a stubby little top-of-the-morning piss boner. He strode over to open the door and let Trooper out. Of course the dog came right for me—they always do—a pit bull terrier, appallingly ugly and primordial in appearance, with short white fleshy hair, and nasty reptilian eyes, its tail stiff and

wagging like a car antenna. It leapt on me, thudding into
my ribs with its clawed club-like paws.

"Trooper!" croaked Dennis. "Down!"

"Fuck me," I said.

I was going to fling the dog aside, but thought that
might only stimulate a more vigorous advance. I made a
move to pat his head. He licked and snapped at my hand.
Dennis knocked the dog to the floor with a two-handed
shiver block. The dog was back up and coming for me again
when Dennis punched him on the snout. I'd never seen a
dog get punched before. Trooper didn't seem too surprised
though. He was up and at it again so Dennis took him by the
collar and pushed him to the floor, pinning him with a knee.
Once he had him subdued, Dennis delivered a stern talking-
to and an additional snout punch. It wasn't really necessary.
I think he just wanted to show off his parenting skills.

I kept my eyes on Trooper when Dennis went to the
bathroom. He left the door open while he took a leak and
bitched out Teddy for crashing into his place at three in
the morning.

"Think this is a fucking twenty-four hour drive-through
or something?" Dennis asked above the sound of the
washroom water works. "This look like Tim Horton's?"

"Oh sorry dude," Teddy said, flopping into a chair. "I didn't
know it was that late. We were at a party. Want to come?"

"Yeah right. Fuck no."

Teddy leaned sideways, stuck his hand down the back of
his pants, and came up with the Colt .45. He put the gun on
the coffee table in front of him and sat forward, hunching
over it.

"Oh," I said involuntarily, weak with surprise. "Oh no."

Dennis hawked up and spit into the sink. "You owe me

money. You got it? Or do I have to keep your phone, which I don't even want?"

"I can do better than money," Teddy said.

Dennis came out of the bathroom. "Nothing's better than money."

"This is my friend Jordan," Teddy said.

"Another Jordan? What the fuck? Jordan and Jordan?"

I was thinking holy crap—Teddy best shoot the dog first.

"I already told you guy. I don't want your fucking guitar."

Dennis was a dark and compact man, only about five-foot six, but with the sprung-steel swaggering menace of an accomplished street fighter. There was a dent in his forehead that looked to be from a nine iron. He stood there rocking back and forth, arms crossed, restless and irate. I realized then where Teddy's terrible Coke Jones had brought us. We were in the presence of the local small town psycho bully, known and feared by all, even the police. Every small town has one. These rugged individualists, with their ready rage, local cult following, surly grievances, and cop-baiting ways, are a part of the very fabric of our nation, so ubiquitous that they merit their own TV heritage moment.

I changed my mind. Teddy should do Dennis first and then the dog.

"That's cool 'cause I didn't bring it."

By then Dennis had spotted the gun on the table.

"What in fuck is that?"

"Oh that? That there's a Colt .45. A 1911, U.S. Navy."

"Loaded?"

"Jordan?" Teddy turned to me, "Do you remember? This thing loaded?"

"Tell you what. You fucking walk in here with a loaded gun I will whip your ass."

"Relax. It's probably not even loaded."

Dennis's eyes flicked back and forth from the gun to Teddy. Like me, he wasn't sure what Teddy had in mind. For that matter, I don't think Teddy was sure what Teddy had in mind. He just wanted to put the gun out there, like a provocative opinion at a dinner party, and see where it led. Dennis was calculating his chances of making a play for it. Or else considering the possibility of getting a hold of something handy and nearby he could use to kill Teddy with. I was doing a visualization of the run for the door I'd make should either of them so much as flinch—stay low, keep moving, run and roll as required, and try not to fall down the fire escape.

Just when the tension was well past unbearable, Teddy said, "It's collateral. I'll have cash tomorrow. There's no way I'm selling this bad boy."

"What makes you think I want to buy it?" Dennis asked.

"Fuck, you kidding me? Check it out man. This thing's worth serious money. Go ahead and Google it. It's totally fucking collectible."

And that's precisely what Dennis went ahead and did. He flicked his iMac on and he and Teddy clicked through gun freak websites in search of a matching Colt .45.

That's how Teddy scored himself an eight ball at three in the morning above a souvenir store on the Victorian era Main Street of a small town in cottage country. Apparently that's how a lot of business got done at Dennis's. Amidst the debris-strewn stinking filthy chaos of his apartment, there were a number of fresh and unlikely items, the flat screen and iMac being but two examples. There was also a Swiss-made crossbow still in its box, three sets of golf clubs, random electronics and computers, a complete set of barely used kids' goalie equipment, and what really caught my fancy—a pretty white with red trim Tommasini road bike that looked like it had never even been wet. These things must have been hawked in trade for the dirty-ass blow, dope and meth that Dennis dealt. I wondered if the good folks in the shop below knew what kind of business was being conducted one floor above them. They probably did, it being a small town and Dennis being its official psycho bully. I noticed there weren't any doilies or driftwood in the apartment.

I wasn't about to relax just because Teddy and Dennis seemed to be getting along so well, Googling and talking guns, then smoking a rock, which inspired them to take apart the Colt .45 to authenticate it. I sensed things could go upside down in an instant. I stayed on my feet with my eyes on the dog and the door to my right. A peek down the hall at last revealed the primary source of smell: taxidermy. In the tub in the bathroom was a moose head. Its magnificent antlers straddled the sides of the tub and kept the head upright so the blood would drip out the neck and down the drain. The moose head looked surreal, stunned, sad, and larger than life, with a halo of lazy bluebottle flies. Were the neighbours too intimidated by Dennis to complain about his unneighbourly hobby?

"What's up with buddy in the tub?" I asked Dennis.

"Road kill," Dennis said. "I mean I seen him on the road so I killed him. Shot him from my truck."

"Cool."

Deal done, Dennis saw us to the back door and followed us right out onto the fire escape to wish us goodnight and make sure we didn't steal anything.

"Yeah, hey Jordan," said Dennis. "Next time you're thinking about coming by here with a loaded gun?"

Teddy stopped and turned to look up at Dennis from the stairs.

"Don't," Dennis said, slapping Teddy across the jaw so hard that it knocked him briefly unconscious. Teddy slowly melted to his knees and would have tumbled down the stairs had I not been below to block his fall.

For the second time that weekend Teddy bled all over the interior of the Pony. That cheap-shot face slap re-broke his broken nose, causing it to bleed profusely. He tore off his t-shirt and held it to his face with his head tilted back. He'd taken a pretty severe knock. I'd half hauled him, stumbling down the fire escape and into the car, and it was only when we were out of town and on the highway that he'd regained full consciousness and realized what had happened. I suggested we swing back and sort out Dennis, but Teddy dismissed the whole escapade as hilarious. Even as he rocked and moaned in pain, he was helpless with mirth, laughing about the stink, the dog, the moose head and the man he called Dented because of that dent in his head. I could appreciate the comedy, but I couldn't get past that farewell cheap-shot face slap, and felt strongly that it demanded a swift and significant rebuke. It wasn't even so much the actual face slap. It was the sense of satisfaction that Dennis would have derived from administering the face slap that infuriated me. I badly wanted to fuck up his sense of satisfaction. But that might also have been due to guilt. Earlier that day I'd kind of suckered Teddy myself.

"Don't worry about it," Teddy said. "Revenge is a dish best served with french fries at the bottom of the lake." Then he reached into his pocket and pulled out a set of car keys.

"For his truck," Teddy said chuckling. "Fucker's gonna find his four-by-four in Red Snake Lake."

"When did you get those?"

"Soon as I walked in. You didn't see?"

"You are a bad man Teddy Chup."

I pulled into the Petro-Can at the crossroads. Teddy was too messed to make a public appearance so he stayed in the car while I went in and bought water, smokes, chocolate milk and a box of baby wipes. Teddy cleaned up in the parking lot, pouring a bottle of water over his head and towelling off with his t-shirt and a handful of baby wipes. He got back in the car and we tooted up. His nose started bleeding again. He tore off bits of baby wipes to insert into his nostrils. I started the car and we roared out of the parking lot and back onto the highway. Teddy chucked his t-shirt out the window and we drank chocolate milk and sang Neil Young's "Helpless" loud enough to be heard over the engine.

Back at the cottage, I swept up the glass on the deck and then Teddy and I went down to the boathouse deck with beer and blow.

I should not have trusted the peculiar sense of euphoria that overcame me that morning. I should have taken it apart and given it a thorough inspection, flipped it upside down and taken off its wheels. I should have scrutinized the source of my contentment. I should have questioned my serene conviction that all would turn out swell. Instead I rode my fine feeling and let all else slide. It's not that I did that much more toot; shit was bad nasty, so I only did enough to avoid crashing. Of course it might have been fatigue. I hadn't really slept in two days, and maybe I was awake but dreaming, in a kind of fugue state, and therefore delusional. Or maybe it was the setting. Dawn on the lake from the boathouse deck was heartache beautiful. The sun slowly swelled up behind us, casting a warm, honeyed glow over the bay. A pair of loons cackled and flapped their wings in the water; your bachelor boyfriend must have found a bride. What a Wonderful World. Roll credits. The End. Maybe that was it. The End. I had this inexplicable feeling that something was coming to a close, a magnificent close, and that this new day was at once the end of one thing and the start of another, bursting with promise.

I was still singing about it all in the shower a little later that morning when you woke up and came in to pee. I stuck my head out from behind the curtain.

"Baby."

"You all right?" you asked.

"Yeah you bet. You?"

"Yeah. I'm okay."

I finished showering and waltzed into the bedroom, happily humming. You were sitting up in bed under the covers, with your knees drawn up under your chin, watching me as I got dressed, clocking my condition, wondering what it was you'd be dealing with this morning.

"I heard the car start last night. I was worried about you. Where'd you go?"

"Had to get chocolate milk."

"Look at you. What a kook. Why?"

"Reason not the need."

"Can we go home now?

"Yeah, just, you know, a quick breakfast, a word with

Harry, a brief signing ceremony. Maybe a swim. Then we're gone."

"Or how about let's just go right now. Please. I can't stay here anymore."

"We're not going to stay. It's just we're just not leaving like, instantly."

"Oh brother," you sighed, pulling the covers over your head and sliding down into the bed. "We're never going to leave. Never, never, ever. Oh dear god. We're here forever."

I sat down beside you and reached under the covers to find your hand. To my relief, you didn't pull away. I feared you'd be cold and bitter that morning, but instead you were warm and sweet, squeezing my hand in return.

"Listen babe," I said, "that thing last night, that was nuts. I didn't know what I was talking about. That was absolute total fucking nuts. I didn't mean any of it. I don't even remember half of what I said, except I didn't mean any of it and I'm sorry. Okay? I really am—really, truly, horribly, sorry. I'm just. It's that, it's you. Leaving, going to Italy. It's making me mental. I can't handle it. I'm trying, but it's not easy, you know what I mean?"

"Yeah," you said from under the covers. "We have to talk about that."

"Yeah, we gotta."

"Okay."

"Come for breakfast."

"All I want is coffee. Just bring me a coffee, okay?"

"Okay. You're sweet T, you are. You know I'm mad for you girl."

"I know."

You told me once that you were the only girl in your high school with leather pants. You'd got them with your older sister on a shopping trip to Grand Forks, North Dakota, for your fifteenth birthday. The vice-principal, a woman, decreed that you couldn't wear them in school, that they violated some arbitrary dress code. So you wrote a letter to the school board to complain, and soon got official permission to wear your leather pants. I don't know what made me think of that then. Maybe because I was feeling so in love with you T and the way in which the world exists for you. I so longed to live in such a world.

Anyway it all turned out to be a morning of major misinterpretations due to this inexplicable sense of joy I was experiencing. I was blinded by happiness, made delusional by optimism. I had you all wrong T. That wasn't sweetness. That was sadness.

Teddy was in the kitchen making a big messy breakfast that no one ever got around to eating, with an open bottle of some kind of traditional East Euro breakfast schnapps to help launch Harry. He'd found the Beastie Boys on the satellite radio, the soundtrack of our teens. He flashed me a conspiratorial grin when I walked in—they were playing "Sabotage."

I made you a cup of coffee, sweet and black, the way you like and brought it to the bedroom. You were up out of bed and dressed for a run.

"Good idea," I said. "A run in the woods and then a jump in the lake—it's like having sex with the North."

From down the hall, we heard Harry yelling at Teddy about the missing Hitler gun.

"Oh dear," you said, as you slipped out of the room and went for your run.

I was already in the lake when you got back.

I was in the middle of the bay, cycling the clear green water. The lake, you must admit, was a smooth jewel that morning. I turned slow 360s, now taking in a view of that side of the lake, now taking in a view of this side of the lake, now taking in a view of you, suddenly on the dock, tiptoeing in a black two-piece, your dark novel in one hand, an iced tea in the other, my beautiful blue green grey lake-eyed TKO.

I was so damn happy to see you.

If you don't mind T, let me stay in the middle of the bay for a moment, seeing you and being happy, because this is the last happy moment I've had in life, a life in which happy moments have been as rare as snowstorm lightning. You, with your balanced upbringing on a prosperous mixed farm, the middle of five siblings—two brothers and two sisters— you might not be able to fully appreciate what happy moments mean to the likes of us with a less certain grip on this fast-spinning orb. So let me be happy there in the lake, just for a moment.

Because what's this? Why it's Teddy Chup, joining you on the dock. He was shirtless in his too-short corduroy cut-offs and black cowboy boots, terrifying skinny white, his tattoos looking like the random graffiti on a truck stop bathroom stall. From where I was, well out in the water without my glasses, he looked like the scariest scarecrow on earth. And what did he talk to you about, with his arms folded and his head tilted in an almost perfect imitation of a normal person? I'd soon find out. You put your drink and book down and slipped into the water like an otter and smoothly stroked out to meet me in the middle of the bay.

"Great, eh?" I said obviously, with a greyhound grin on my face, doggedly paddling.

"Yeah," you said. "Great. Come in. Come to the dock. We have to talk."

"Let's talk here."

"No. Not here."

"Say it in the lake or not at all. That's the rule."

"Oh E. Please."

"What? What's wrong?"

You were trying hard not to cry.

"Please," you said.

"I'm the loon. Talk to me here."

"If you. Okay. Oh E. I only want to say this once 'cause it's really hard, okay? This time I mean it. It's over. For real. I just can't keep doing this. It'll be better for both of us. You'll see. I'm sorry. Okay?"

You looked at my face, which was bruised with shock, my eyes brimming with lake water. I looked away and said nothing. I wanted my silence to serve as a wall that would make your words bounce back at you and that you'd take them and put them away and forget you ever said them.

Instead you said, "Teddy says it's time for you to go do Harry, whatever that means. So I'm going to go now. I'm getting a lift to town from the neighbour. I'll take the bus home, okay? So goodbye. I just can't do this anymore. I'm sorry."

I turned to see you crying.

"That guy shoots crows. For sure he'd shoot a magpie."

"Oh Earl Jonathan Boyle, you make me cry."

"Oh Theresa Katrina Ovseenko. Same here."

As you turned to swim away, I said, "Wait. Just. Wait."

You paused and I came to you and draped my arms over

your shoulders. Words are important. I say draped, but you might say clung and dragged you under and the water shot up your nose. T all I did was stop cycling to let you feel my weight. It's a matter of bone density. I'm a sinker by nature. So we sank together into the lake and I held you tight. You, misinterpreting my meaning, fought against it. Your nails clawed my chest and face and arms, your knee hit my hip, but I held on as down we went. You rolled and pushed off with all your coiled strength, your foot striking my throat. I came back up.

Your face broke the surface a few feet away, opened wide, eyes and mouth gaping. There was fear and surprise in your face, but that wasn't the worst of it. The worst of it was the cold quick calculation I saw there. You looked at me as though for the first time, seeing me at last—big and scary, dangerous but clumsy, out of my element in the water, like a panther fallen from a tree into the lake. Your hard appraising eyes flicked over me and past me, to the safety of the dock. You fluttered backwards when I made a move toward you.

"No T," I said, "I was—"

But you were already swimming around and away, strong, smooth and fast, and got to the dock, where you gathered your novel and towel and disappeared and I haven't seen you since.

That's the worst thing of all T—your face, looking at me like that. It's the last face of yours I'll ever get to see. Think of all the faces I've seen of you T. And now I'm stuck forever with that one final face, a face that says: You're trying to kill me.

That's not me you saw T. I'm not a killer. I was only wanting to hold you in the lake for a moment, but I'm a sinker and you're a floater, light and buoyant and gone, and it was too late to explain. So the last face you have of me is a killer's face. That's why I so desperately needed a trial T, for a change of face.

That's what this has been all about. That's why I wrote all this.

Then came the crash. Long forestalled and feared, it came with shocking suddenness. I puked and sobbed and gagged, everything coming out of me all at once. My head weighed a hundred pounds. I've never felt so monstrously tired, so deeply blue. I wanted to sleep forever. I wanted to stay in the middle of the bay until the lake pulled me under. I wanted to be food for fish. I stayed out there, barely treading water, drifting to sleep.

I was awoken by a car horn. Right away I knew it was Teddy in the Buick Electra. I tried to ignore it and resume committing suicide, but there it was again—the horn from the shore, a trumpet of doom, bleating and insistent. He wouldn't stop until I came and made him stop. I'd have to commit suicide later.

Dog-paddling for the dock, it struck me: It can't end like this. I can't allow it. There'd be no girl going to town with the neighbour to catch a bus back home. The girl rides home with me, in the Pony. We've been through things before. This was no different. We just needed time to talk. But you were long gone when I got to the cottage. I'd been shocked by your words in the water and then astonished by the speed of your escape, so swift and certain, as though you'd been planning it all along. Our room was vacant and you were gone. And Teddy would not stop honking that fucking horn.

I yanked the car door open and said, "Fuck. Right. Off."

"Get in," Teddy said, from the front passenger seat.

I slid into the backseat. The big machine was alive, engine throbbing and air conditioning whistling, the chilly liquid air pouring from the dashboard, pine scented. The cool brocade chaffed my wet skin. It felt like being in a jet gathering itself for takeoff. Father and son were in the front seat, the proverbial apple and apple tree, side by each. Teddy had mixed high-octane martinis in pop cans for the ride.

"Road jar?" Teddy asked, passing me a can while snapping on his seatbelt. I did likewise.

Harry was at the wheel, no seatbelt I noticed, in tennis whites with a curious lemon-coloured stain on his shoulder and a crude bandage on the back of his neck. His head was purple and wobbling. What have you done to him? I wanted to ask Teddy. But I said nothing and the big car meandered down the narrow driveway and spilled out onto the twisty gravel road.

I thought about getting Harry to drop me at the neighbours, where I could confront you and make a proper spectacle of myself, in shorts still wet and anguished from the lake, begging you not to go. Would that have worked? No. Context is everything. I'd save my begging for when we were both back in town, sitting out back of the shotgun shack in the Junction, quietly watching the freight trains roll by. I didn't know which neighbour you'd meant anyway.

"You dig Lithuanian music?" Teddy asked me, as he slipped a disc into the stereo. The car abruptly filled with The O'Jays harmonizing on the theme of backstabbers. Conversation was now impossible, which suited me all over, but Teddy talked non-stop, pointing out I know not what local points of interest. Perhaps he was recollecting summertime follies from his wretched and chaotic childhood. Then he pulled his cowboy boots off and propped his naked feet atop the dashboard. He became quiet and introspective. I can still see his bone white and black haired legs jutting out from the crude brown cords that looked as though they'd been shortened with a butcher knife, and his strangely small feet there on the caramel coloured dash. He was the straw man who'd broken my camel's back. He held a camera on his lap.

We weaved out and onto the two-lane blacktop, Harry making use of the entire road surface to negotiate the ponderous automobile up and around the hilly bends and curves of good old Shield Country. And then, as though he'd become bored with waiting for the car to crash of its own accord, Teddy lowered his window, undid his seatbelt, reached over to the driver's side, took a hold of the steering wheel, and yanked hard right.

Now it was a carnie ride. We plunged into the deep ditch in slow motion violence. A big bang exploded in the vast plush interior, followed by the crack of glass as we rolled onto the roof and the airbags deployed, and then another big bang as we rolled right over and dropped heavily onto the wheels, the car's momentum grinding it halfway up the other side of the ditch before coming to a slamming halt, hung up on a rock. All systems went dead. In the sudden quiet my ears rang like church bells. The car filled with airbag angel dust, the smell warm and plastic.

I got knocked around pretty good in the tumble, but the seatbelt had done its job and I was harnessed tightly twisted at an odd angle, alive and with nothing broken. One of Teddy's cowboy boots was on my lap, and a gurgling pop can was at my feet. I felt like an astronaut after a crash landing on a strange planet. I anticipated finding everything different out there.

Harry was slumped unconscious half across the dashboard. I figured he'd been knocked out by a combination of schnapps trauma and airbag shock. Hindered by his airbag, which had failed to deflate, Teddy produced his box cutter and punched a hole in it. It hissed and sagged across his lap. Then he pulled himself out of the car through his open window. My door was stuck shut so I crawled over the seat and did likewise. Neither of us said a thing. That's strange to remember—how we didn't talk. We were both soaked in sweat and panting like dogs.

I realized then that Teddy had been angling to get tossed out of the car. Suicide by drunk-driving dad. He'd forgotten about those airbags.

I went up the side of the ditch to get some distance from the Chups and gain a perspective on the scene. I was right: It was like being on a strange planet, and everything did seem different. There were no cars on the road. The weather had changed. The sun was barely visible, like a flashlight behind a gauzy grey sheet of clouds. I looked down in the ditch. Harry was pulling himself out the open passenger door window. Teddy came over to help. Harry flailed at him with both fists, his lower body still in the car, and then fell forward and toppled to the ground. He tried to get up, but couldn't. He crawled away from the car and Teddy walked alongside, bent over talking to him. I couldn't hear what he was saying.

I don't have a hundred percent clear recollection of what came next. I'd been hoping that my trial might sort some of this out. Obviously that's not good. When you're relying on surveillance footage and a criminal trial to help clarify what happened on your weekend, that's not good at all.

I do remember slipping into the ditch. I was woozy and wobbly so I lost my footing and slipped, sliding into home plate beside the Chups. In the process, both sandals came off. All at once and at first inexplicably, Teddy hooked his bare foot into my vacant right sandal. Then he stood on Harry's neck with it. More than stood, he stomped, bringing all his weight down on the back of Harry's neck repeatedly, with a shock of damp black hair hanging in his eyes and a whistly whine whistling from his nose.

I merely watched, submerged in a dreamy state of detachment and dazed incomprehension. By the time I snapped to, realized what was what, got to my feet, pushed Teddy off Harry, and regained control of my sandal, it was too late—Harry was dead, killed with my sandal, although I wasn't the one using it at the time.

The next thing I remember was putting Harry in the trunk. When I opened the driver's door to pop the trunk, the key in the ignition indicator chirped—stupid, happy, normal—as though we'd just swung by the Beer Store for a two-four. I won't tell you of the horror of hoisting Harry's dead weight and heaving it into the trunk.

Then we squatted beside the car at the bottom of the weedy ditch and smoked the Benson and Hedges Special Mild Menthol cigarettes plucked from dead Harry's pants pocket. My cigarette was cracked. Teddy pulled his cowboy boots on and started making plans; I remained barefoot without any plan. Teddy was spent, calm, and at ease, as though waiting for a helicopter evacuation after a fierce jungle fire fight. The warm and heavy greasy grey sky, accompanied by the electronic buzz of the insects in the ditch evoked a suitably tropical mood.

Teddy's plan was to get the car towed back to the cottage.

Then we'd take both boats out to the island and dump Harry
in the lake. We'd leave one boat out there, so when they
found the body, they'd think he got pissed, fell out, and
drowned. We'd torch the Electra and report it stolen.

It wasn't a bad plan, when I think about it now. Not that
it would have worked. And not that I wanted to have
anything to do with it. I was hardly listening.

Harry's cellphone rang from the trunk—"Knock Three
Times"—and I nearly fainted with shock. That was it for
me. I was out of there. I didn't want to have a role in Teddy's
thing anymore. The show was over. Up the side of the ditch
to the other side of the highway, walking away, Teddy calling
after me.

Sorry to say, but here comes a cliché: I'd never felt so
alive. Walking barefoot down the road away from that scene,
it felt like the world was pulsing with life in a brand new
way and I was pulsing with it. I was barely able to contain
the life that pulsed within me. I think that must be how
human sacrifice works. We kill in order to more keenly feel
death's opposite.

That also explains how I fucked up my feet. I had a
broken toe already and now I was walking barefoot over the
broken glass and debris on the gravel shoulder, just tripping
along oblivious. I walked for hours before realizing I didn't
know where I was going. At one point, I saw Tim the tow
truck man from Barrie in a flatbed truck. I tried to wave him
down, but he only stared and blew by. I figured it was a race
thing. When I'm in the city, I'm mixed and mixed in and no
one thinks much about it either way. But the further north I
go, the blacker I get. I was far enough north to be quite
black. Because of what you'd done to my hair, people driving
by must have first thought I was a platinum blond white guy

with a mad tan. Then they'd get a little closer and see and go, nope—it's a scary Negro with dyed hair, walking down the ditch barefoot in swim trunks. What's amazing is that the OPP never rolled up to have a chat.

It was dusk by the time I found my way back to the cottage. It was dusk and I was wrecked—fatigued beyond words, bug-bitten, ruined feet, thirsty and hungry, utterly whipped. All I wanted to do was to tumble into the Pony and go home. Too bad Teddy was there. The Buick Electra was also there, sitting on the back of Tim the tow truck man from Barrie's flatbed truck. I'd snuck up to the cottage and hid in the bush by the driveway, taking stock of the situation. I figured Teddy was going to wait for me to come back to help him execute his plan for disposing of Harry's body. It was a two-man operation. Meanwhile, Teddy and Tim had been bonding. They came out from the cottage, put their beer cans aside, and got busy getting the Electra off the flatbed, with a great loud ruckus of chain rattling, ramp banging and winch whining. I overheard Teddy talking about prepping the car for the demo derby in Betterham next weekend.

"Might as well do her," Tim agreed, "frame's fucked anywho."

I hung in the bush watching them for what seemed like forever. When they finally went down to the dock, I snuck into the cottage and grabbed my stuff and car keys. I feared Teddy would come back up and foil my escape, so I pushed the Pony down the driveway and onto the road, as far away from the cottage as possible, not wanting to start up and have the sound alert Teddy.

I don't know how I managed to drive back to the city. It

was madness. It felt like I was trapped inside a dark roaring cave. I had to scream to quell the engine noise in my head. The worst of it all was when I started calling for my brother Douglas and of course got nothing back. I drove to our place, but left the instant I realized that you'd been and gone and taken Ronnie with you. I suppose you were concerned that I might still be looking to kill you both. I had similar but much more legitimate concerns about Teddy. So I went to my mom's to hide. The stricken look on my mom's face when I showed up at her condo was matched only by the stricken look on my mom's face when, two days later, I was taken from her condo for questioning by police.

As soon as Teddy saw I'd been and gone from the cottage, he must have jumped into the Electra and pointed it at the city. I can picture that big wrecked car limping down the 401 slant-ways like a crippled dog, and then Teddy dropping it for dead in Harry's driveway in the suburbs. Then he took his camera equipment and footage down to his studio and went to work. The cops came by there to pick him up later that afternoon, after a call from Harry's lawyer and best friend, who'd been trying to get a hold of him all weekend. Early that morning he came by the house looking for Harry. The lawyer-friend was standing in the driveway, puzzled by the wrecked Buick Electra, when he made another call to Harry on his cellphone. That's how they found Harry in the trunk.

The reason why Harry's best friend and lawyer had been looking for him was that he had some bad news. Harry's business had collapsed, brought down by the debt he'd accumulated in his effort at diversifying into the home security system sector. Apparently, everyone who ever wanted an automatic garage door already had one. Harry's attempt to launch a new enterprise had only pushed him into ruin. His creditors were calling in their chips. Harry was bankrupt. He was done. So the whole weekend had been pointless.

I'm sure Harry's creditors would like to get a hold of that Hitler gun.

I want to clear up that gun thing with you T, just to finish all things off here. I watched you on screen with that gun. I watched when you first found it on our bedroom floor, and how you stashed it in your bag. You held it all that day while we were looking for it, for safety's sake I think. Then when you left, I watched you walk through the kitchen, bag over shoulder on your way out for good, and stop and flip the gun on the kitchen counter like an afterthought. I watched you hesitate. Leave. I watched you come back. I watched you pick it up, shove it back in your bag, and disappear forever. I can't see your face in your hoodie as you do all that. But here's what I do see: Love. I see an act of love. You took the gun to save me. The rest would be up to me. That's how I want to watch that.

So thank you for that T. Thanks for that loving goodbye.

It's only because of that I'm sending you these notebooks. I've got them here now, full and done, my Hilroy notebooks numbered one, two, three. I'll mail them to you, c/o the family farm, as soon as the post office at the Shoppers Drug Mart opens.

I'm in the kitchenette at my mom's condo. Outside a grey dawn light is bringing the ramps and expressways of the basket weave into focus. The traffic is building and beginning to bog down. I am Stayed.

Love,

e.